THE
TORTURER'S WIFE

ALSO BY THOMAS GLAVE

Whose Song? and Other Stories

Words to Our Now: Imagination and Dissent

*Our Caribbean: A Gathering of Lesbian and Gay Writing
from the Antilles* (Editor)

THE

TORTURER'S WIFE

Thomas Glave

City Lights
San Francisco, California

Cover design by em dash

Grateful acknowledgment is extended to the editors of the following
publications in which some of the works in this book, each in different form,
first appeared:

Callaloo: "He Who Would Have Become 'Joshua,' 1791" and "South Beach,
1992."

The Kenyon Review: "The Torturer's Wife."

The Massachusetts Review: "Invasion: Evening: Two."

Stone Canoe: "Milk/Sea; Sentience" and "Woman   Impossible Task."

"The Blue Globes" first appeared in *Black Silk: A Collection of African-
American Erotica* (Anchor Books; ed. Retha Powers), and was reprinted in
Best Black Gay Erotica (Cleis Press; ed. Darieck Scott).

LIBRARY OF CONGRESS CATALOGING-IN-PUBLICATION DATA

Glave, Thomas.
  The torturer's wife : stories / by Thomas Glave.
    p. cm.
  ISBN-13: 978-0-87286-466-5
  ISBN-10: 0-87286-466-9
  I. Title.

PS3557.L354T67 2008
813'.54--dc22

                                    2008020488

Visit our web site: www.citylights.com

City Lights Books are published at the City Lights Bookstore,
261 Columbus Avenue, San Francisco, CA 94133

To
Nadine Gordimer —
comrade,
but also,
always,
beacon

Contents

Between
1

The Torturer's Wife
33

The Blue Globes
75

Milk/Sea; Sentience
87

Invasion: Evening: Two
97

South Beach, 1992
129

Woman   Impossible Task
155

He Who Would Have Become "Joshua," 1791
171

Out There
209

BETWEEN

DAVID
Now walking. Alongside the other. His shoulders raised to their highest. His shoulders nearly touching his ears. Walking alongside Jonathan (but not too close). Jonathan, whom he has dared, for the first time, to bring into his neighborhood. It feels very daring, for him. Daring, as he wonders if the neighbors — the people here and there sweeping off sidewalks, bending briefly over front-yard garbage cans and casually glancing up from clipping and pulling up persistent weeds in narrow flower beds as the two pass — will look at him, at the two of them, and say anything. Or rather, will their eyes say anything? Will their eyes ask (as he has long feared, upon bringing Jonathan into the neighborhood, they would) what the hell *he* is doing with *him*? (Of course none of them will yet know Jonathan's name.) Will their eyes ask, What is he doing — What are you doing, David — with one of *them*? Will their eyes say, Oh. Oh, well look at this. Isn't it bad enough that you're . . . isn't it too bad that you had to go and become *that*.

Bad enough that you had to go and shame your mother and your entire family. Make them all sick. Wasn't that enough? But then now you have to go and bring one of *them* here? Bring it all right into the neighborhood? What would your mother have said? Would you have dared to bring him here if she were still alive? Would you have dared to walk so close to him, making it so clear to everyone that you and he —

Trying so very hard now not to touch Jonathan in any way, touch being the thing he loves most — at least one of the things he loves most — when they walk together in a place that feels . . . safer. A place, though small, where two like them can walk with some ease some of the time —mainly in the early evening as lights soften and dusk beckons. Someplace far from here, where an easy touch of wrist against wrist or knuckle briefly brushed across knuckle will not tighten shoulders or further narrow eyes already moved to slits. Trying so very hard now to maintain a space, a well-defined space, between them, he thinks briefly of that part of town — remembering it and knowing that right now he really wants to —

Disgusting, he fears their eyes will say. (Looking straight ahead now as he walks next to Jonathan. Feeling that he just cannot bring himself, just now, to do what, in cloaking darkness, he is certain, he tells himself, he still would do, has done so many times before: look fully into Jonathan's face.) *Sick*, he fears their eyes and shoulders and backs will say, are saying, as they turn back to their assorted daily tasks.

(The two of them walking down this street, one of them determined not to touch the other, are still relatively young, youngish: nowhere near "middle age," but old enough to have learned to be aware of — sometimes even cautious about — the self-absorption that complete youth, and the world always brought to its knees by youth and beauty, permits. They are old enough to have learned that the visible differences between them, visible also to others, cause at least one of them to raise his shoulders up to his ears when walking in his neighborhood with the one next to him whose mouth and arms — whose everything, just about — he knows so well.)

That's David, walking with his shoulders like that. The one who's known in these parts. Tomorrow, some others — a few of the young men who know him, who grew up with him, or at least nearby him — young men who have gradually come to realize that there are in fact many things about him that they've never known and would hardly have guessed, although a few long ago did guess it (*come on*, they'd occasionally said or snorted among themselves, look at the way he walks; *come on*, one had sometimes murmured, can't you just look at his *mouth* and tell that he's . . . yeah, right, uh huh) — tomorrow evening three of these young men, remembering having seen him in the neighborhood in the company of the other who now walks beside him, will narrow their eyes, suck on some more of their rage, remember well how they were taught from early years to regard him and his kind as *disgusting, sick* — and surround him near a vacant lot. With little time wasted, they will hurl profanities at him, then begin leveling repeated blows on him — using, among other items, a heavy piece of splintered wood close enough in size and shape to a baseball bat; appropriately thick-bodied construction boots; a good-sized silver hammer; a shining screwdriver; a rusty bottle opener (an odd tool, fetched from the cluttered garage of one of their parents); and, of course, their own fists. Whether or not they actually kill him will be learned first by the late dog-walker who will happen by not long afterward and discover the mess, oozing over the dirty sidewalk, that remains of him. (In actuality the dog will discover it, sniffing in sudden heightened alarm and distress as he and his owner near the spot.) What remains of the person who, not so long ago, had been a fully functioning human will sprawl across the sidewalk in a dark, spreading, sticky

pool of still-warm body fluids, the purple-bruised eyes swollen
and closed and the face completely unrecognizable to all who
might have known him. David. (Because of the furious skill with
which the hammer will be wielded, it is possible that what will
remain of him will also end up missing a few teeth.) On that
evening — tomorrow — just before he loses consciousness as
the hammer slams for the first time into his left eye and the
screwdriver, jabbed and then twisted, rips open a jagged path
through his neck, he will remember. Remember one word. A
name: Jonathan, he will think, at the very beginning of his descent into asphyxiating darkness and, shortly afterward, silence.
(Not long after this, he will know in the deepest part of himself
— the part that clings ferociously to life even when faced with
the most ridiculous odds — that the silence that surrounds and
fills the movement toward death is not at all peaceful, no matter
how desperately the living insist on believing otherwise. Moving
much too rapidly through that silence, aware of it and aware of
his arms flailing so uselessly and frantically in that darkness that
none of the living, watching his unmoving form, will be able to
see, he will know for all time until the end of such time that the
silence that fills the journey toward death is nothing less than
utterly terrifying, unmerciful, and — no matter how many worrying hands of the living world fret and flutter in their frantic
attempts to pull the descending one back up to consciousness
— unkind. *That,* he will know in that deepest shrouded place
that will cling to breath for as long as it possibly can, until either
death or rescue — that will be true death, the movement toward
death. And so immediately after the ceasing of the violence and
the strangely calming sound of retreating running feet, aware of
the astonishing unpleasantness of his own blood in his mouth
and its thickness in his throat, he will, very weakly, call out that
name one time —
   —Jonathan—

— after which he will close his eyes, in surrender to whatever sequence of things, with or without him, will happen next. But none of that will happen until tomorrow evening. Today, here, he is still his complete, unharmed self.

His shoulders still very high. His face still not turning, not once, to regard Jonathan walking quietly beside him. Jonathan who seems to have sensed that at least for now, walking here, David cannot be entirely his; all subtle intimations of possession, even or especially the suggestive or provocative glance, forbidden. Later, in a quiet place where, between them, space is made for the movement of limbs, they both will remark (with their bodies, if not with words or the eye-expressions they have come, with each other, to understand and mostly trust) how quietly they walked through the neighborhood toward David's house; toward the house in which he grew up, inherited by him after his mother's death three and a half years ago. The slightly ramshackle wooden house, some of its outer paint peeling, its window frames weatherbeaten, and each of its sagging gutters beginning to fall. The house in which, since just after his mother's death, he has lived alone, not with Jonathan. —Just because we haven't really taken the time to get you moved in yet,— he sometimes tells Jonathan, pushing his face into that warm neck as he wraps his arms around him in a bar, in a café — anyplace they feel it's all right, even approved, to do things like that in public. *Just because you know damn well we never will,* Jonathan does not ever answer; savoring with closed eyes David's smell so close by, and the feel on his skin on David's face, that smooth face with its beautiful arching eyebrows that always suggest some mild astonishment.

Neither of them will comment — not with words — on the run-down state of the house and the raggediness of its front yard. (The kind of neighborhood, David once told Jonathan, in which the people who have always lived there in raggedy-yarded run-down houses, raggedy children screaming in the yards and from the front porches in summer, will always be the people who will live there in raggedy-yarded run-down houses, always with raggedy children screaming somewhere. Mostly big-bellied, thick-armed people — *fat* people, Jonathan thinks, eyeing them with almost completely concealed distaste — with someday-to-be-fat raggedy children drugged on Kool-Aid, Coke and Pepsi, potato chips. Fattened on hot dogs, french fries.) Jonathan will say nothing about the house's unkempt lawn and deeply untidy flower garden, both of which he knows reflect David's occasional anger, ambivalence, about feeling *obligated*, David has lately frequently said, to maintain this house in a neighborhood that — even though he lives in the house — no longer feels part of his skin as it did when he was growing up in it as a watchful, and even in those early years cautious, child. Nor will Jonathan comment in that moment about the old woman across the street, who, beneath the awning that shades the front porch where she sits with a very young child playing with something at her feet — a tin can with the label peeled off, or a piece of foil — watches them from deeply narrowed eyes as they enter the front yard, keeping her unwavering gaze on him in particular. Later, David, not so willingly, will tell Jonathan a little more about her. He will learn that she is — was — a dear friend of David's mother and grandparents. (And so that was why, as they had entered the house, David had finally turned and waved and called to her, despite the woman's chilly glare that Jonathan had felt like a corkscrew in his spine from a distance of twenty or so yards.) *My mother thought her husband used to beat her,* David said, *well, there were signs: black eyes, and sometimes a lot of bruises. He died in a car accident a few years ago. A fucking alcoholic. That was her grandson on the porch, but nobody ever sees her daughter, at least not in the daytime.* Not irony in his voice, but . . . then Jonathan recognizes it: a smidgen of disgust, coupled with David's customary quiet anger and, especially when he talks about the people around here or the place itself, sadness; the edges of longing and loneliness not easily assuaged by intimacy or the rustlings of affection. From all that David does not say, and from that tightening at the back of his neck that Jonathan knows so well, he will figure out that she too, like most of the neighborhood, has been privy to some of the rumors about David and his personal inclinations — indeed, his tastes, among which, Jonathan knows, is included (primarily, he and perhaps David would like to believe) himself. As David closes the house's front door to the street behind them, Jonathan will see through the curtained living room window facing her house directly that she, like the people whose reactions David most fears in his daydreams, does not even attempt to veil the scorn that, in this minute, to his eyes, appears far too caustic — far too scalding, severe, as the wash of acid over tender skin — for her withered, cauterized face. The face of a woman perhaps once beaten savagely by a man with whom, for some reason presently inexplicable to him, he wants to imagine she had once been in love (if she had indeed been in love; is it ever really possible, he wonders, to be "in love" and be sensible, not stupid, reckless, completely selfish and self-centered in it?): that face, the face of a woman who may have been beaten by a drunken man, now partly ruined by the ugliness of . . . but whatever it actually is, he quickly backs away, in his mind, from the painful word. The word that conjures for them both all sorts of fear, outrage, and (yes, *admit* it, his mind insists) agony. As neither of them can know just now, it is the vitriol presently searing the most human parts of her face, rendering them both tragic and destroyed, that will exactly match the acid that will appear on the faces of the three young men who, weapons gripped and at the ready, will surround David tomorrow evening.

Jonathan

His shoulders are so high. I feel them. I can almost see them, even though I'm not looking at them. But then mine are, too. High and tense. Tense because — I guess — I really can feel them all looking at me. All these people out here, doing their different things. These people, wondering. Wondering why he's with me. —With one of *them*,— they're probably thinking. Wondering, maybe, how *he* could possibly stand to —

I don't care. I don't care what any of these people think. I know that's how these people are. They're narrow. I mean ignorant, I mean. . . . Most of them have probably never even left this neighborhood. Some of them are probably living on welfare, or . . . I *mean*, public assistance. Just look at the houses around here. The — these yards. And the sidewalks, so . . . well, they're filthy. But what else could you expect? That's how these people are. He told me a long time ago about them, about how he felt growing up here around them, but I had my own ideas about these people long before he told me. And so . . . all right, I'll admit it. Admit that I don't like the fact that he's — well yeah, he's one of them, in his own way, kind of. I mean he comes from them. That's just a fact. This place produced him. He can't help that. (Although thank God, thank *God* he doesn't *act* like them. He's not fat. He's not lazy, just sitting around living off welfare or whatever they live on, if you call that living. He doesn't sit around all day and eat and watch soap operas. And he speaks like an educated person. He forms whole sentences. Not like one of them.)

Yes, he comes from them, and I'll bet they think of him even now as kind of one of them. But I —

No. I told him once, and I'll say it again: I don't care if any of these people talk shit about us. About me or him. I don't. I don't care because . . . well, first of all because we don't live here, in his mother's house. At least I don't, and one day he won't either. I mean, look at this place. It's a shithole. Who would want to live here if they didn't have to? His mother didn't really have a choice. She wasn't educated and she never wanted to leave the neighborhood, but he — well, he has lots of choices. He'll sell it and maybe, maybe we'll get a place together or find something. I don't know. We've talked about it a little. I know he wants to. I'm sure of that. I can say I'm sure of it because in spite of everything I feel him, I mean really feel him. Feel him like in not a day going by that I don't think about him. I think about . . . well, that doesn't really matter. All that matters is that he knows it and I know it too.

I remember the first time I felt him. When he put his hand on me. I mean *on* me, in a way like . . . it was like he didn't even have to say "I want this" or "Yeah, I do want you, and I'm thinking about doing this to you," because he knew before he even touched me that I wanted it too. Wanted the touch and all of it. The heat of his hand and the squeeze of it where he put it on me, holding. It was only a couple of hours after we first met, in a club, in the city — a club that's far, I mean like *really* far from this shithole. The way he tells it, it's always like, the J and me, he says, we met at this house party, and I'm always like, No, D, you got it wrong again, it was in that club, how could you forget, don't you remember? *I* remember, I tell him, looking at him, so why don't you? But that's him, that's D That's how he is.

When he came over to me in the club that night (he was going to ask me to dance, you could see that all over him, especially in the way he held out his chest), I laughed. Other people were watching, the way they do in clubs sometimes, you know . . . watching like they want to say, okay, now what's this shit all about? And I was like . . . what the fuck is this now, I thought, even though he was —

Well, yeah. He was cute. Hot, even. His face, and his mouth. The muscles in his shoulders and arms. The way that t-shirt looked on him, the way it showed his nipples pressing up under the shirt, and the way his ass looked in those jeans, like . . . I could get myself into *that*, I thought. Cute, yeah, I thought, even though . . . and then somewhere in all that, somewhere in the middle of all that even with some people watching when we began to dance, I felt him. Hot. Close. Trying to get closer. I could feel him, even with all the noise in the club. The music. And could smell him. That t-shirt that he wore, starting to sweat in it as we danced, with his arms getting shiny . . . I saw him, smelled him, and then I felt him. There, pressing against me as we danced. His hands on me and mine on him.

That was the first time for me ever getting that close to one of them. I mean, so close that I could smell him.

And — well, fuck it. I'll say it. It's true what everybody says: they don't smell like us. No, they don't. He had a smell like nothing I've ever smelled before. It was just . . . different. Very —

And the whole time with him getting closer and looking at me like that and then pressing up against me, I was like, *oh shit*. Thinking like, here I am, in front of all of my friends, dancing with this dude. Dancing with — I mean, what can I say? I had *never* danced with one of them before.

No. Not ever.

But Jesus, the way his arms felt around me. Oh God. I mean, *yes*. So warm and so strong. And the way he smelled, with all that sweat . . . I just wanted to keep smelling him. I wanted to lick the sweat off him, *taste* it, taste him, because he looked so hot, dancing like that, throwing his head back with his eyes closed and still holding on to me and letting me squeeze his ass, I mean *squeeze* it, as I pressed my hands into the back pockets of his jeans and felt him, felt his hard parts as he let go of me and then came back again, let go and came back to hold me again, always throwing his head back, and I was like, *oh my God, hold me again*, I thought, but wouldn't ever say to him, oh no. And then — well, you know. I began to be kind of shy about pushing against him the way he kept pushing against me, because then he would . . . well, you know. He would feel it. Feel me. I felt his arms around me not long after that. And mine . . . well, it was just sort of like mine just found their way around him. Found their way feeling him, feeling . . . but even now don't ask me how, or —

And — can you get this? — even with some of my friends watching, in spite of what I knew they'd say later, I just . . . I didn't fucking care. Even when he put his mouth on mine — and he did have the nerve, I mean like *the nerve*, to put his mouth on me first — and later when I put mine on his, I . . . didn't care. I honestly don't know how, but I . . . didn't. Didn't care about the color of his skin, or the way he smelled that was so different and still got me so hot, or how people in my neighborhood would look at me, Jesus, how they would look at me when he came home with me only a few days after that. (Yes, he did. Of course he did. I brought him into the neighborhood. But you can see why it would be *sort* of okay. Just look at him. He looks respectable enough. Not dirty like some of them.) Because they did stare. Whispered. Snickered. Talked shit. Of course they did. A few of them looked at us like they hated us, like they would have liked to have seen us (or especially me, or especially him) dead. I know all some of them could think was what the fuck. What is he doing. What is Jonathan doing, bringing one of *them* around here. Is he out of his mind? Doesn't he know better? But I didn't care. I tasted him. I felt him. The way I feel him now, even though (but now we're at his house) my own shoulders, like his, are raised so high.

So much of the paint on the houses around here is peeling. Peeling off like even it wants to get away.

So many old people, too. And (but I see it where I live, too) fat people. Just sitting around. Lazy ass motherfuckers. But guess what — I can tell you this much: it's time to get a fucking job.

You can hear the sound of the trains in the distance. Freight trains. Loud. Echoing.

The people around here don't — no, they do *not* — look happy.

David
That was the first thing I thought when he took me home to his neighborhood: that the people around there didn't look happy. They looked . . . heavy. That was the only word I could think of to describe it . . . heavy and kind of — I don't know. Hollow, maybe? Or just empty, or . . . even now I can't figure out how exactly to describe it. A few of them spoke to him when he passed, but most of them didn't. And I kept wondering . . . well, of course. Who wouldn't? I wondered if they didn't speak to him because he was walking with me.

The first time I went there, I was like, *whoa*. Welcome to Porktown, I thought. Pork as in like, fat, I mean like *really* fat. Everywhere. But no, not like in my neighborhood. Fatter. I mean like waddling down the street. *Waddling*, like pigs, or something else like a pig. It's something about their skin, how the fat looks underneath their skin. And how it makes them smell. And then they'll have the nerve to talk about us. Talk about how we're always doing this and that, causing trouble, always causing trouble for decent people who just want to work and live a quiet life. But some of these fat motherfuckers probably couldn't even get a job, know what I mean? Fuck, they probably don't even *want* a job. I mean, some of the women, Jesus Christ . . . but have you seen some of the men?

He told me about some of them. About some of the ones who watched — who watched us. Who seemed to watch with the most burning. Kind of like the most snarling from behind their mouths. He told me how some of those same ones, the younger guys who still looked good, not fat and gross like the older ones, used to want to — to do him. To sneak with him. Even one time tried to force him, a few of them. When he was like around thirteen, fourteen, and they were; when he was a little older and they were. —Just suck on it a little,— some of them had said. —You gonna swallow it for me tonight?— one of them had asked him, laughing.

—Did you ever do it with any of them?—I asked him when he told me about it. I was holding him. We were lying down. I asked it softly, a whisper in his ear, with my face against the back of his head and one of my legs thrown over him. But he didn't answer just then. Just kind of fluttered his eyes with that look he gets sometimes — yeah, *that* look, like deep water — and I left it at that, though I wanted to know. Well, yeah, of course, I wanted to know.

Two brothers in particular, he said, had talked a lot of that kind of shit to him, and made it clear to him that they were interested in something. Both of them had since gotten married and moved away. Another guy who'd talked like that to him, and done things like rub his own crotch and half-smile whenever they saw each other (though not when any girls were around), was one I remember: a real handsome dude who'd been sitting out one day when J brought me over there again. Sitting on the front steps of someone's house (his uncle's house, J said), with that beautiful girl (well, woman) on his lap. Wearing a baseball cap turned almost backwards, to the side, on his head. The girl had been playing with his chin as he nuzzled his nose, every now and then, between her breasts. I remember the white tank top he'd had on, the curling hair on his chest, the gold chain around his neck that had ended in a little gold cross, the way his knees had pressed forward out of his jeans underneath her legs, and how his cheeks had hollowed inward when he sucked on the cigarette he'd been sharing with her. His stomach was flat, I mean fucking flat. Not an inch of fat. And his arms, with those muscles

. . . yeah, he looked good, and he knew it. That's how some of them are when they know they look good. His name was Chris, J said. Years ago when they'd both been around sixteen, he had tried to get J to suck him, and had wanted to suck J too. In fact, J said that the guy had even wanted them both to do a whole lot more; he'd tried to get J to go all the way into him. It had always been like that, J said. A few of them back then had always wanted to put it inside him, and he had let them. —I let them,— he said, —because sometimes it felt good, even though sometimes I was scared. But sometimes I really wanted it, like they did. And sometimes, later on, mostly, I put it in a few of them, too.—

—Did they like it?— I asked him.

—Mostly everybody likes it,— he said, —so long as they have a choice, you know what I mean?—

—A choice . . .—

—So long as it's not *rape*, they're not being raped, and no one ever finds out about it.—

(I closed my eyes for a minute and tried to imagine what it would be like to be raped by one of them . . . like what would he do to me first . . . would he grab my ass and tell me he was going to fuck the shit out of me . . . would he talk about my "pussy" and say that he was gonna fuck my pussy now, bitch, because now you're my motherfucking bitch . . . haul out his thing and try to force it up between my . . . would he want me to swallow it first, then try to push it into me . . . but then what if I wanted to do it to him . . . what if I wanted to rape his ass and get him under me, yeah, *under* me, and push it in him and keep him down there, crying . . . screaming . . . what if I wanted to make him my little pussybitch *because that's all you motherfuckers are good for, that's all you've ever been good for, feel me? Do you feel me now on top of you slamming into your*)

Was I jealous? (I began to hold onto him more tightly as he was telling me all this.) Maybe I was jealous.

But then I had been with him, I thought, for a long time. Except that he'd never been like the rest of them. He knew how to — I mean, you could take J anywhere.

Those guys he talked about were some of the ones who'd looked up when he and I walked past that first time, I remember. The ones who, like Chris the good-looking one, had watched us walking together, or watched me walking with him.

Going inside . . . oh, *hell* yeah. I'd always loved going into him. That's one thing I can swear to God. The first time he asked me to, asked me to without asking me to (his eyes; the way he looked at me then looked away, but he was still *looking* — and oh fuck, *fuck*, his hands). And . . . I could feel myself almost groaning. Groaning as I got high, *high* on top of him and moved his legs so that I could feel him. I mean really feel him. He wanted me to. He wanted it. Wanted me. He was holding on to me and saying (but without saying it), *Okay. You can. I'm ready.* Looking up at me with his eyes like that, saying *Yes, you can.* Gripping me. My legs. Holding on so hard, hard, to my hands. I almost couldn't take it. I almost . . . and I wanted to be inside him, *in* him, and not ever (uh huh, I swear it) let him go.

The first time I went into him, I didn't even know that I was thinking it until I heard it, the thought, come back out to me as I heard him groaning under me: So this is what one of them feels like, I thought. This is how it is with them. Tight. And hot. And gripping. And this is how it feels to be inside one of them, I thought. This is how they smell, like him, *and how they taste,* I thought: like him. Just like him, I thought, as I went in, and went deeper. Deeper, still deeper, with him crying out quietly and holding on to me. *Do you feel me slamming into your* Telling me, *telling* me he loved me. —. . . *love you, D,*— he called out in that quiet way to me in the dark. Called out and held me, as I held onto him tighter too and bent down over him and took his mouth into mine . . . covered it with mine, and thought,

Now. Now you're completely mine. All mine because I'm inside you. On top of you. Covering you . . . no one can see you now because you're underneath me. Underneath me, feeling me deep inside you. You'll always feel me inside you, I thought. *Because I'm possessing you now*, I thought. *Possessing you, uh huh, and completely in control. On top of you and —*

Jon, I thought. *I really love you, Jon,* I thought. Wanted to think. *Love you, yes. I do.* And smelled you one more time.

Jonathan
Well — yeah, I did. Not long after we first met. I took it out and held it. Squeezed it, and continued to hold it. His.

I took it out, and stared at it. It was hanging there. It . . . *hung.* Heavy, the way I knew it would be. Thick, the way his pressing against me even with all of his clothes on had told me it would be.

Bending to the left, the way he'd told me it did. What he hated, he'd said. Was so ashamed of. —But nothing to be ashamed of,— I told him, —why would you . . . ?—

—Because it's ugly,— he said, not looking at me.

When he said that, I wanted to say . . . I don't know what I wanted to say, or what I would have said. I ended up not saying anything. I just looked straight at him, in silence.

The truth is — of course this is the truth — that I wanted *him,* only him. But that day, that afternoon, I couldn't stop staring at *it.* At its color, like nothing I'd ever been up close to before; and the way the skin looked over its tip.

Well, this will be my first time with a — with one of them, I thought. First time tasting one of them that way.

He'd already done it to me. Twice. Three times. —It's . . . but it's *beautiful,*— he'd whispered the first time and the second time, and then the third: looking down at it, at me, while whispering that. Looking down with that look on his face, almost as if he was surprised by what he was looking at while holding it, me, in his right hand; surprised but something else too, that I couldn't figure out and it looked like he couldn't figure out either. Then using his other hand to cup it underneath as he lowered his face to it, right there along the middle: the middle, where he kissed it. Kissed it, squeezing it a little underneath, until he pulled it all along between his lips, so soft and smooth, and back to the back of his throat. (I remember his teeth on the side gently pressing. Pressing, and his mouth holding so tight so strong because he didn't want to let go. *And don't let go*, I thought but never said.) —Beautiful,— he told me again later. —No,— I told him, —You. You are.— Meaning it. Meaning it very much, I told myself. Closing my eyes and wanting to see only him. Trying to. And holding him.

And then kneeling. In front of him. Kneeling as he sat on the bed and threw his head back.

As he threw his head back reaching with one hand reached around to the back of my head, to my neck, to push me closer to it. To him.

Then pushing more deeply into my mouth. Into my —

And oh my God, I thought, *I'm really kneeling. On my knees, in front of one of them.*

But it's David, I thought. Not just. . . . It's David. Him.

That skin, I thought, *and that smell. That hair, and those lips.*

I was kneeling, but closed my eyes. I wanted . . . only to taste. Didn't want to see.

I don't — don't know why I wanted to keep my eyes closed. I just — I *wanted* to. It was private. I mean private between us.

I only heard him groaning and calling out my name as he held the back of my head. But I didn't see him. Didn't look. (No, wouldn't look. No, *didn't*.)

No, and couldn't. Not that time. Not at his face. His body. Because the whole time I was kneeling in front of him, all I could think even while swallowing him, especially while swallowing him and tasting him, oh Jesus, tasting all of him (but I'll never tell anyone this, I'll never tell him and I swear to God I won't even ever tell myself this), was that —

Yeah, no avoiding it. All I could think of as I was swallowing and breathing in and out with my eyes closed was that one of them was actually in my mouth. Actually in it, all the way back in my throat, as I tried, tried *really* hard, not to gag.

David
What he does not tell Jonathan: He will never tell him — does not imagine he can ever tell him — about the dream of rage: the dream that he does not know is a prescient one. The dream that, since they have known each other, has visited him two, three, four, even six times, and is always the same. After each dream's visit, with their tones of violent sunsets and maroons, he sometimes recalls the dream-sounds of particular taunts. Shrieks. Then the feel, received in deepest sleep, of blows.

In the dream, the young men in the neighborhood confronted him: blocked his path one evening on the sidewalk only a short distance from his mother's house, near the highway overpass; in an alley near the one diner in the area that still operated (open all night) within whistling distance of the freight yards. They must have seen him with Jonathan, the dream insisted, in some other part of town when, unawares, the two would have been walking one evening, feeling themselves safe from the scrutiny of familiar eyes — not troubling themselves to think in those moments that people from the neighborhood did travel sometimes, that people from the block did get out and around far enough when least expected, to see and understand immediately just what it was that moved between the two of them walking and occasionally looking at each other that way, and what the something-or-other actually was in the way they walked in *that* way together, and what it really meant when the knuckles of one occasionally brushed against the other's, as one pulled the other back to the curb with *that* grip on the elbow, to keep him from crossing the street too soon. That grip, followed by the most fleeting squeeze, but still a squeeze, that told anyone who happened to be driving by what all that was really about. The witnesses' outraged observations were followed not long afterward by the confrontation, words hurled at him: but what the *fuck*. (Amazing how words like that could sound even harsher in dreams, he'd thought upon awakening, wet from forehead to belly and shaking everywhere.) But what the fuck *what*, he had dared to respond — trying, though with unquiet hands, to move past them. What the fuck are you doing, they'd replied. Shouted. *Doing*, they'd shouted, with one of *them*. As if it's not bad enough that you are what the *fuck* you are, but then you go fuck around with one of *them*. (All shouted. Shoulders taut.) How the fuck, they'd screamed, are you out of your fucking mind. (Fists suddenly more than raised.) How you can even show your fucking faggot face around here, they'd shouted. How —

But then, that quickly, he begins to feel himself drowning, going down: down in the dreamwater with all that water in his mouth choking him. As he does his very best to paddle frantically upward, he feels that familiar terrifying tug somewhere south of the knees: the tug that will make sure to rip out the heart of his private parts. Is it then that he also feels that burning sense of cloying shame, because — as they snarl and shout again in the dream, he knew it and still knows in his deepest most hidden place that everything they shout is true: Jonathan is exactly what they shout Jonathan is. Is, with that skin, that hair, and those things that pass for lips. Is, with his way of walking; with his way of acting so completely different, from a totally different world, as if the world had always been that way, had never changed into all the other millions of its parts. Is: Jonathan, the one he cannot imagine not always having there somewhere to wrap his arms around, to press tightly against, to watch and touch so quietly in the darkness and think, or say silently, things like *You* or *God, look at you*, as that face, unmindful of his steady gaze upon it, slowly sighs itself off to sleep, sometimes nuzzling itself into his welcoming chest. That was the face whose breaths and sleep-sighs he knew as well as he knew it belonged to one of those who really *were*, weren't they? — really *were* filthy, nasty. Never to be trusted. So from his own very earliest days he had been told and told and told, so from his earliest days he had (in that deepest place) believed but not wanted sometimes to believe but had believed. Don't ever turn your back on one of them. No, nor even *think* you can ever count on one of them. They can't help it, it's just how they are. How they've always been. Sneaky, liars, users. Just don't let them too close, he had been warned and warned. Everything that he had learned from those earliest days is still true, he hears himself thinking in the dream and later after waking. The hotshame and sudden unexpected disgust that accompany the words charge through him in the dream and will charge again long after he realizes that it's just a dream, that's all, and finds himself soon enough holding Jonathan asleep in his arms once more.

Is it then that, along with the shame's hot rush and the disgust, he finds that one of his fists, then another, connect like the bricks they suddenly become with the screaming faces before him? Then, for the first time or the fifth, that he feels the smear of warm red, redness on his knuckles, hears the crunch-sound of injured bone, and then the blows, the so severe blows and kicks and unceasing pummels, all about his own head? It is most definitely then that he falls, hard, to the sidewalk; then looks up and, seeing all of them gathered around him, above him, snarling, he cries out, and shields, with both hands, his head. In slurring dream-words, he begs them not to pick up that heavy piece of wood lying nearby. *A nail sticking out of it.* Please, he entreats them, don't. No. They move toward it. They pick it up. He begs . . . but. But please. *But how.* The fluids from his body . . . he feels the fluids from his body warm; — warm; — warm — on his face. Is it then that he passes out, perhaps soon to — (but *no,* he manages to think in a sudden panic, *that can't happen. I'm way too young. Not yet).* Just before he goes under into that darkness, he remembers one word, and says it: —Jonathan,— as if it is a name someone else wishes and even needs, very much, to hear. He descends into that darkness . . . but not entirely. (*And fuck,* the voice at the very center of his being down in that darkness hisses, *it hurts . . . it* really *hurts. —Jonathan.—* This time the voice at the very center of his being says it. He hears it, and, from way down there where he seems to have fallen even farther than into mere darkness, he tries to reach out what he can — a fleck of blood, the smallest glob of spittle — toward the word and the face and flesh behind it: the face and flesh he wants so much to see and feel hovering next to his own now so that he can touch it, hold it: the face and flesh that are not there.) Some sounds of laughter above him, but also someone's frightened comment: —*Whatup, did we kill him?*— He feels himself *drowning, going down, choking and coughing in all that redwater of shouts, punch-es, kicks: shouts of fucking faggot, homo. Cock*sucking *little bitch.* The dream always happens this way: with him drowning, go-ing down while thinking or trying to think *Now I can't breathe, now the water down here is all blood, now I can't see my skin even my skin for all the red*: it always happens this way each time the dream returns to him, each time before he sees J's face bending over him once more in some deeper notch of the dream past the screams of *What the fuck* and *you let one of* them *fuck you in the ass you fucking sick fuck That's why all you bitchfaggots get AIDS* Drowning in it now deeper but somehow impossibly managing to lie on his side, on his side that hurts so much, *it hurts so much*

Jon he whispers to the face above him that he is certain now is there as he feels the wetness on his face that might be his own, he thinks, but could be someone else's too: the wetness because he knows once again that whatever else happens now, whether he lives or remains shuttered and silent in all that darkness forever, Jonathan won't let him die, the J with that skin *you can't trust them not ever* won't let David his David die. But then even though he is certain that (in the dream at least) he is dying, it is exactly there, the place on the dirty sidewalk stained and sticky with his various body fluids where those who attacked and beat him left him to die (he still cannot know on this particular night how prescient this dream is) that he feels the kiss: himself kissing J, he thinks in that darkness, and Jonathan kissing him. For just a moment, either underneath or above, he feels himself inside Jonathan; then Jonathan above him, beneath him, inside him. *Well can you keep me here*, one of them says. It sounds to him like Jonathan's voice, but could be his own. *I mean hold me here, not let me go. Oh don't let me go*, one of them wants to say so much but does not dare to — too vulnerable even now at the edge of all that darkness. Too scary to admit to someone else, even *the* one, that you want so much — always — to be protected by him. To be held and kept safe, sheltered within the embrace of his shielding arms that smell of him and that not long after his holding onto you that way for so long will smell of you too. You want those private things of yourself to mark him, want to put your mouth on his and taste, *taste* yourself on him, but can't, no, *cannot* let him know all those things even though you can feel them: that's just how things are. And now they kiss again. *I am Jonathan*, this dream or something like it tells one, tells the other, *and you are David. No, you are. I'm one of them, you're one of them. No. Yes. We are. Here.* David, lying on his side in darkness. Feeling J's breath, breathing, on him. Jonathan lying beside, or behind, or on top of, David, in darkness. Each one conjuring the other's face. Each imagining the other inside him. *In me,* one of them thinks. Which one thinks that? Some things to be said only into the other's chest. Whispered, just like that, so very quietly, into his neck. Whispered before awakening, and — if possible — before death.

Jonathan
One time — once, I remember —
     When I had my mouth all the way around him, in the dark, all I could think was: *I've got him in my mouth now. Again. I've got his skin in my mouth now, again, and this is how it tastes.* I was holding onto him with my left hand and cupping him underneath with my right hand and playing with them a little, weighing them like they were pebbles or smooth shells that I could kiss or suck on slowly or even sniff. I did sniff them. I kissed them over and over but gently, you have to be gentle with them — and all the while I kept thinking *when it happens, when he finally throws back his head and grips the back of my head the way he always does and calls out my name and jerks forward and gasps the way he always does, I'll taste that part of him too: hot, or warm. Thick. Strong. I'll taste all of it, because there's nothing wrapped onto him tonight. He's bare, exposed, the way we've always liked it: no coverings, no sheaths. I'll taste him warm (or hot) and thick, before he even reaches my throat. Some of him will stay on my tongue, so that when I kiss him afterwards the way we always do he'll taste himself, still warm and strong-smelling on me. In me. And all of that, maybe especially all of that on my tongue and in my throat where it hasn't all gone down yet, will taste to me like his — well yes, Jesus,* fuck! — *like his color. His color that — that turns me the fuck* on, okay, *but that sometimes also makes me sick. Sick, I mean like sick to my stomach, I mean like I can't believe sometimes that in spite of everything I couldn't do better than (but don't you fucking think that, don't you ever fucking think that). Just like I think*

sometimes about what some guys who know me would say if they knew. Guys who don't know D Things like Hmmph, they would say with that smirk, that nasty curving smirk, so you're into that stuff, huh. As if they know what you're thinking, know exactly what you're thinking and who you are, when the fact is, even friends, they really don't know shit. It's hard not to hate some of them sometimes, it's hard not to wish that they'd fucking *die in a car accident or worse* — I mean die, motherfucker, I mean drive off a *fucking* cliff and crash and burn and let me be there, oh Jesus *fuck* let me be there to see what gets left behind. Hate. With people who say they're "friends" but judge you and talk shit about you, that's when it feels good to fucking hate. But sometimes too even now when I take him in and look down and see his skin sliding in and out of me, back and forth filling up all the space in my mouth and moving back and forth over my tongue, I know that I do feel like I could get sick, throw up even (especially) with him in me, even as I feel myself hard,* hard, *tasting him. Squeezing myself around him. Feeling him. Feeling you, David. Turned* on *because of you. Turned the fuck* on, *baby. Yes, always. But also because of your* —

But I already said it. I'll never say it again.

T
But I'll say it. Say the truth: that I'm surprised to find I still have so much to say, after so long of not saying anything at all. After everything else that happened, I didn't think that I was ever going to wind up talking about it, what happened between one of them and me and all that. But after thinking about all that they've said (and all they haven't said, God knows), it came to me that this would be a good place — maybe not the best, but *some*place — for me to ease myself in and what *I* have to say about it all, for once. For just this time.

Everything considered, you could see how hard it would have been to have been such a good friend to both of them like I was at that time, back then. A really good friend, the best kind, in fact, even though the truth is that now, right now I'm feeling way past the time that was *then*. *Then* was when I knew them, not that long after they met: the J and D I knew them for a while, a couple of years, actually. But what happened to them after that, well . . . your guess is as good as mine, maybe better. I don't know if D died or not after those guys came after him that day, or what the J ended up deciding about anything — about D, the future, his own life. I hope that D did survive that beating, the kind of beating that practically nobody could survive, or survive without some really fucked-up aftershit. I mean like brain shit, I mean like . . . I don't know. I was out of there by then. When I say "out" I mean like *far* away, I mean like gone for good. I hope that if he did live through it, he and the J stayed hooked up. They should have. I mean, you just had to see them together to know what that was all about, no matter what else was going on. But the truth is that I don't have any way of knowing any of these things . . . and even if I could know, I'm not sure I'd want to. The truth might be too — scary, maybe. Or just too raw. And the plain truth is that I haven't lived near them for *years* now, I mean like years and years. I got the fuck out of that fucked-up place years ago, and put *it* and all those people I wanted to forget, including the both of them for a while, far, I mean *way* far behind me. Believe me when I tell you that I was only too happy to get out. Happy to leave, to change my name, and to start working on like, I don't know . . . becoming somebody else. Somebody else trying to think for a change of other ways to make money in other ways than how I'd mostly done it there, like mainly on my knees or with somebody else's what*ev*er, plus his sad story, in my mouth. You think you'd catch me dancing on a bartop now, pulling ten-dollar bills into the crack of my ass when those old faggots would sit there grinning or just staring and holding the money in their teeth for me to catch? *Lower* *your ass over me, prettyboy. Let me kiss it, let me suck it, let me put my face right in it.* That's what their faces would say. But now I don't think so. Let me say it again: I don't *think* so. D and the J knew these things about me, but, well . . . that didn't stop what happened from happening. And now for all I know D could be working on his house, or in that ugly shitgarden that surrounded it, with the J heading over any minute for some more of their (yeah, uh huh, all *that* again). I don't know which one of them liked it more, but . . . well, I won't even get into that now.

I won't get into it partly because I don't always like to remember all that. I don't always like to remember the way he used to look at me and put his hands on my (yes, he did, and yes I did like it most of the time) while the other one was only a few feet away, I mean like in the *next room*, I mean like watching TV and saying shit like *Baby, come look at this.* Right there, had no idea, and us carrying on. And I don't like to remember it partly for other reasons. Reasons like the way it started to get so fucked up, I mean like scary, like *real*, when I started to feel that way about him and the way he smelled when he came to me, I mean actually *came* to me when, later on, I began having all those dreams: the dreams that always had him in them looking at me and touching me like that. Dreams that started out as dreams and ended up as him in me, him sweating and breathing on me while inside me. I used to think, Jesus Christ. When I think about those dreams and all that happened after I know I won't call his name even now. I won't tell even now how he did it to me, did what he'd always dreamed of doing and hadn't had the chance to do, I mean *really* do, up til then. It really bothers me even now to remember how we did it, all of it and more, behind the other one's back. How he lay down on top of me like that all those times, covering me completely and pressing down so hard and grinding, *grinding* with his face in the back of my neck, every time gripping my shoulders or my hips and asking me didn't I like it, *like* it: You love it, don't you, he said. (Even now, after all that, I can't figure out if he was the one who liked doing it to the other one, or if the other one liked doing it to him. Or if they flip-flopped. You never can tell with people no matter what they look like. But anyway he never wanted to talk about that.) *Come on*, he whispered every time into the back of my neck, *tell me how much you love it.* Gripping me. Almost forcing, though I always said Yes. *Tell me how much you want it.* Grinding. I cried out then sometimes and sometimes I pressed my face into the pillow, it hurt so much. I think he liked that: knowing that he was hurting me sometimes. Knowing that he was *killing* me sometimes. Yeah, he did, because he knew that he was — what do people say, the shit they always say — he was having an *effect* on me. Like when I did stuff to him that he liked and he would grab me and hold on and cry out *T*, or groan my full name, but even then I wouldn't stop. And I — . . . well, yeah, why not admit it? Fuck it. I did. I wanted him to hurt me. Yeah, *hurt* me, I thought. *Go on*, I thought every time, *do it until I can't take it anymore*, and one time I even thought *Yeah, make me your* fuck*ing bitch* (and he liked calling me that), because he was *in* me then, in me all the way and I knew he was mine with me holding on to him like that even if he thought the way he liked to think that he was the one always in charge. *All right, bitch*, I used to think, *but I got you inside me, you want to be inside me more than you want* him *the other one touching you and that makes you mine more than you'll ever know*, I thought. Then he would put his hand underneath my throat and squeeze, squeeze and hold onto me hard and say *Of course we're not ever going to tell him about this*, meaning the other one: waiting to hear me say, *Naw, of course not, we won't tell.* As if I would have. Or could have. And I haven't. I'm not telling partly because I did know the truth, exactly what he didn't think I knew, and what we never talked about: why he wanted me. Not somebody else, but me.

He thought that I didn't know the secret part of it even though I used to always catch him looking at me, *looking* front and back and up and down even when you-know-who was right there — I mean *right* there, standing between us talking about some TV show or movie and whatnot or sitting down somewhere not far off looking through some magazine like he didn't have a clue, which he never seemed to. Fucked up. I got the looks and felt his hands on me when he could get away with it — and that was hot, okay, I admit it, very hot, because it was a secret between us, it was a secret *right there* and *no one* else ever knew — and as soon as all that shit began to happen with his hands and I began to think about what it might be like to feel him in me I knew it was only a matter of time before I would get underneath him to taste him and swallow him all the way and look up at him from underneath and show him in my eyes and with my arms wrapped tight, tight around his neck that I wanted *him*, him and nobody else, him and nobody else pushing into me and hurting me but kissing me at the same time and caressing my neck because he and me, we were, we had always been —

Yeah, because. Because we were the same. The same color. The same skin. That was why.

He'll deny it now if you ask him (but he'll never tell), but that was the fucking reason. The truth.

The same color, the same skin, and *oh Jesus*, I thought, *what the fuck were you thinking to go and put this boy in front of me and put that look on his face when he looks at me, when he stares? What were you thinking, God?*

He did admit it once. One night: he told me when we didn't have that much time but had a little time — just a bit — before he and the other one met up to go out. The same color, he said, but really quiet: the same skin, you and me. It's just so nice, he said, for once, to. . . . But I don't want to talk anymore about it, he said right after that. And so, grinding on top of me again, he didn't. He didn't say anything about how the whole thing, everything he felt about the other one and did with him, made him sometimes feel so ashamed. Ashamed, sometimes really torn up inside, because, well, people did stare when they walked together in some areas of the city, didn't they? People did give weird looks, or smirk or whatever into the collars of their jackets and winter coats, when they saw the two of them walking. He never said too much about all that, but I knew. Shit, you could kind of tell just watching them together when they were out in public — something about the way they kept a kind of space between them or whatever. I don't know how to describe it exactly. But anyway when someone grinds into you in secret and hurts you and then calls out your name and leaves his stuff inside you (yes, because we didn't use latex, he never wanted to use latex — I think you're fine, you look healthy, he always said to me, and I thought the same about him — and who wouldn't, really, looking at him?) — the same person that looks you in the eye and wants you to swallow him in a dark room that you use for that occasion and nothing else — when all that goes on, you know things. You know that he likes the way your skins look together even as (though without saying it, because no one can ever talk about any of these things) he wonders what it would be like, for once, to have it easier that way: same skin, no problems. Same skin, and it's easier — and it looks better. I thought so. He thought so. Same skin, and you don't always have to *talk* about this and that: about where I come from, and how we do it, and why it's like this in your fucking family but not in mine, all right? When someone presses his hands into your shoulders and grinds into you in a dark room and whispers in your ear, sweating on you like you're sweating on him and talking all kinds of crazy shit about how he wants to smell his most secret smells on your breath and taste them when he pulls that part of you into his own mouth, you know that, at least for the skin part of it, he'd really rather, I mean *really* rather be with somebody like you. Somebody who doesn't look anything like the one he's with. Somebody whose smells are closer to his own, and whose family and friends won't raise up their eyebrows like that when they meet you, see you. Because here's the truth, and we all know it: there are words for people like the other one. There are words for how they look and for everything else about them. But we can't say those words, at least not now, not out loud, because everything's changed, everyone says: things are supposed to be different now, aren't they? We're not supposed to use those words to talk about them, although we can still think them. Thank God we still have that, *all* of it, way deep inside, where the blood goes on and on, beating. The one place where we can still feel whatever the *fuck* we want deep inside and no one, *no one*, can know . . . uh huh. Thank God.

THE TORTURER'S WIFE

*B*UT IN THE EARLIER DAYS, THESE DEADWOMEN ARE saying (sitting in a circle, in a muddy field far from any homes or people, long after dark) — *in the earlier days, she truly had not known. No. Of course not,* they say. *A young laughing girl like that, as she had been when she first came to* Him, He *to her? And what a figure she'd had!* one woman says, sighing out of what remains of her face. *A gorgeous young thing she was back then, even while falling in love with* Him. *What do you mean "even while"?* asks another. (The Lost Whore Without Arms, they call her. She is remembering now the feelings on her fingers of rings. Her fingers, like her arms, now somewhere at the bottom of the sea.) *Especially while, you mean to say. Oh yes, well,* He *had that effect on her. On every woman,* another says, known among them as the One Who Never Stops Sobbing. (And it is true — since her death twenty-nine days ago, she hasn't. Sobbing now and still wearing the necklace of blood that He had given her.) *On every woman who survived* His *attentions, you mean,* says an old, toothless one, bent over to the point that what remains of her forehead touches the ground before her. *Yes, and the same for every man He favored also*, laughs another. They all laugh. And laugh some more. But they soon grow quiet, knowing that they will not be here long — for they are dead, after all, just a bunch of deadwomen with scars over their rotting flesh and amputations in a few places. If this is a dream — and tonight it is, once again, as always, her bluewashed dream of them — who can stand to gaze upon them for long?

In complete darkness, they sit in a circle, in this muddy field that changes color minute to minute from brown to black to blueblackbrown.

Those who still have complete faces try, from time to time, to look at each other.

Soon, all of them will feel a terrible, stabbing pain in their breasts (in what remains of their breasts, for a few). The pain will sear their decaying flesh to consume them utterly. The flames will come then — bright orange licks that will roast them unto blackest ash. They will scream, will feel unimaginable pain — worse than the pain that, in one of the secret underground places, had finally killed them. But how can they know that the flames that will finally incinerate them will, at least in this dream, be the rage of the dreamer? How can any of them know how much she, even while suffering their deaths and obliteration, hates them? *So many dying and deadwomen beneath a naked light bulb suspended far beneath the ground. The women who are gathered there now in complete darkness, sitting in that circle.*

The women who try from time to time — those who still have complete faces — to look at each other.

Being a witness is never easy, one of them thinks.

They return frequently. (She tosses on the pillow. Lying next to Him. Listening, in the deepest passages of her dream, to the sounds of His breathing next to her. He is there. Do the dead-women now watching her chest rise and fall, and her tossing, quail before the sight of Him?) Frequently, among many other voices. Yes.

She truly had not known. Hadn't known, when, younger, still a laughing glowing creature, about all those secret rooms. Twisted limbs. Eyelids sewn shut. Lighted cigarettes pressed into — but oh my God, I can't take anymore, one of them screams out. (She tosses on the pillow. He breathes. She registers His breathing. She tosses. Where, right now, can there be a place for her hands?) *And so the laughing glowing creature she had been had soon disappeared over the years, hadn't she, as the knowledge slowly, inevitably, became more, more . . . more* inescapable, *she herself came to think on the heels of all those increasingly thick-blue-dreamed nights, those hours lying beside Him . . . hours filled with listening to Him breathe. In. Out. Wondering what it would be like to hear Him breathe no longer. In, out.* The words once known only by deadwomen and deadmen (and who knew how many deadchildren) had finally been carried into her nights even by the things she had trusted for so long: the reliable evening breezes, seasonal rains, and the spreading sea that she had so long believed to be her friend. But at last even the sea had betrayed her — reviled her, when, on that afternoon not so long ago, in an hour when she had sought its caresses against her tender skin, it had thrown out to her from its depths that sightless chorus of mermaids. Those voices obsessed with
"falling,"
they had sung, gazing directly at her out of those sightless eyes,
"from planes."

But do not blame her, one of the deadwomen beseeches the others, even as she begins, with them, to feel the first fire licking at her flesh. *For who can know exactly what she will do when, soon enough, that rainfall of most secret parts clatters, in moonlight, upon her roof? How will she feel about the sea* then?

And about Him, the others murmur as the flames, in the field and beyond it, begin to roast their flesh —

And So Once Again Hating (But Really Fearing) Moonlight.
With Difficult Breathing, and Skulls

Yes, it is true. She abhors the moonlight.

Lying next to Him, breathing in His nightscents and the sweat glistening on the back of His neck, she does her best to close her eyes against it.

It frightens me, she thinks, *the way it shines so brightly, insistently, on skulls.*

(*The skulls that return every night,* she dare not think.)

It terrifies me, she thinks, *the way it exposes all those skeletons out there in the garden — in the garden*, she thinks, *where all those skulls are or soon will be. Out there*, she tries so desperately not to think, *where I know all those hands lie waiting. Waiting* —

(But tonight is still weeks away from the time she will send the maid out there to sweep up that most unbearable rainfall of hands.)

It is hard to breathe, she thinks, lying next to Him.

I'm afraid to breathe, she thinks. *Afraid to breathe in too much of Him, all of those things that made me so wild when I was a young girl. Oh God*, she thinks —

Afraid to see His face in the faces of my children.
Our children.
(*His*)

The moonlight, she knows, reveals skulls. Gleaming. Grinning. Skulls of bodies dumped "somewhere out there," she thinks, "in the secret places that everyone pretends don't exist." The moonlight reveals "teeth," she thinks (but trying so hard right now not to breathe Him in), "knocked out by truncheons. Scattered like dice. And fingernails," she thinks (but how can she bear to think of *that?*), "— that the men, working down there, in all those secret rooms everyone says don't exist, wrenched out. With pliers," she thinks, screwing shut her eyes, clenching her fists.

Moonlight, she thinks, listening for the clattering of the first skull's teeth outside, surely, in the front garden. One of them will soon come. One of them always, in the dream-hours, comes. Hangs. *Hovers. Moonlight*, she thinks, *reveals too much. Like the most vulnerable kind of face*, she thinks, *capable of hiding nothing*.

Song (But from a Chorus of Mermaids). The Madwoman, in Flight

But now here: of an afternoon in a place that she will insist is part of another dream, although today she actually is here: a long narrow beach of sand and salt, salt and all that water, that so-enormous water she had once (but why?) believed to be her "friend" and somehow "protector" — pulling her legs down. *Down*. It is here, in what she has managed to convince herself is this afternoon's dream, that she will refuse to see them. Refuse to see the women whom she had seen long ago in the bluegreengray waters of so many other dreams. The same women whose bodies, this afternoon, will shortly surface and surface again from beneath that sea's curling waves. She is here, alone (and so happy for once to be alone — out in the sunlight so much is easier) — on this beach: not the dirtier, more dangerous public beach accessible to all, but this private one where she and people like her can come without care to bathe, laugh; to delight in the unexpected pleasures of an afternoon. A beach surveilled, sometimes unobtrusively, by His uniformed men. A place where women, women like herself, even alone, can feel safe: no catcalls, no ogling, nor (but she will not think of it) anything worse. It is an unlikely day even for someone like her, a woman of relative leisure, to visit the beach — a weekday. But only two hours ago or so she had ventured forth from His house (their house) so high up above the city, to "escape," *yes, it had definitely been an escape*, down to the beach to bathe in this surf that, as she will later recall (though right now still completely unsuspecting), had, on her arrival, so blithely licked its lips, and beckoned her with those soothing if slightly odd refrains of *Return   Come   Return*. She lies on her back now on the blanket she has brought, feeling something sublime; feeling actually vaguely "happy," she thinks; noting the freewheeling dives and swoops of seabirds as, her eyes just barely closed against the moody in-and-out sun, she recalls the faces of her children — the faces she will see again in only a few hours. And so in this repose she is at peace, she thinks: *I am at peace, I am nobody. I am alone. . . .*

Who will ever know exactly how she knew to sit up so abruptly in the next moment as she did? If the sky had any idea, it discloses nothing now to the sand and the water so far below. It continues to gaze down at her with a blank, impassive face. Gazes down at her as she jerks to her feet with a cry, because she *does see them*, she thinks, *but how can they be here?* All those women out there, in the surf. Out there looking directly at her but as if they are blind. All of them, rising up out of the waves and standing. Standing there. Dripping. Naked. Sightless. Clutching their breasts, she sees: clutching the places where their breasts should be. Crying. No, singing. A tuneless song. A chorus of blind mermaids singing

"About the planes," they sing,
"the planes, so full of us, and counting,
laden with bodies and counting,
drugged bodies and counting,
bodies dying, unmoving,
parts twitching, soon to rest
as they lifted off and *up*, the pilots,
with us all inside and counting,
took off to bank sharply out over the sea,
always at night, the darkest hours,
the time when (yes, it is true) some were pulled —
pulled out,
out
from their homes,
blindfolded,
gagged,
manacled and bound,
along with others to whom that all had happened long ago,
then loaded into the (yes, into the planes)
(counting)
the fingers of a few officers on board even then
diddling more than a few of our
cunts,

drugged cunts,
deeply asleep, unspeaking cunts,
unanswering-back cunts,
officers' cocks dipping into drugged flesh for one last
(yes, with all of us)
before they took their final count and
dumped us,
pitched all of us, some still living,
still breathing (though drugged),
into the so-far-below sea.
The planes, the planes," they sing,
"and us falling beneath the waves.
So far down beneath the waves.
Those waves —"

But then her absolute refusal. Refusal to admit, before their sight-less eyes, clasped hands, and all of their wounds, that a scream at last explodes out of her; impels her feet beneath her; provides her with the speed with which she hurtles so fast so far from them from the song from the waves from the soldiers guarding the sands the redsun redsun redred beach. Away from all of them still standing there naked sightless but seeing her somehow (yes, she knows it) and holding each other's hands above the curling returning waves *oh all that foam* as she flies, as she: *Because no,* she insists, flying, *No. I never saw them.* As she had screamed and screams now. *In the beach in the dream but today. No,* she insists now *(what is the way out —?). I was never there.*

Her eyes tightly closed. Screwed shut. Locked. Because of course some of the mermaids hadn't washed up headless. Handless. Headless and handless to elude dental records, fingerprint trac-ing. How very clever, she dare not think. How impossibly clever of Him, His cover-ups. *How invincible* (but she is not thinking this, she tells herself) *the machetes of His soldier minions.* Ah, but the sun. How it still shines, she sees: now yellow, not red. How the trees flare green, gold. How the day — in dreams, in actuality — still beckons. Life, she thinks, then mouthing the word, "Life": something perhaps still possible, as — not entirely to her surprise — she runs. Feels herself running. Still. And faster still. Racing —

Later, gathered in market squares beneath retreating light, or plaiting their children's hair while daydreaming about the whirr and secrecy of hummingbirds, assorted watchers in the small town that is not far from that sea (a place soothed in twilight hours by the sea, by its crooning, those same curling sighing waves and their perpetual call of *Return, come, stay*) will recount to each other in hushed tones that afternoon's vision they all had shared: that sight of the madwoman racing through their midst, screaming what had sounded to them not like a scream but a toneless song. *Like a song of long ago,* one of them will say. *Long ago, no,* will say another. *As new as the last hour's whispers.* A song without tone of deadwomen standing before her there and still so red, she had screamed, in the surf. A chorus of dead mermaids baring before her and the waning afternoon the evidence of their lacerated breasts. A chorus singing of what had happened to them in secret hours of blindfolds and handcuffs (and of course, she had guessed: interrogations), and most of all what had been done to them as they had lain drugged in the planes — *the planes,* she had screamed, running. What had been done to them that *He,* only *He,* she had cried out, could have arranged. Out of the sky, into the sea, to form a redchorus of once-were-women, with missing parts. Once-were-women with too much shame, she had screamed to the retreating sky, or none at all.

The Country Itself. But Also She

As a place of beauty? But unparalleled, of course. A place of dark, lean-flanked mountains with sturdy shoulders, more than willing to accept the sea's reliable fawning at their feet. A country busy with trees, birds — birds of which there are many thousands, even millions, all of which (perhaps having received news of the excesses of the evening patrols) make certain to sequester themselves after dark.

Beauty and majesty in this place in every type of flower, every sort of butterfly, and in the most fantastically designed insects known to inhabit the sphere. Lushness in rolling hillocks everywhere, and meadows only too pleased to preen beneath the sun that adores their wide-open bellies. A guaranteed rainy season, and — for at least the past two hundred years — none of the devastating betrayals of volcanoes. Nor those of earthquakes. Broad fields ripe with crops whisked quickly enough to the teeming capital, and a surfeit of cracked hands only too willing to work them. Better roads than ever before. Telephone service in almost every village.

And freedom — for the country is, certainly, a free one. So free, so filled with so many choices (flee or remain; survive or die; remember or forget; laugh loudly in daylight, or sob in deepest darkness until a fearsome pounding at the door, accompanied by the growling of waiting jeeps and the clicking of long rifles). So many choices that none of the citizens need even believe in freedom, and in fact are encouraged by those presiding not to do so. Why entertain the need to believe in it, this thing called "freedom," when it so clearly abounds? the citizens are asked. You might as well believe in air, they are told, or in light; you might as well believe in the passing of time, as if such belief would make any significant difference. You need not *believe* you are alive when you so clearly are. Do snakes *believe* that they possess skins, fish *believe* that they sport fins? Does the sea *believe* in its perpetual embrace of the shore?

Similarly, those presiding remind the nation, one need not believe in things that simply are not true, and which, here, have obviously never been true: that in this, our beloved and gorgeous country, extrajudicial executions are regularly carried out in secret; that innocent people are kidnapped nightly from their homes, to emerge from other places some time later as assorted hands, legs, feet, and arms in small black plastic bags; that more than fifty secret mass graves litter the country, especially the lowland rural areas and the more remote mountainsides in the north; that the most promising soldiers in the nation's sleek army were trained abroad in an infamous school in the most ingenious practices of "detainment" and "innocuous interrogation"; that the very young children of those allegedly kidnapped people — infants and toddlers, mostly — have occasionally been sold on a so-called black market as "orphans" to childless couples; and that He — known in most quarters simply as He — in His splendid uniform, an official of elevated rank just below our cherished President, is, with our President and so many lieutenants, commanders, generals, and soldiers, "behind" it all. "Behind" that which, of course, never occurs.

He: as everyone knows, of magnificent shape and height. Promoted to his rank only five years ago, at a still-useful age, after sixteen sterling years in the illustrious armed forces. (No, of course He hadn't worked for the secret police during those years. How could He have done, when — remind yourself now, please — such a thing has never existed?) He: blessed with a house of enviable design and size, flanked by an Elysian garden, well situated in the palatial suburbs high above the teeming capital, with that ever-matchless view of the boundless sea. Blessed too with His children: two adorable dumplings, who, naturally enough, resemble Him, and whom, laughing heartily,

He bounces frequently enough on His knees; and blessed most
noticeably with His superb wife — known by many as She, but
more commonly, among many, by her actual name. A lovely
name. A name that brings to mind swaying bluebells, lilacs, and
the scent of roses glancing off lithe trellises in sultry-houred afternoons. She who had first encountered Him in her earlier days
when still a young laughing thing. Encountered Him as a girl at
that time bedazzled by His beauty and His force — as, shortly
thereafter, He, gazing upon her, swiftly enchanted by the lively
glow she had invariably brought in those times to dulled faces
and dim corners alike, had felt rapidly genuflect within Him
that thing, that indefinable whatever-thing, that, so tripped unawares within Him, compelled Him whenever in her presence
in the time that followed those first gazes, and for years after, to
adopt both before and beside her (at embassy parties, at so many
required functions of state) the precise adoring position: a sometime (though subtle) bowing of the head, an occasional lowering
of the hands, and an always murmuring of her name, followed
in His deepest mind by the word "She," He had thought; by the
word "Mine," He had thought, and always by
    Exactly. By the word "Yes."
    He who had built for them and the children they would
soon bring forth that enormous house so far up above the city.
She who, on His magnificent uniformed arm, lifted high in one
easy swing by Him and carried across the threshold, had moved
into it with Him and a flock of servants ready for her (surely)
imperious command. He who, on so many nights and even during the days, had steadily risen and fallen above her there; had
panted and, in earnest desire, conjured her face beneath Him;
had imagined the conquering and plundering of continents
as — though she had not, at the time, felt so — He had in
fact conquered her; subdued something in her; quelled her, of
course — but had also somehow tenderly come to know some

most indefinable and secret part of her, a part not easily given to surrender. He marveling all the while as she had lain beneath Him at what had so unquestionably become, without significant contest, truly His. Spoils. Endless riches. A fertile plain for the planting of much seed, and seed planted again. She who, as He had labored and panted, risen and fallen, had gazed up at Him and clung to Him, her arms about His broad back, in adoration, fulfillment, absolute wonder.

She who had not, at that time, turned her face to the wall in darkness and pondered the flesh of deadmen. No, nor feared the power of moonlight to bear witness.

She who, at that time, had had no fear of skulls or stones raining down upon their (His) roof.

Nor had she felt anything then about what she had not yet discovered: all those other deadwomen who had begun to infiltrate her dreams.

She who, like Him, had always appeared to love the gorgeous, spreading country so completely free it need not concern itself with freedom. The same she, who, lovely to the eye as she had appeared during those early years, rapidly began to fade sometime in the last . . . but who can remember, in a place where remembering is anyway never wise? Sometime in the last whenever. Began to fade, as if, plagued by unfortunate dreams, she became, at first, slightly — ever so slightly — haggard; then, over time, more so. More thin about the mouth, some thought, and darker than ever in those depthless eyes. Oh, those eyes. And legs. Yes, even now. Even now such overall form. A body still capable of outdressing every other woman in the nation. A being still capable, despite a fuller knowledge of who exactly, in the nation's long history, He has been and continues to be, of grace. Elegance. Style, in spite of all those things brought to her by gradually more insistent dreams, whispers, voices *out there*: secret underground chambers, and blistered testicles set afire before the next round of shouts and punches beneath the naked, dangling light bulb. Ah, yes, some of the citizens had long murmured and sighed, for years, a model of *haute couture*. Utter aplomb. She.

Garden, Morning Sun; Keeping at Bay Thoughts of Killed Children

But then let her have it: this most secret, nourished hatred. For it is now, after all these years, what she most reliably possesses. What she possesses as, from day to day, pondering her impossible thoughts, she meanders the spreading garden of that house; as she envies the ignorance, simple destinies, of birds. What she possesses aside from her children, who remain — like everything else — part of Him.

Allow her this private, cherished, solitary time in the beckoning garden. He far off in the teeming city at work ("or something," she thinks, feeling the grimace).

Allow her to feel the sun's soft nuzzle along her exposed shoulders, the breeze from the far-off sea carrying to her today the scents merely of sea, not of a redchorus of ruined mermaids.

Allow her, as she strolls, to register that great relief — the relief that comes when, gradually cajoled (seduced) by the sun, she is unable to think. Unable to recall deep-throated dreams. The relief a sojourn that she knows will not last.

Allow her not to summon the very late night, or the very early morning, when she just might — yes, just possibly — murder her children. Murder them perhaps because "they so resemble Him," she thinks, and because she also fears "what they might become," she thinks, "carrying His blood." (She will not dare, right now, to look down at her hands.) What they might become "as they grow," she thinks, "and as they —" but she cannot finish that thought. *What they might finally have in them*, she thinks, especially the boy, who just might (but who really can ever know these things? Who can ever —) "just might have all of *that* in him from *Him*," she thinks, shuddering-nearly-trembling in the sun. "All of *that* in him," she thinks, "my God. And so much more."

Her head hurts. Too much to think. Too much sun. And no, she thinks, *no*: she has not, absolutely not, lost her mind.

"But even now," she tells the deadman lover who visits her regularly in the hidden room of her most desperate hours, the deadman whose face she can never forget — the deadman who wraps her securely and warmly in what remains of his arms: what the soldiers, before running over his prone body with their jeep, had permitted to remain of his arms, "— even now, sometimes, I really do. I want to —"
    "To kill them," he says, stroking her face with a decayed wrist. "Your children. The two of them. Yes. I know."
    "I want to kill them not because I don't love them," she says, pulling so hard on his withered cock — pulling on it a way she could never have dared do to Him *— "because, in truth, I do love them. They are my —"*
    "They are your —" Pressing ruined lips to her throat.
    "My most precious —"
    "Your most beautiful —"
    "Yes," she whispers, squeezing his mutilated testicles against her belly, "my most precious beautiful gorgeous things."
    "Except for the flowers in your garden," he whispers, massaging her breasts.
    "Except for . . . yes, but they are the flowers in my garden. They remain so."

"They always will be."

"Oh yes," she says, moving down to kiss his withered cock. "For all time."

Years later, the walls of that hidden room of her most desperate hours, the walls of that room filled with the stench of a decaying deadman and the misery of a still-beautiful woman, will still remember: recall how, in that next moment, she rose up to climb onto and sit on the shimmering tip of her deadlover's cock. It was there, swaying backward and forward, that she began telling him, through all those tears, what he already knew: how

They are her children,   *"Yes, mine,*

But to have to see, every day,   *"Always,*

His face in theirs,   *"Can you imagine the horror,*

His laughing in theirs,   *"Oh my God, as if I,*

And His smile, those teeth,   *"'Close your mouth, children, don't smile,' I sometimes tell them,*

So that she does sometimes, yes,   *"Of course,*

Want to obliterate them,   *"Eradicate them,*

Wipe clean from the earth's face   *"Annihilate them,*

His finest creations,

And kill myself too,   *"Yes, rip open my own throat,*

For how frightening it is — is it not?   *"Of course it is,*

That they, her most precious somethings,   *"Might grow up to be a something like Him,*

And that their Father, in addition to all else,   *"Yes, all else,*

Betrayed me, lied *to me, with*	*"Lied to you,*
so many others,	*yes, and to*
	others,
And then there are also the	*"Of course*
moments	*there are,*
of perversity,	
Moments when she thinks,	*"When I think,*
Ah, and now how will You	*"To come home*
feel,	*and find Your*
	children
	dismembered,
Your boy's little mushroom,	*"Yes, ripped out*
	and stuffed
	down his throat,
Your daughter's budding	*"Yes, carved.*
breasts,	*Sliced. Forced*
	down into her
	deepest part,
All because, like those others,	*"All those nameless*
	others,
they would not tell,	*"They would not tell,*
they would not	*"Oh no. To the soldiers.*
	Tell."

*She weeps out the tale to him once again: the confession, rocking
back and forth on his cock: grateful to be able to tell him again what
she has told him so many times before: grateful to be able to tell
someone — even a deadman who, she knows, by the time she comes
(if indeed she comes this time), by the time she looks down fully from
her rocking and crying, will be gone, gone again: I am bereft, she is
bereft, I wanted to murder my children unable to bear the thought
of His face growing in theirs, I could not stand the idea that one day
they and the boy especially might grow to become like Him and oh*

*my God to bring about more redchoruses of mermaids thrown out
of planes into the sea and so many daughters incinerated (but first
raped) and so many sons raped and carved up their remains fed to
the pigs the goats the dogs the:*

    *but I cannot bear it but he the deadman who always came to
me in that hidden room kept every time my hand from striking
them down slicing open their throats shooting them in the head as
they slept shooting them with the pistol He keeps in the house in that
room in that cabinet for our "protection" and: no she thinks I did
not kill them I will never kill them I will*

*— she thinks, coming; gasping: holding onto the hips that already
are no longer there; holding fast to the cock that has already vanished
beneath her and the thighs that already are no more, as the walls of
that room that does not quite exist will remember many years from
now, as she sobs, sobbing, looking down now to see without doubt
that he who on so many afternoons like this one, through so many
dreams like this one (but not quite a dream), provided her with both
pleasure and comfort even in the midst of his remorseless decay: he
who, as so many times before, is "gone," she thinks, slowly sliding
down off the mound of her conjure, to lie there once more alone and
finger herself in the sorrow that flushed through her coming: "gone,"
she thinks, "the way he must have gone when His men came and
took him away from wherever it was, and took his wife, too, and
children . . . the grandparents survived because he had long before
sent them into hiding abroad. Gone," she thinks, fingering where a
deadman's cock had just rubbed against what He had always half-
playfully called her "rose" (ridiculous, she had always thought, what
a ridiculous term for a part of the body that was), "and who knows,"
she thinks, lying there so alone in the room that is now slowly becoming another one, one of light and billowing curtains into which
she knows the children she has not killed will soon race, shouting,
with news of school and the day, "who knows," she wonders, turning*

*her face away from the billowing curtains and back to her fleeting
entertainments of death, "who knows when, if ever, he will come
again?"*

Parties; A Smile; Astonishment Regarding the Body That Is Not Hers

But how could she not despise them? All those stupid laughing
women? The women so brightly attired in silver. In gold and dia-
monds. The women whose hands, at the last shining party, had
fluttered like the sparrows' wings that have never, not ever, come
to comfort her. Fluttered as their mouths sipped red wine, champagne (imported from "the continent"), and asked in those so
bright voices how she was doing these days, darling, and doesn't
she look di*vine*? Divine, darling, and how jealous we all are of
you looking so splendid, so lovely with that gorgeous uh huh
absolutely *beau*tiful husband of yours. Yes, my dear, you know
He is. And in that uniform . . . a few epaulets make all the difference, don't they . . . in the position He's in at his age, and so
tall, so grand, well . . . you can only imagine the things He'll be
doing in this country in another five years. . . . But then wait.
For how could they not have seen? Seen the rage and contempt
in her eyes, and the loathing, even though her hands, her very
own hands, also had reached for this tray or that one of champagne flutes carried about with perfect balance by the ever-silent
white-jacketed, white-gloved waiters . . . how could they all not
have sensed that her whinnying laughter was merely a response
to their own? Could they, none of them, not see how much she
abhorred Him? "My dear, they look *so* good together —" (yes,
well, they always had), "and before you know it, she'll be carrying another one." "Of course, with a man as virile as Him, and
that body of hers. . . . " "*Made* in Paris, my dear, as if she just

stepped off the Champs-Elysées, like nothing you would ever see in this country, except at one of our parties, of course. . . ."

They had never known. Her smile, so well held in place by the accustomed muscles, had revealed nothing, hidden everything. "But who *is* that woman, standing next to you, smiling like that?" — so she, not quite awake, sitting half-upright in bed, had asked Him one morning on glancing at that photo — god, not another one! — on one of the newspaper's pages.

"Who," He had half-absently responded. (He had already dressed and inspected Himself, but something had momentarily distracted Him: a button missing, God forbid, from His uniform; a bit of lint on the cuff.) "Why, you, darling," He told her, laughing, looking down at the photo over her shoulder, "who else? What an odd sense of humor you have sometimes, my sweet." Bending down His towering form to kiss her. To press His freshly shaven face close to hers. (She had caught the scent of shaving cream: lime, one He liked and had reminded her earlier that morning to make sure and remind one of the house staff to pick up that week; something so *masculine*, she'd thought, not quite permitting her lower lip to curl and disclose the clenched teeth prepared, given the right circumstances, to snarl.)

Me? The word formed without form in her mind. *Me?*

She looked carefully at the newspaper. Blinked. Then, in the photograph before her, regarded her own smiling, if glazed, face. Blinked again, then thought . . . but what she thought she could hardly say. For her thoughts just then formed not words, but colors.

She felt His mouth touch her skin as, still utterly dazed, she sat on the bed amid rumpled sheets and a comforter, her mouth half-open in that way He had always, even from the very beginning, found so "adorable," He'd once told a lieutenant. "Just like her, you know? Always so in her own little world, and still so innocent." Her mouth had hung half-open, suggesting in her face the beginning of the slightly stupid look she had habitually, when taken unawares by it before unexpected mirrors, despised; and her brain — well, "frazzled" had been the only word she'd been able to summon in those moments to describe, accurately, the sensation: "I am 'frazzled,'" she'd thought, "to see myself smiling that way, in that dress that looks so ridiculous, at some embassy party or the other, holding onto His arm as He puts His face next to mine (bending down as always) to plant a kiss on my cheek."

Even with that half-dazed expression still on her face (one of the maids would soon come in to make up the bed and tidy up the scattered nightclothes), she had been pondering — though far behind her veiled eyes — knives. Knives, of course. One or many, right there, in her smooth though trembling hands: hands awake or dreaming or (as was so often the case) someplace restively in between. Any large shining knife that, securely grasped, would complete the necessary task as He slept beside her; as, between shiftings, twitchings, rapid eye movements, occasional teeth-grinding, he called out to the darkness or murmured indecipherable things, memories not yet revealed. She envisioned His naked back, so smooth and broad, hairless, as He slept; or, better yet, His chest. His chest into which she. Into which she would. His chest into which she now feels trembling at the thought: trembling over the danger, utter cruelty, *daring,* of the thought. She feels that swift leap of her eyebrows that means *I have transformed,* she thinks, *no longer she but* She . . . but, feeling the slow trembling now quaking throughout her, the trembling that could so easily (*but pretend it isn't so*) carve up her children and rip to shreds the entire world's living fabric, she drops it. Drops the knife that is not there in her hand. Banishes it. Banishes all of them — butcher, cleaver, bread knife. Banishes them to the place where dead lovers disappear, where deadwomen and skulls do not, at least not so insistently, call her name. She is startled, of course, when He whom, in this reverie, she had long ago left behind, walks up to her still sitting there on the bed with her mouth half-open ("So innocent! Always in her own little world"), and pats her on the head, does something like kiss her on the head; says something now like

—*Goodbye*—

and

—*Have a lovely day, I'll see you later tonight*—

as she sees and feels herself lift a hand, an all at once weary and fragile hand, in adieu: adieu, my love, her hands seems to say. The illusion must go on, she knows, like her condemnation: it must continue.

She sits there for some time. ("Not now," she tersely tells the maid who puts her head around the door to inquire if Madam is finished, if she may tidy the room, "in five minutes, please.") She visits, once more, rooms that do not quite exist. Inhales in them the forlorn scents of dead lovers. Deadmen who, in the very worst of times, can always be relied on to make ghostly love to her on creaking beds wrenched out of blue (but, thank God, not red) dreams. Some time later — only minutes later, possibly, or hours — she understands the truth. The truth as to "What I know now," she says in a room that is not quite there. "The simple fact that I am not living in my own body. So that when He kissed me," she says out loud, "or kissed that woman who had my face and was smiling in the newspaper photo as she held that glittering champagne flute, I was completely unaware of it because I wasn't there. That wasn't my body," she tells the room that gazes so dully back at her, "nor was it my face, or my mind behind those eyes so full of laughter in the photo. That's why, for so many years now (and who can count them?), I have never felt Him when He has touched me, because He hasn't touched me. No, not me.

"Them," she thinks, feeling the knives once again in her

hands, "His face so close to theirs, underground beneath a naked light bulb, and the sound of other men's laughter. But not me.

"I live in dreams," she tells the not-there room. "In those dreams (though I would prefer that most of them were different) is where my body, my truest body, truly begins.

"And as for this," she tells the room, looking down at the body covered in pajamas, "well, I don't know.

"I do not know who *she* belongs to or even — sometimes, yes, sometimes — what her truest name will finally be."

A Rainfall of Hands, A Nineteen-Day Sweep

MAID:
"Well, yes. She did. It's been nineteen days now, and she did ask me on that day, or, no, *commanded* me, to . . . but wait. I want you to listen. I mean listen carefully. Because — well, because I would never say a word against her. I still love her with all my heart. Oh yes, I do. I've been with her and the Sir fifteen years, right from the time they got married. (Such a gorgeous bride she was, and He! — He looked so handsome in His uniform! So happy!) And, well, never in all that time until now — never in all that time did she ask me to do anything so, so —

"So *outrageous*. Yes, that's the word. Outrageous, unbelievable, what you see me doing now. Right here. Always. Alone. In tears.

"'Come here,' she called to me that morning. And, well, no . . . in truth, she didn't look so good that day. She didn't look like herself. I mean, you know the Madam! She was always made up so beautifully, with her hair just so — everything just so . . . like a true . . . I don't know, majesty, she always was. Perfect, I mean. And the loveliest dresses, and shoes . . . yes, even at eight o'clock in the morning, always when the Sir was ready to leave for the city and the children were packed and ready to be driven by the chauffeur to school. . . . But that day, well —

"All right, then. No, I don't want to say it, but . . . well, it's true. She did look as if she hadn't slept in days. Deep, deep rings under her eyes, there were, and her beautiful skin looking so . . . I don't know. So sickish, sickly, as if she really was sick. And — well, you know, she really was . . . was *swaying* a little bit. Looking a little unsteady on her feet. But her eyes were bright enough — almost as if she had fever, or something. . . . And so she called me. When she called I always went quick. Why wouldn't I? I loved her. She was the Madam. She . . . yes, I loved her. I still do. With all my heart.

"'Yes, Madam?'

"She was shaking. I saw that as soon as I got up close to her. But in sickness or health, well — far be it from me to say anything to her, except what I tried to say, which was only:

"'Madam, is anything —'

"'I want you to sweep up all those hands outside. Every single one of them, in the garden and on the walkways. There are even some in the — in the *pool*,' she said in that shaking voice, as she covered her face for a minute. Standing there before me, swaying, and looking more sickly than ever. Looking like she was about to be ill.

"I — well, no, I didn't think I'd heard her right. Hands? *Hands?* You mean like *people's* hands? I thought. But I must have misheard her. She must've said 'ants,' or —

"'Why are you standing there looking at me like that?' she said. Her voice louder. And more — I don't know, like it had a — a pistol in it? Something. Something about to snap, or crack, or —

"'Madam?' I said. Staring at her.

"'I *said*' — she took one big deep breath then, as if she didn't want to repeat in any way what she had just told me to do.

"'I. Told. You. To go. To go sweep up. To go sweep up those — those *hands*,' she said, truly beginning to shake then. That was when — I'm sure of it — I began to get — to get really scared —

"'Madam —'

"'There are *thou*sands and thousands and *thousands* of hands in the garden!' she began to scream, moving closer to me and stretching out her own hands toward me as if she intended to (but she couldn't have, no; not the Madam. No!) hit me. Hit me! And I —

"'Hands all over the place,' she shouted, pulling me over to the hallway window. 'Look! Down there! Don't you see them?'

"'Madam, I —'

"'Burnt hands. Severed hands. Melted. Hands stuck all over with cigarettes. With lighted cigarettes stuck *into* them. With their fingers broken at the knuckles. And with — my God, but how could He — how could anyone have —

"'With their *fingernails* pulled out,' she whispered. Putting her own hands up to her face then and covering it. Shaking, her hands. I remember. Trembling.

"'Oh yes.' Very quietly. So quietly, she said that. 'Smashed by the hammers they use in that place. By the *wrenches* —' She covered her face again. 'They all fell down last night in the rain-storm.' Talking through the fingers covering her face. 'A rain-storm of hands clattering all over the roof and keeping me up all night. Some of them are already — look, girl, don't you see? — are already becoming, becoming —

"'Becoming skeletal,' she whispered. 'Down there.

"'But no,' she finished, turning away from the window and wrapping her arms about her shoulders and squeezing, squeezing herself that way as she began to rock back and forth: standing there in the morning sun streaming in from the window. The same sun that was shining over the garden below, where there were — I'm telling you honestly — *where there were no hands*. Only the forward lawn and the hedges and all the flowers she had always loved so much. And the marble statues. And the pool.

"'No,' she said, still turned away and rocking herself, 'not this. Not a rainfall of hands. Anything but this. Even the skeletons reaching to me out of the dreams I could take, up to a point. Even the deadmen who wanted me to do all those things to them as they told me one more time what He and His men had done to them I could take up to a point. But not this. Not hands. Not here. Not in this house. Not where my children — my children . . . *live*. No. *No*,' she said, and —

"She was moaning. Groaning. Sounding as if she needed so desperately to . . . to sob, cry out loud. But no sobs came. None that I saw.

"I — well, I was so terrified I couldn't — no, honestly, I just couldn't move. I couldn't —

"That was when — well, when I just went up right behind her and tried to — tried to, to just —

"To touch her. Hold her. Put my arms around her and say, Madam. Madam, please. Madam, it's all right, Madam. Whatever's bothering you, it's — it's all right, Madam, all right. You don't have to worry, Madam, I wanted to say — yes, so much! I wanted so much to say I'll take care of everything, Madam. You won't have to worry about anything. Haven't I and the others always taken care of everything since you and the Sir brought us here? You just rest now. Yes, rest, Madam. Madam, we all love you so much, I wanted so much to say, if only you would let me, let us —

"But that was when she did it. The moment my hands touched her, she jumped back from me and —

"Yes. She did. Struck me. Struck *me*, who had always loved her. Who had *worshipped* her. Who had sung songs to her children at night, through so many long afternoons, and comforted them and kept them company when she and the Sir were out at one of those parties. I'm telling you. She. Struck. *Me.*

"'Don't you — don't *you* ever put your hands on me like that again,' she said. Or no, she *hissed* it. Hissed it like a garden snake, or . . . and looked at me. Kept on looking at me that way.

"'Do you hear?' she hissed once more. Shaking as if she might break into pieces right there in front of me. Her eyes so bright, as if with fever.

"'Don't *any* of you ever touch me again. Not you, nor *Him.* Especially not *Him.*'

"'Madam, I —'

"But she had already turned away and, with her shoulders so caved in that way, in a way I had never ever seen in her before, slowly shuffled — she, the Madam, shuffled! — down the hallway, back toward her and the Sir's bedroom.

"'Just make sure that you get *every last one* of those hands cleaned up,' she called back, without looking back over the sunken shoulders. 'Do you hear?'

"'Madam, if you —'

"'Don't stop until you've cleared away every single last one. Otherwise . . .' — but her voice became even more faint then, like the whisper of —

"Yes, I thought. *My God,* I thought. Like the whisper of a ghost.

"'Madam . . .' I tried calling once more. But she was gone. Mumbling, whispering, then nothing. She was gone.

"What could I do? This is the only place I've ever known aside from my home. Both of my parents and my two brothers — that's right, and my grandmother — are all dead. In the countryside, that's right. Well, the northern mountains, really. My parents were taken away one night by some men in a jeep, after word reached the government about some kind of 'uprising' in our town. Uniforms? No, in that time they didn't always wear uniforms. Only the soldiers did. . . . The soldiers, three of them bearing enormous rifles, came for my brother much later, and my grandmother . . . I was a very small child then. On the night they came for my parents, I had been sent to sleep in the house of a woman who lived down the road, not far from where the forests begin. Everyone in town heard about what happened to my parents — well, of course, they weren't the first — and someone — no, I still don't know who, though I think it might have been the woman's young nephew — hid me underneath some dirty clothes in a basket. The next day, they both sent me across to the other side of the country to live with some of her people, who themselves vanished one night a few years later . . . yes, she herself is still alive . . . and her nephew . . . but no, I don't. Don't get involved in politics, everyone always told us. You never know who you might be talking to, or —

"And so I did. Of course. I had no choice, did I? I followed her instructions. Followed them with a broom in my hand, while weeping all the while in my most secret place for the Madam I once had known. That one. The one who had laughed and told stories and jokes to her children, and had always looked so happy when her husband, in those earlier years, had come home to her . . . both of them so young together and lovely. . . .

"And every few days — well . . . I wish it wasn't true. I *wish*. But it is. She comes out from her bedroom looking more exhausted than ever. She walks out to the garden, past the marble fountains, and asks me: 'How are you getting on?' 'Fine, Madam,' I say, 'just fine.' But I'm not fine at all. I never let her see how now I'm almost always crying. 'Ah, well,' she says, not quite looking at me but at something else, something that you'd think she sees in the garden there, from the way she frowns and then shudders, then closes, so tightly, her eyes. 'You missed one there, and one there, too,' she always says, pointing over to the manicured hydrangeas, or beneath the huge crouching pines. 'Yes, Madam,' I always say, turning my face away from her, and continuing.

"I don't know if the children have noticed, God save them. No, really, I don't know. Or the Sir. I don't know what they would say if they did. The angels. The precious little dumplings. A boy and a girl. They smile, and tease me: 'You're sweeping so much!' they say, 'like forever!' 'Like forever' is what it feels like, I can tell you. But mostly I — I miss her. The way she used to laugh. I want *her* back. Not the ghost. Not the — the *thing* that she became. That she still is.

"And so . . . well, now you know all of it. Now you know why you see me here in the garden perpetually crying, holding this broom in my hand. Holding it and sweeping up the hands she's so convinced are scattered everywhere about here. '*Decaying*,' she sometimes screams out at me. '*Curling*,' she sometimes screams, 'with their fingers broken at the knuckles. And the — the fingernails . . . pulled . . . no, *wrenched* —'

"And so that's why. Why I've been here all this time. Sweeping without end. Holding this broom and moving it back and forth, back and forth across the grass and beneath the trees, for these past nineteen days. Every day now. Always. Yes. Alone. In tears."

A Clattering; Transformations; The Sea

In years to come, before all of the events recounted herein are completely forgotten, another voice living or dead (or somewhere in between) will rise up out of the spreading sea and tell it: tell the truth about how it was the strange deluge of that night and no other that would finally propel her. Propel her into flight as soon as, so very late that final night, she awakened out of the sleep that as usual had been plagued with "dreams" — so came the word to her, abruptly, where, on that bed next to Him, she had lain perfectly motionless for hours, eyes wide open and fists and jaw clenched: "Will I never ever be free," she had wondered, those staring eyes focused on the dark ceiling, "of all these choking dreams?" Never be free, the ticking silence whispered back to her, aware of her shallow breaths, but nothing even in all those shadows and those that had come before could have prepared her for what happened next: the sound of clattering, outside, on the roof just above. A clattering as of insistent heavy rain which that night was not rain at all, but rather a rainfall of mutilated "vaginas," she knew instantly on hearing them. "Vaginas that, right now, this very minute, are raining down on the roof, in the very same way that all those hands did only weeks ago — hands, and now vaginas, filling up the garden."

It took her only a moment to spring, half-clothed, from her bed, to peer with that expression on her face out into the moonwhite garden. And so yes, she thought, believing the evidence of her eyes; for there, below, across the moonlit grounds, were indeed a scattering of "vaginas," she thought, "without question vaginas, nothing more nor less." Hundreds of them. "No, thousands," she thought, gripping the windowsill and not yet daring to glance back through the shadows at Him asleep. Vaginas everywhere. And, in long curling rivulets from where each one fell onto the grass with a thud, redness. Redness everywhere beneath the moonlight. Vaginas that had been "slashed out," one of the shadow-voices that always came to her in those hours whispered into her deepest ear just then, "and tossed into secret places. Secret graves. Or burnt. Chopped out," another voice among the shadows whispered to her. Vaginas clattering down out of the sky and filling the moonlit night; but how much more did her face change and change again when she began to see that, unmistakably, there could be no mistaking it, every single vagina falling out of the sky all at once changed upon its hitting the grass of her garden? Changed without any effort at all, to a face? — or, rather, changed from simply a vagina fallen from the sky to a vagina fallen and with a face at its very center. A face with eyes, lips, mouth; a face with a nose that surely, she thought just then, could scent her very blood; as those eyes, all those watching eyes and growing as more plummeted down onto the house and into the garden, gazed upon her "like the ruined mermaids," she thought, "except that these faces can see."

Staring down at them for one minute or two but no more, she soon apprehended that more than one of them, red and wet as they appeared in that without-mercy moonlight, began to mouth her name — to call her name as the sea might have done on a distant afternoon, with refrains of Come. Return. Come. She watched them upon the grass as more continued to fall, thudding upon the grass between those already moving, shining, glowing. Moving like spiders, some growing (but extremely quickly) the short, dark, bent limbs of spiders; clambering over each other, or tearing with the small teeth in their small mouths at the dewsoaked grass. A few of them scurried over the ground to devour unsuspecting night insects. But more than a few lay still — panting, gasping, as if in that moment, in all moments yet to come, nothing more for them could be possible. As if everything possible had ended long ago.

But then now, here, is especially what the voice either living or dead (or somewhere in between) will recall when, years later, it rises up out of the sea and recounts the events of this night: how, in this very moment, she sees and feels her body moving directly toward Him, still sleeping. Finally. Sees and feels herself moving toward Him as, amid the clattering outside and all those noises down on the garden grass, she feels within the hand that is somehow astonishingly her own the thing, the cold, hard, sharp, shining thing that cannot possibly be in it, she tells herself; the thing that, in regard to Him, she has dreamt of one day or night holding and using over and over again; the thing that cannot possibly now be in this hand that is somehow mine, she thinks, for how could something like this ever happen? Yet she feels it, that thing, ready and sharp in her amazingly not-trembling hand, and her hand knows it. Grips it. It had always been there somewhere, hidden not far from where, looking through *the darkness at Him sleeping, she now stands. Holding it, she moves closer to Him. Looks, briefly, at Him. Then looks around in the darkness. (But does not, will not, turn to look over her shoulder out the window at what continues to fall from the sky out there.) Looks at Him sleeping again; then moves closer, as the noises outside rise.*

Rise, as she, now standing over the sleeping Him and watched only by the lengthening shadows, sees with her very own eyes what happens next. Standing in the shadows, she sees that woman who so incredibly resembles her raise a hand, the hand holding that long, sharp, shining thing, and plunge it into Him. Once. Twice. Three times. Then her ears hear that noise. A gurgled cry. She sees: those arms, flailing. Grasping, uselessly, the air. Then the head above the arms turned, jerking, its eyes all at once widely, terribly open. How is it that her eyes suddenly know the danger of looking at those eyes? She looks at them. Into them. (But she is not there, she thinks all at once. No, though she feels herself standing there, utterly still, watching with her face also utterly still, she knows that she cannot possibly be there.) She sees how the woman looks steadily down at Him with that expression on her utterly still face, unflinching, not moving, as she herself, watching and feeling that thing pressing so hard against her hand and feeling her face still so completely still, does not flinch. Does not flinch despite His violent cry, despite His useless arms. Despite all that coughing, spitting. The gurgling of a throat engorged. She sees Him grab out wildly again at the air and attempt, jerking with that terrible gurgling sound, to sit up in the bed with that look in His eyes, that look, as she watches the woman again plunge the thing into Him. Plunge it. Twist it. Pull it out. Plunge it again. And again. Now, deep beneath His left armpit. Now, just below His collarbone. Now, in spite of the gurgling and His wild hands reaching, grasping, directly into His navel. At one point the thing, shining, gleaming, gripped so tightly, she feels it, the other woman feels it, the thing gripped so tightly in the hand that simply cannot, no, of course not, be her own — at one point it accidentally runs right through one of His hands, ripping open His palm, but by the time He can even manage to get out a small gasp (the sound of bubbles churning louder in His throat), she, that other woman, has run it, that thing, directly into His throat. Stained, wet, but still so sharp and shining, it emerges on the other side of His neck. Now, His form falling heavily back on the bed, His eyes do not close, but He ceases, all at once, to thrash. He lies there, unmoving. She watches, and feels her hands. Watches also the other woman who, standing exactly as she does and wearing that expression that is no expression, watches her.

All movement stilled, but for what continues to happen outside.

How warm her hands feel, she thinks. Warm and wet, as if she had recently dipped them in a summer sea. The sea. But how cold, too. There is coldness there. Somewhere.

She watches the other woman look down at Him as she feels herself looking down at Him. Then, when the woman turns away, away back into the shadows, she feels herself do the same.

But she has not forgotten the voices outside that continue to call. That continue to grow. Louder. More of them than before.

She feels her body moving. Down the hall. Down the stairs. Through darkness, though not yet through (toward) light.

The voice that will rise in a future time from the sea and recount this entire night will remember how, now, she stops outside the boy's room. Stops, and gazes with that expression that is no expression at that other woman, reappeared, who gazes back at her. Who now soundlessly opens the door to the boy's room as she feels her own hand on the doorknob, as they both walk into the room.

No, she cannot possibly be here. Of course not. But how long this dream is. And how wet.

There are voices, so many: inside her, outside of her, and out there, in the garden. Voices begging her now please, not to do it. Begging her to leave him, leave him, please. The boy. The precious sleeping little boy. Please. Do not. You cannot. Do that. No. But why are they all begging me, that smallest voice within her asks, when I am not the one doing any of this? Why do they not beg her, she wonders, that woman now standing over his bed, holding that thing in her hand and preparing to do to him what she just finished doing to Him? And ah, sighs the night, it is anyway much too late for begging of any kind, isn't it? Much too late for Do Not, No, You Cannot. The future voice that will recount these events will remember all that useless begging, and know that, as the vaginas continue to plummet outside and transform to faces on the dewsoaked grass, it is too late: for her, and for all of them.

Now standing completely still, she gazes silently upon her sleeping boychild for not long at all — for barely a minute, if that. Gazes, remembering His face in his. His blood coursing through his. The boychild, the seed of His loins. Bloodfury. Bloodrage. Vicious. She gazes, before watching what happens next: that other woman, the one with her exact face and even her hands, bending over him swiftly, drawing so quietly across his throat the shiny thing still held so tightly in her hand. Watching, she feels it in her own hand; feels her grip tighten on it as she (no, no, the other woman, the one who is doing all this) draws it across his throat; feels her hand pull away as the other woman pulls her hand away. In the small, soft place where the boy would have screamed and now cannot runs only wetness, warmth: "On my hands — no, on that other woman's hands — and on him," she thinks, looking neither to the right nor the left. Looking not at that other woman she feels looking back at her. Then looking down to see him looking up at her. Seeing his eyes widen, then dim so rapidly. Hearing his last muffled attempts to speak. Noting that he, like Him, cannot speak, for the choking. Watching him grab briefly, very briefly, at the air — at her — before, shortly, his arms, incapable, fall back upon him; then become still.

She is so relieved knowing that she cannot possibly be here. So happy that the boychild, before those movements of his arms, did not call her what he always calls her. That word, that most now unbearable word.

"The voices outside," she thinks. "Rising."

"Yes," she hears the other woman say.

"And all the vaginas," she thinks, "still falling. By now there must be millions of them on the lawn, throughout the garden, all transformed into faces. Millions of them."

"Of course," she hears the other woman say.

And the enveloping night, knowing what will happen next, pleading: Do not. Please. No more.

But the girlchild has His face and blood too, she thinks, turning to that other woman, who nods back at her. (Later, on her way to the sea, she will recall how strange it was to see a face so like her own nodding back at her.) The girlchild who — one day, like all of them — will grow up to be a woman. A laughing crying woman. A woman, but with His flesh and face.

And so she does. Must, she thinks. With the sleeping girl also. The girl, who, immediately on feeling that thing slicing into the warmth of her throat, awakens to look up and see the woman standing and looking down at her that way: looking down at the girl as though she is not looking at her but rather watching someone else do what her own hands, holding that thing, just did, then did again. The girl feels herself drowning in the warmth that is entirely her own. This is what she, girlchild, knows in the final quiet place where such things are ultimately known: that all that spreading warmth and wetness are entirely hers. That warmth, spreading its broad creeping shawl over everything. Sinking into the deep water that she all at once feels sucking at her feet and the entire bed. The deep water that for her will be of all time and utter silence, through which she manages to get out only one word: the awful, unbearable word the boychild had not murmured, that they both had always used when talking to the woman standing over her. That word, mouthed before falling asleep and not long after waking. Mouthed, shrieked, or whispered in all moments of affection, weariness, need. It is the last word she hears herself say before, understanding nothing of what all this means and why those hands above all others did that thing to her throat, she sees the woman standing over her swoop down like a great tall thing. A tree. A great tall tree, though slim, holding to its chest a pillow. A pillow, as, between all that warmth still spreading outward over the bed, spreading, the small head now pressed firmly beneath the lowered pillow attempts to fight, push upward, though feebly, for the first few seconds; then finally goes limp. Its tongue, pressing against the small teeth within, suddenly loses all sense of purpose, as its eyes, rolling back, confirm beneath the pillow for the darkness what the night and the voices outside already know.

"And now," the woman holding the pillow in place thinks, "He is no more. Here," she thinks, "in both of their faces, He is finally gone. All of them are gone."

She looks through the darkness over at the other woman who, as always, looks back at her. The woman: crying, she sees. Sobbing, her shoulders shaking softly, but with that strange light across her face; sobbing, her face lit that way, standing there holding a pillow bearing the stains of so much warmth released. It is then that she feels in her own hands the thick thing that is the, the — yes, that, clutched; as she feels that movement in her shoulders. As she feels the wetness on her own face.

Now, she tells the other woman, but without speaking the actual words, go. Go away, she tells her, and do not ever *come back.*

Go, she repeats without speaking when the woman makes no move but simply continues to stare at her, her face shining wet.

I mean it, she tells that staring face. Get out of here. And don't ever come back.

Weeping, still clutching the stained pillow, the woman slowly moves out of her sight into the shadows. Slowly out toward all the voices out there. Then, all at once, more quickly out into the night. "Yes, vanished," she thinks. Gone.

In this hour, while the moon-filled night still fills its belly on the dreams of the restless living and the dead (and those somewhere in between), let it be known throughout every corner of the moun-tain-filled country that there will come a time when all of the events recounted herein will, by even the most steadfast, be completely for-gotten. Yet let it also be known that long before that dire time, on a future moonful night, a voice shall rise up out of the yawning sea and recall it: recall how, on this night, with all those shadows licking so closely at her heels and her hands in that unspeakable condition — her hands holding still some of the warmth of Him, and of the boychild and the girl — and with her back so impossibly straight, her face so unmoving, her eyes staring straight ahead (yet still seeing somewhere else that other woman, watching her with that face), she walked in the first moment of her waking (for a kind of waking it certainly was) directly out of the house. Walked, and did not — no, not even once — turn back. Moved casually and cleanly out into the garden to find herself, in that moment somehow not trembling, among the thousandfold vaginas that had almost en-tirely transformed to those enormous mongrel-spiders, littering that always-impeccable garden — scuttling in every direction across it as their open mouths, tearing at the dew-damp grass, continued to move and stretch from side to side. It was then, in the precise hour of the heavy moon's beginning its slow crawl back down into the sea, that she began her own walk toward that water: quite like a sleep-walker, some of the shadows would later attest. Like someone in the deepest and most irretrievable of dreams. Toward the black stretch-ing water, past the sleeping houses and the faithful late-hour patrols always accountable to His command but that night evidently lost for all time in a thick (though useless) dream of their own, or simply stone-drunk on the job; for, though armed with their submachine guns and rifles and ready for a fight with any hapless late passer-by who might be up to some evil business against the magnificent nation's peace and order, they noticed neither her nor that grotesque parade of spider-vaginas crawling, some mutely and all with their mouths wide open, at her heels. "She was without question walking toward the sea," the night observed, wrapping its slinky arms more closely about her as it continued to whisper profanities over those skulking mountains.

Yet here is where some of the shadows that witnessed the next moments became confused. For, upon her reaching the shore in the company of all the strange creatures following her, did she in fact step out into those dark waters, into the arms of the blind mermaids who — according to some watchers — rose up just then out of the churning waves to surround her? The sightless mermaids who, singing their tuneless forever song, then descended beneath the waves with her, their unseeing faces to the last all turned up toward the lowering night sky, to be seen no more? Their arms all about her, pulling her down between them as, her face also turned unseeingly upward, she — evidently willingly — went down with them? Went down stretching out at the very end her hands still bearing the evidence of what that other woman, the woman who had borne her exact face, had done? Or, as others later insisted, did she in fact rise above and walk on those waters out into the dark? Walk, followed by those innumerable strange, spider-like creatures, farther out, still farther, until no trace whatsoever could be seen of her or them from land by those who, improbably in those last moments of the final moon, convinced themselves and others that they actually had seen her — yes, had fully witnessed her journey?

But now here is all that any of those who remain — remain amidst occasional rainfalls of severed hands and other parts, including tattered vaginas — are willing to commit to memory: that by and by the night, in collusion with the heavy moon, shrugged, snapped shut its eyes, and lowered its weary head against the retreating shore. By and by, as the sun edged up out of the sea and daylight stuttered in, the news spiraled and rose, then charged, of a woman known to many somehow gone missing — vanished, voices began to murmur, then repeated in loud whispers (but not too loud), with God only knew how much of Him and two others on her hands.

The boychild and the girl . . . but the maid, yet condemned to sweeping up the garden where the torrent of vaginas had plummeted only the night before, would be the one to find them. All of them. And the funerals — but of course. In the next days to come first for those three. For all of them a monarchical procession of state wreathed through with weeping cascades of flowers, during which actual human weeping was both expected and required; then, not long afterward, ceremonies for the several who had worked directly beneath Him and who for expediency's sake, on rapid orders from high above, had been quickly "detained," accused, and summarily secretly shot. For she could not possibly be connected with any of it in the public memory in any way, the higher voices had insisted; whatever had actually happened, it remained critical that she not be linked to it in any way — for obvious reasons, one of them had muttered to a comrade-skeptic, you know what He meant to this country, to everything — why do you even need to ask?

More funerals would be held over the next several weeks for those who continued, as many had all along, to struggle, cry out, and ultimately succumb, red-mouthed, to terrible dreams.

And the final rainfall, about which that future voice, ascended out of the sea, will tell? It will happen. On the tenth day after the last of these events, the entire country will be nearly overcome by a literal deluge of assorted parts: throats, fingertips, and the smooth undersides of chins. The storm will continue for an uncountable cycle of dreams, well into the time of the new He appointed to replace Him; well into the time of unfathomable dark water and a returning chorus of blind mermaids staring sightlessly, heads bent impossibly back and open-mouthed, so far beneath the waves. Well beyond even the memories of this recounting and the echoes of the sea-voice that will tell it all and tell it again, until the inevitable time when the faces and flesh of the living and the dead recalled herein will, by even the most steadfast, long have been forgotten.

THE BLUE GLOBES

B UT FIRST THEIR SECRET. THE BLUE GLOBES. WHICH are always blue, as they always were. In the beginning. When he was thirteen years old. When I was twelve
years old. When we were
                        sixteen and seventeen
years old

But yes. Beginning with their secret. That of the blue globes, their secret and his, which was also mine. "Smell," he said, smiling down. "I want you to —" "Smell," I said. Smiling up. My jaw feeling the (but yes). My face moving toward what he wanted me to smell. Toward what was his, until I made it mine. Until I breathed it in. "I'll never tell," I said. Said to him. To his laughing, smiling face. His face that smiled as (in darkness, in light) the blue globes came closer and closer and "Smell it," he said. "Just like that. Now. That way," he said. And laughed. Both of us laughing, laughing now, and no one will ever know.

I am calling
his name. I am looking up and calling
his name. I am calling his name as he looks down at me and
then
"Oh, Jesus!" I say. *As he pulls that part of me closer to his (yes) and
I am Oh I am and I
am and Oh.*

*He wants me to breathe. To inhale. To take in all of it and carry
it "to your dreams," he would say. "I want you to smell me in your
dreams." But yes.*

*If they had ever known — any of them, the ones who were never
there when we, the ones who never heard when we, in that time
or this one — if any of them had ever known, "They would have
laughed," I said, "they would have said —" "Uh huh," he said, "they
would have thought —" "Of course," I said, "they would have —"
"Exactly," you said, "and we wouldn't be —" "No," I said. You and
me. You and me who were and are he and I, and who if any of them
had known would not have (no, not ever). "No," I said.*

And so they who were we
will never tell. I will never. You will not. No.

*Years later, they will look back. Both of them. They will see them-
selves holding
each other. See themselves smelling
each other (yes, and laughing).*

*"Do that to me," he said. You said.
"Like that." Dusting off furniture in the secret place they kept, the
place no one ever knew
about. Where they could go sometimes and "Underneath?" I said.*

"Between the —" "No," he said (you said), *"right there, next to*
— yes, yes, that's it. That's it," you said.
Looking back. With so much ahead.

And so the globes. All of this having begun when I was in summer camp. When we were in camp. When there was no one
around. "They're all swimming," he whispered. "In the pool
down by the —"
    "Getting wet," I said, pulling at the —
    "Yes," he whispered (you whispered). And laughed.

In camp. Right there. Lying on my back. "On your back," he
said, quietly. "Stay there." "Why?" I asked. "Because," he said
(you said), smiling. But I didn't have to ask. Because that would
the first oh yes the first time that he would ask me to do that.
To do just that. To put my face there, in that way, near the blue
globes.

He liked the color blue, he said. His mother bought it for him to
wear when he was in the water, he said. Which was often. He liked
the water. He liked the blue thing his mother had bought him. He
liked the way it fit so nice and tight around his (yes, me too). He
liked the way it slid so slowly off his (but of course, and I did too).
He liked the way the blue shone in the sunlight and glistened when
he dove into the water. When he parted the water, moving his legs
and there was no smell, no sense of smell, only his open mouth and
his legs, arms, moving. Only watermovement. His belly flat between
the strokes. His open mouth moving through the water. Tasting it.
Between strokes. His mouth moving above the water's mouth in
darkness, yes, and light.

Smell it, you said
Why, I asked

THE BLUE GLOBES

Because you like it, you said
Because you like it, I said
Yes. Yes, I really like it, you said
You want me to smell it. You want me to breathe it in, I said
Jesus, yes, you said. You groaned. Jesus yes. Yes yes. As I did, and you
did,
and no one ever knew. Because we won't ever tell. Oh no.

And so a dance. A two o'clock in the afternoon dance, a moving
out of dusty corners. When all the others were away. Away swimming, wetting their mouths, soaking their thighs. A dance that
began when we were thirteen and fourteen years old — began
not yet with the blue globes, though they were there, but with "A
skirt!" I almost shouted. Lying on my back, on that small camp
bed that fit only one. "Where did you get that?" A skirt that you
had stolen from — from her? The one whom you would later
kiss while I watched? From her? "Do you like it?" you said. "Jesus Christ," I said. A skirt. The blue globes (though I didn't know
it then) beneath. Shining. Beckoning.

Yes, I liked it. Just that way. The way the blue thing your mother
bought you fit so slyly around your (and always has). The way
it breezed, ever so slightly, when you did what you always did.
"Wear it," I said, quietly, very quietly, as you watched me. Lying
on my back. "Wear it," I whispered, as you climbed over me,
stood above me — dancing over my face. "Look up," you said,
"and tell me what you see."
    "I see everything," I said.

He was dancing over my face. They were all away, away at two
o'clock in the afternoon. Splashing each other's backs, each other's
chests. Away as he danced over me, as the skirt he wore swished. As
I saw everything. The blue globes, beneath the skirt. And everything

pressing beneath them. His ankles, his thick-to-thin ankles, on the bed on either side of me. His feet without the high heels that, years later, while again dancing over my face, he would wear, in that secret place we kept. I could see his ankles as I would see them years later, when, on those nights that were still to come, long after camp and the bed that fit only one, long after hidden afternoons when they all were away, getting wet, with their shouts and splashes, long after the rings we would each eventually place on fingers in pledges to other people who would never know, long after the children we would each beget who also would never know, he would come to that place, that secret place that had begun long ago with a dance whispered out of dusty corners at two o'clock in the afternoon, and once more dance over my face with a skirt that swished, swished to reveal — only now and then — the blue globes, and all that pressed behind them, beneath them. He would dance again, as he danced only yesterday (but I will never tell), now with those black patent-leather heels. Those shining high heels close enough to lick. He would dance, and still he would command me to "Smell it," he would say, and I would. Clutching myself. Smell it, oh my God, smelling it as my face disappeared behind the blue globes and they became all. Became everything.

No, we can never tell. He can never tell how much he enjoys when I "Smell it," he said, and "I'm smelling it," I whispered, and "I know," he groaned, holding my head there. Keeping my head there. He can never tell. Not ever tell the one who delights in the rings on their fingers, nor the many others who share the spreadsheets of his days — the days when he thinks of me, I know, and of how, on some night soon to come, far away from the children he begat and the she who bears the ring that match-es his, far away from the children I begat and the she who loves my smile as I delight in her face, I will smell him I will smell him I will — "But just kiss it," he will say some night, "just this once, or twice, or three times." "What would any of them say if they knew?" I ask one night as he dances over me, trying to aim everything for right there, just there. "If they —"

"But they'll never know," he says — and though I cannot see him entirely for the darkness of that place, I know that he is smiling, that he will soon laugh — laugh the way he always does when he comes down over me, when the skirt billows over my face, when he knows that I am closing my eyes as he closes his and smelling it, taking it all in, about which we will never tell "anyone," I say. Say to the darkness. To the globes, that will become (but not for the first time) my mouth. Open my mouth.

The first time, you wanted me to touch them. You put them in my face.
They were wet. And I
Yes. Was thirteen
years old. Was fourteen
years old. You were
fifteen (sixteen?)
years old. You were
"swimming," you said,
"swimming. That's why they're wet."
"They're blue," I said. "Blue like —"
"Don't say it," you said. "Just put your face there, and —"
"Smell it?" I asked.
"Yes," you said. "There. Right there!"

That was camp. When we were twelve or thirteen or fourteen years old. By the time I was seventeen and you were
"Eighteen!"

I thought with purest secret pleasure as you danced over me and I thought about doing so much more — so much more than merely kissing it. You were eighteen and had graduated

from lifting first one leg, then the other. From laughing so up-
roariously when you did what you did, and I breathed in. From
sticking it out so that the blue globes, especially when it was
time for you to do what you did, touched my face. From balanc-
ing over me just that way, gently, ever so gently, so that, when it
was time, when you next wanted me to, I would inhale all of it
and reach up just that way — still lying on my back — to kiss
the blue globes that would be "wet," you whispered, "For you,
always wet. Like the first time when I came in from swimming
and they were —"

"Soaked," I said, remembering.

No one else ever inhaled. Ever smelled. You promised me that
they wouldn't. You promised me that you wouldn't do that with
"Her," you said, "no, of course not. Are you crazy? How could I?
She would think that I'm the ultimate —"

"Pervert," I said. "I know."

"Exactly," you said, blowing out the candle next to the place
where we stretched, fully prepared. And then it happened, you
did it, did it without lifting a thigh or arching your back (even
while lying on your back), one of your most reckless moments,
and you commanded me to "Smell it," you said. And I did, of
course, as you pressed down upon me and kept me there. Covering my face. Covering. Ensuring that I thought only of you and
what your she or mine or any of the children would say if they
could "see us," I thought, closing my eyes. Sucking silent air.

But don't worry, I said years later. When I was forty-one years old.
When you were forty-two years old. When we were
"in secret again," I said. "Um-hmm," you whispered, taking that
part of me in your hands and smelling it. "Absolutely."
Don't worry, I said. No, I said, squeezing that part. You don't
need to worry, I said, for (but how powerful it felt in my hands!)

there will never come a time when the globes are not blue and you do not wear that thing that makes them blue, as you did when you were

fourteen

years old. There will never come a time when I will not want to smell their secretmost things, those things shared only with me, about which I will never tell. You will never tell your her, I whispered into one of your parts last night, and I will never tell mine. I will take my finger that bears the ring that pledges my self to her and put that finger in your secretmost place that is only for me, and never (but no. How could I?) tell her that I did so. You will take your hand that bears the ring that pledges your self to your her and do that to me as severely as you can, please, once more and again, just like that, with those circles, those spirals, all of those circlings around the secret part — you will do all that, I will command you the way you command me when I smell you and open myself up to (uh huh), but you will never tell her — she whom you never ask to smell anything as you ask me and have asked me since the two o'clock dance of that first afternoon. Don't worry, I said, because you are — of course — deep, deep down inside my lungs. You've been there, deep down, for every year of all these years. The way I've been in your dreams and you've been inside my (exactly) and we both in all the secret places for all of these years. The way no one will ever know about it. No one knows about it. The way your ring shines and I can still smell you because the blue globes are only inches over my face. The way the globes move when you dance, the way they shudder. The way the children you begat laugh when you come home. "Daddy," they call, delighted. "Daddy, daddy!" The way she smiles at you when you're tired. Smiles, not knowing not ever knowing how you have been smelled for years, and how another face that smiles at her ("How are things, baby? Looking good, baby!") has disappeared within your secretmost parts for more than (fill in the years). The way you dance over my face, wearing that skirt (last week it was

*a Scottish kilt, with pleats) and those shiny high heels prance close
enough to lick. The way —*

No, no one will ever know. Nor see. Nor hear. Nor smell. Smell
that smell that is for me. Me only. Only mine. In darkness and
in light.

Close to my face. As you do that. Yes, please do that. And that
and. About which we will never tell. Never tell as I am smelling
you. As I am fifty-one
years old. As you are fifty-two
years old. As you are

*Above me. Dancing, yes. And the globes. Shining, full and round.
Shining, before they descend. Descend to cover my face and I inhale
and*

Laughing. We who are laughing. We who are —

MILK/SEA; SENTIENCE

THE STORY, AS IT HAS BEEN PASSED DOWN TO US, HAS always gone like this: all the women in that village were dreaming, still dreaming, and in fact had never once ceased dreaming in over one thousand (at least) years. Their village — this one, of course — was, indeed, that old. As everyone who knew the story knew, the village had been that old for a very long time, for much longer than most in our time could possibly imagine. It was known by all far and wide that the women really could not stop their dreaming, for if they ever did so, or tried to — well, but what would happen instead? What would they face? What would they become, and how soon? Where would they live? And how — the most pressing question — how would they live? For the village by this time, our time, had become a place of utter dryness, total ash; devastation. Starvation. Little from the realm of the living could sustain itself there, except the wavering figures of those in dreams — shadows, mostly, wandering without place or claim — and spiders, cockroaches, and (now and then) various forms of mold. Soldiers from a powerful distant country had invaded them some time ago, as soldiers from more powerful countries were always inclined to do, and decimated most of the men. The men who had not been killed — flayed of their skin, incinerated, or simply shot dead through the eyes, through the back of the head — had in most cases been run off to the outskirts — the *very* outskirts: the highest hills to the north and west of the village, where, as everyone knew, they were certain to be killed by the enemy guerrillas who instantly targeted for annihilation anyone who came into their midst. In a few other cases, the men run out of town by the invading soldiers were simply forced into the hands of varying bands of mercenaries, who used them for their own ends (rectums, mouths, and any other possibilities) and then discarded them in a storm of bullets.

And so the women dreamed. Dreamed with their children clutched fast in their arms. Perhaps better to dream for all time and evermore than to awaken out of those depths and find that *that* was being done to them again — done to them in the same laughing way they it had been done before, using everything within reach. Using even — no, especially — things with sharp edges. Very — sharp — edges. Sharp, but the entire experience indescribable. How could they possibly make anyone understand that? How could they possibly make anyone understand the feeling of the laughter outside, then the feeling of those things moving inside? Then only to find, because they were awake, not dreaming, that the same thing, or worse, was being done to their most precious thing: to this daughter; to that son. They would remember then that some had been stretched; others carved. Knowing all that, it would be better, wouldn't it, to stay in the realm of dreams, where all was safer? *Where it was safe*, many of them murmured among and to each other in those twilit realms, still clutching to their breasts their also-dreaming children. There, in the indefinite region of not-quite memory, not-quite sentience, where all things remained mostly deep blue-tinged, where the skin could rest intact, where the softest parts could relax uncarved, where the hour just before sundown never ended — *never* ended — and the sky, up there, way up there, always bore one of the steadfast colors of the sea — there, where no one would ever look up into midday's harsh light to see unimaginable things (Is that a part of my child, lying in all that mud at the side of the road?). *Stay here, stay here*, the women intoned in their dreams without speaking; and stay there they did, for (as the story has been faithfully recounted after all this time) more than five thousand years.

The "story," of course, is much more than a story. We know that it is — always has been — much more than a village tale. It is in fact a known reality. A documented reality, the core and substance of which need not be questioned by those who know nothing of our village, nothing of the we who are "We," and nothing of how all this dreaming, and so much more, ultimately came to be.

But then here is another fact, little known to those who have passed the story down through time: a fact that has to do with the oldest, most ravaged woman of the village, who had borne to men — it is still unclear how many men — not two children but twenty; who had lived in that village not forty years but over one hundred and fifty. An old woman who knew well the taste and texture of salt, whose thighs had (but unwillingly) rubbed up against the brutality of tree trunks, and whose fingers knew secrets unimaginable even by the shrewdest sage. A woman who, for reasons of her own and more, dreamed like all the rest. Dreamed with as many of her grandchildren locked against her voluminous chest as she could manage; with as many of her children, though most of them long grown into vaulting saplings, as she could possibly manage. They all slept in a pile, breathing deeply against her withered breasts. And so, all sleeping, all moving as far as possible from the sentience of actual memory into the safer, calmer regions, how could any of the other women, eyes tightly shut, with their children so tightly clutched against waking, possibly understand her awareness, even in those twilit depths, of great thirst? *For the village is thirsty,* she dreamt, *and has been ever since, ever since . . .* but she could not recall a time when it had not been terribly thirsty. *And the ground,* she dreamed (but here she turned, tossed; briefly clutched, in sleep, the air made misty, thick, by dreams) *is dry. Dry, dry. The ground is dying,* she dreamed, *and the children have nothing, not even water, to drink. The village,* she dreamed . . . conjuring, even if somehow against her will, the sense of great thirst. It was possible to do that. Possible, but even she, brave woman that she was and always had been, hardened-by-life-and-knowledge woman that she was, did not dare, though she conjured dryness, to dream of fire.

(*People burning in trees,* someone lying near her dreamt, stirring uneasily. *That smell. The sound of crackling, the sound of limbs breaking, and such great thirst.*)

And so many in our own time, the time of now, who had not known what the story would later disclose, finally divined it: the next part. Divined that it was she, that same woman aware in dreams of thirst, whose breasts, of their own accord, began to flow. And flow. And flow, without end. Flow, those withered breasts, with milk the color of clouds; milk the color of honey; milk new and fresh as the newest leaves in spring's first blush. Milk warm as desire before the long, hot day's end and dusk's curl. Milk flowing: rivers of it everywhere. Entire lakes. Milk flooding valleys, canyons, and (though this certainly came as no surprise) the village itself. Milk raising to its river-surfaces all the still-sleeping women and children, and some of the men who still dared not awaken — no, not yet; for though the rivers and streams and lakes of milk portended something altogether new (and what that new thing might be not one of the dreamers could possibly guess), no one yet dared, even floating so effortlessly on those milk-currents while still dreaming, to awaken — no, not even rocked so lovingly by the milk-streams; for who knew what, upon awakening, they might remember? Who knew what they might see that more than a thousand years of dreaming would still not have obliterated from memory?

Milk finally everywhere. Above the trees. Covering the tops of shacks, huts, even the occupying soldiers' quarters. Covering mountains, and even reaching up to the highest hills north and west of the village where, years later, the twisted skeletons of the guerrillas who targeted for annihilation everyone who came into their midst were found, in precisely the places where their living breathing bodies are to be found no more. Milk in all colors, all tastes, drowning the unsuspecting soldiers. Choking them. Putting an utter end to them for all time. Soldiers drowned in milk. Subsumed in milk. Men of arms vanquished in unrelenting tides of milk. . . . Why the dreamers themselves did not succumb to the rushing tides about them and beneath them no one — certainly no one today — can say; but it was known at the time, as it remains known today, that all of them — every single solitary last dreamer, every child, every woman, every man of that village who had lived there in peace long before the invaders had arrived — soon began, though still dreaming, to descend, eyes closed, beneath the swirling eddies of milk; to sink down, down, to the deepest depths of the milk; to travel into the most hidden parts of those tides produced by an aged woman's decrepit breasts, she herself still dreaming. Descend, never — as far as anyone knows — to be seen again. Never to be seen again in the region. Our region. Vanished forever. Down, down, into the milken sea, all of them. Motionless. Eyes closed. Perhaps (for who could tell? Yet so it was believed) dreaming. Dreaming for all time . . . dreaming without end. . . .

Never to be seen again? But why do people say such things?

And that voice is, of course, the voice of the child — this one: the one now crawling on his hands and knees up out of the sea. Up out of that sea that appears in the sentient realm, the realm of complete recollection, only sporadically. The same sea that is (and how, given all the preceding events, could it have been in any way otherwise?) composed entirely of milk. A sea composed entirely of milk and one that, unlike other seas, does not necessarily end at the sky. He crawls, the child, to attain the shore; to stand upon the shore; to grasp his small, shriveled penis; to shake it in the now-building breeze as he shakes out the wetness in his hair; to begin to piss upon the shore — and it's all right, you can look at him; he doesn't mind, he isn't shy. He has never been and never will be shy. He does not mind if you look at him as he pisses left to right, left to right, up and down, up, down . . . back and forth. He pisses, now pissing stronger, and why does it come as no real surprise to anyone watching that he pisses a steady stream of milk? He belches milk; he breaks a wind of milk; and even his tears, when they come (and they will, rest assured, come later), will be composed entirely of milk. (If you simply look into his eyes . . .) It does not stop, his steady stream of piss; it cannot stop once he has begun; the truth is that it will never stop. He begins to walk, turning now to the East and pissing; casting before him a steady stream of milk fresh from his penis, fresh from that sea. From a past that, though he is apparently now awake, he might never have known outside of dreams. He does not look back at the sea behind him; nor does he waver in his walking. He walks, and soon, we know — *I* know, I who have witnessed every single minute of this and more with my own eyes — soon his milk-piss will fill up the entire world. The entire world, awash in milk; the entire world, guzzling and sputtering in the piss that is the milk that began in the desiccated breasts of an ancient woman who, like those around her, steadfastly refused to cease dreaming. *Cease dreaming,* I myself think; but now I am watching the child; I am watching the child make his way and piss; I am watching the child make his way all over the world that will soon, one day, at the end of his journey, become all milk; become all the milk of dreams and what the story told us had been feared in that village, in all the villages: *do not dare to open your eyes because of the danger of waking and what will be there; do not open your eyes, for what milk can possibly save you now in the midst of these flying limbs? In the midst of this fire and the stench of your own burning flesh?* I have not forgotten; I, but not only I remember partly because of an ancient woman's breasts that would not — will not — cease in their milk. And now . . . now *he* is walking. Clutching his penis and still pissing. Pissing milk. Walking . . .

But so many villages, he thinks as he walks, *where still some (nay, a great many) are dreaming, and still are thirsty . . . so in need of water, of milk. Now, please, they mutter in those dreams: water. Yes, they gasp, but softly, very softly: and milk. For we are so very thirsty, they say (but still dreaming). Yes, utterly parched, they repeat, amid all the burning trees. Amid all the limbs smoldering in the trees. And all the faces. The faces that maybe even now,* he thinks, *are somehow dreaming. That are staring,* he thinks, *with their mouths open, but saying nothing. No, nothing at all,* he thinks. *No words nor —*

INVASION: EVENING: TWO

NOW, UTTERLY EXHAUSTED BUT ALMOST COMPLETELY past the initial stages of panic, they are there: in that place from which further running will be impossible, they both know, at least for tonight. There, some time before the *but how?* disbelief and the gradual prickling that will come just before the slow creep of orange light; still trembling slightly and each convinced that, though they barely know each other, they have at last left everything behind: faces, hands, and all the recollections — smells, touches; the way a pair of lips had sometime grazed a neck, and the shy crawl of fingers along a clavicle. Recollections with which their memories and wills to survive, though they do not yet know it, will later engage in battle. Now, in this partly sheltered place that they know they are fortunate to have found in the city that once, like the country itself, had been theirs — the city that minute by minute is becoming flames, smoke. Rubble. An inferno of bombs. Grenades. Of rifle shots aimed from roofs, and exploding missiles. While neither of them yet knows if they will survive to hear news of the aftermath —

information about post-invasion political trials and guerrillas' impassioned appeals to international tribunals; updates about the fate of tortured dissidents, about those who were permitted to leave the country (or managed, inconceivably, to escape) to testify before "truth and reconciliation" commissions ensconced in safer countries of placid snows, and who among their associates, families, and friends had or had not been rounded up for the detention centers (but, more likely, decimated by way of clandestine extrajudicial executions) — they do know that tonight, this evening, they have only "Now," they simultaneously intone, breathed not quite to themselves nor to each other. "Only now. This moment," they each think, gazing out at the rumbling tanks in the distance; each half-turning in the direction of the voice not his own, as if one, or the other, though scarcely daring thoughts regarding comfort, seeks a presence somehow sensed. This moment, they both think, in this abandoned place. (It is in fact a bombed-out storefront, littered with debris — planks of scorched wood, lengths of twisting corrupted metal — now essentially no more than a dim room thick with ash, soot, and barely maintaining what had once been an intact ceiling.) This place in what has rapidly become a forsaken corner of the burning city. Here, from which — though they must exercise great caution in how they peer out onto what once was, out there, before sailing bombs, a principal thoroughfare — they can see the impossibility of what cannot be, but is: the swirling lights and fires of what neither of their straining imaginations can now deny: simply, undeniably, invasion.

Two men. One young, the other not so young. The not so young one with gray hair thinning in places, a high forehead scrawled with lines, a paunch that spills indifferently over the belt line of his filthy, dust-covered pants (though in less frantic times he had been given to impeccable self-presentation), and a pair of heavy-lidded eyes, filled with too much remembering.

The young one already stooped, sunken-faced, given to excessive sweating and trembling hands — trying his best right now, his long arms at his sides (and he is lean, in truth knife-thin — the refugee's life, in this regard, has not helped him), attempting to still his eyes darting between their poles of stunned disbelief and bewildered rage. Two men who met — or, with the force that panic occasions, actually slammed into each other — only a few hours ago, running in the company of equally terrified others: first one direction, then another, after frantic shouts of *Emergency Invasion Bombs Get out of here with your* before one shouter lost his entire face, and much of his exposed flesh in the culmination of a superbly timed detonation. As they now move slightly closer to each other, the slightest physical shift unacknowledged in the moment by either, they will do their very best not to recall how what remained of that man's body had fallen — crumbled — to the ground, among those screams. *The little girl who saw that,* one of them will do his determined best not to recall, *only seven years old, or eight. Her mother — had that woman been her mother? She had looked very old to have a child of that age — had tried to run with her toward the market (but why there? One of the places most exposed), toward the market and the square, but the bayonets . . . — The bayonets,* the other will try hard not to remember as he begins to rub his elbow with an urgency that, for the moment, he will not notice, *and all those people running…that woman with the little girl,* he will insist, as he sees it once more, he did *not* see with his own eyes, *and the — when they knocked her down and put the bayonet down into the girl's*

But no, they both think. *No.* As if "No" were ever enough. As if that sort of *No* could ever be more than the last clutching grip on the smooth rock of the precipice before it gives way beneath; more than the hooved prey's last desperate backward kick before the predator's expert lunge. That *No,* that was always the unabashed clinging to life that even — especially — now, here, rebuffed all reason, logic, reality, and probability, and directed its steadfast gaze only toward the brain's implacable demand for the blood that, for the body, made "Tomorrow" possible.

That *No*, that now clenches itself more deeply across their shoulders as they both struggle not to recall shining bayonets dripping after repeated plunges, and more small girls running, beneath the flashing lights of explosions, into imposing structures once believed by the righteous and devout to be impregnable. Girls running into buildings crouched heavily beneath stars, crosses, domes. Girls, mostly still possessed of the correct number of limbs, running into whichever structures so piously dedicated to holiness and the inflammatory words of prophets had been left intact in the invasion's first hours, miraculously still erect and fairly unscathed amidst the smoking rubble; their tenuous pardon from destruction (until the next morning or the next wave) occasioned either through great fortune — a trajectory overshot, miscalculated, by the slightest of degrees — or by the refusal of those who, though familiar enough with hatred's unslakeable thirst and the joy of witnessing manacled rebels first "interrogated" and then dispatched by an AK-47, balked, even in the glow of ideological fervor, at destroying the sacred houses of beings in whose propensity for terrible vengeance they had from childhood been so passionately taught to believe. Believe, in order to understand without question that both gods and men could be capable of such acts. Capable of (but now feeling even more strongly that *No*'s tightening clench; feeling the precipice's slight give and the slow raising of a single hoof) what those soldiers or whomever they had been (they had possessed much of the invariably bellicose bearing of soldiers, if not the actual uniforms and finer grade of American-made and -supplied weapons strapped to their torsos) had done yesterday, last night, this morning: done without any trace of facial expression — something neither man, even now, here, can fully bring himself to believe. Done in the simple driving of a jeep, reversed to run its wheels over the backs and legs of four men who had been forced, at gunpoint, to lie face down, handcuffed one each to the next, in a public square; a square that, six hundred or so years before, had numbered as only one among several of the old city's sites dedicated, on varying days, to the thrill and spectacle of public executions.

The older man, just slightly conscious of the precipice but fully aware of the hooves now galloping apace in place of his own feet, will swear to his innermost being a simple *Of course not* — imploring his heart as, briefly, he shuts his eyes to ward off a mortally affecting case of the bends. Of course not, of course he hadn't. Hadn't, *couldn't possibly have* seen in the light of that same day's early afternoon a man, his hands smeared with shit and his entire face screaming indecipherable obscenities, attempting to shove into a latrine as shit-covered as his hands what had appeared to be a newborn infant. The man had staggered drunkenly out of the latrine (the mother of the child, dead or alive, nowhere to be seen), and had been summarily shot directly through his right eye by a passing phalanx the moment he stumbled into their view. *The stench of fresh remains*, he strives so ardently not to recall, pleading with the *No, and the baby's feet, so very small, sticking up out of the latrine*. Later, when the approaching night has stretched to its thinnest, he will recall the astonishment he felt, and the shame, following the success of his retreat from that scene. Unwanted memory of the retreat now impelling him to another place where the *No* will soon descend: the place of scent-thickened remembrance of his wife and three children. (Two sons, one daughter.)

In the remembrance, among them all again and only a forearm's length from the curve of his wife's neck and his daughter's ever-beatific smile, he absolutely *will not*, he tells himself. No.

Will not pray. Will not pray now because — *Because I just can't do it anymore*, he tells himself, while reassuring himself that those are not his words, could never be: *of course* not one of those words had been uttered in his mind. And so certain that he cannot possibly be thinking what he actually is thinking — clenching between his teeth the power that he knows resides in the resolute denial of truth, the ultimate power and respite of those who ultimately find they have none — he refuses to pray that his wife and children made it to the border safely; that none of them were intercepted by either the reliably snarling roving patrols or the always-unpredictable guerrillas; that his wife would not be required to do what she had threatened to do, if necessary, to protect their daughter and sons from the men: all of those men, out there. *There was never any question of your coming with us, of course you can't*, his wife had not needed to say to him; her face, with its customarily unflinching gaze, had told him even more than that. His face, known throughout the nation and hated by many because of his work — principally, over time, that of struggling, with determined others, to counteract the violence of soldiers and despots from both within and abroad — bore an unthinkable risk for all of them were he to be discovered in their company: the catastrophic fate invariably visited on those who, earlier in life, had opted for the comforts of love and family before becoming radical dissidents. Now, passing a slightly trembling hand over that part of his head where the hair is thinnest, he remembers her hair, like his, also beginning to retreat. Closing his eyes in order better to smell her neck against his face, he remembers what, on the point of their parting, had registered with him as utterly new: the way her face, beginning to wrinkle more (though not nearly as much as his own), had offered him that rarity: before their parting, the force of her unblinking stare directed at him — that hard, unyielding stare that he had previously seen her level only in the direction of laughing soldiers who, passing by in the streets during the last invasion, had riveted their scanning eyes just a little too boldly on their daughter's body and face. Her face had been naturally too soft for such an unrelenting stare, he had always thought; as it had been too gentle, he had believed or needed to believe, for the unaccustomed hardness of her hand in his that morning of their parting — the hardness that had revealed to him in that final hour its utter disdain for consolation, as (and this really had frightened him) it had impressed on him how with scarcely a twitch, with barely a trace of concern whatsoever for the body that owned it — hers — it easily could have sliced open the throat of one man, or two. Five. Twelve. *That* hand, integral part of the woman with whom he had produced three children and much laughter and tenderness, and whose scent now taunted his nostrils.

Until the stare and that hardness of her hand in his own, he had never — not even once through so many earlier attempted occupations, territorial raids, even post-insurgency states of emergency — stopped to reflect on whether or not he would ever have been prepared to do what she had plainly resolved to do to save any of their children. He saw before him just then the "boys," as he and she still called them, though both, like their sister, were nearly fully grown, nowhere near children. It was the summoning of all three of their faces — the girl's, the boys' — that stretched his mouth wide, a soundless motion, and tightly shut his eyes. He did his utmost to grasp securely the *No*, to feel its assuring weight in his hands, but it eluded him. Eluded him to abandon him on the precipice, visibly trembling with his mouth open to the most impossible possibility: the one, he now realized (but how could he, embroiled in the underground political realm as he had been, have lived in this country, in this world, all these years and not realized it? How could the *No* have so ill-served him and blinded him, incredibly, unforgivably, to the precariousness of what was most dear?) that was *that thing*:

that act of violence that people committed on those over whom they had control in times like these and others, and had done with wild pleasure since time immemorial; *that thing* that *could* actually be done to his children, his most precious creations and hers, in a time like this — anytime, he now realized, but especially now. And when they were ready for his children (amazed at his own daring in asking this next question. Grabbing wildly for the *No*. Feeling it dodge him), would they, the bayoneting ones and the drivers of jeeps, press the handles of their bayonets, and then the shining blades, into his daughter's hips? Laughing, would they squeeze her throat to the point of her choking? Between punches and kicks, would they pull on his sons' hair while demanding that the boys make it smooth for them, no teeth in the way and no gagging, as they pushed themselves all the way in? Would they shatter the boys' jaws into fragments after the desired tightness and then slam them both, with his already-torn daughter, into a wall?

(The precipice crumbling. The predator's hot breath close upon him.)

In the way he will not acknowledge that freezing sweat now dripping down his spine, he will also not say Yes. Yes to his wife, followed by *I know. I know now why your hands*, he wishes he had told her, *like your face, have hardened.* Regarding through closed eyes the burning city he can still see and smell, orange light now edged by deepening dusk, he stares in the blackness behind his eyes at the shame, the, the (but what word?) of what, in his deepest parts, he, like her, had always known: that with a daughter, despite the *No*'s enduring power and seduction, one had always known about the imminent possibility of danger, but simply refused to face it, think about it — but still one had known. The world as it was and had been since the species' amphibious origins in the primordial slime would not permit it otherwise for the wary mother or adoring father: neither the dubious peace of ignorance, no matter how adamantly the heart clamored for it, nor the blithe collusion of (perhaps occasionally privately acknowledged) self-deception. With a daughter, from her first hours, her wrinkled form pulled by skilled hands from the heaving canal, one immediately understood the realities of danger and vulnerability, even — especially — when she was that ridiculous size: a wizened, shriveled thing bent only on pursuit of the nipple. One knew and, in the early parenting hours, in the most secret place where the imagination permitted the envisioning of vengeance and its atrocities, one did occasionally, on witnessing cruelty (a defiling shout at a young girl in the street, the screams of some woman beaten to waste by some man), begin to nurse fantasies of putting to an agonizing death he who ever would dare to impose his perverted lust or rage on that blessed body; one dreamt, but never countenanced the dream in daylight, of torturing in the most excruciating ways possible the known or unknown *he* who would have tried to defile and leave in sundered ruins *her* body. As the parent, often hapless but ever ardent, one knew, secretly, how easily one could — would — *rip* apart that man's vitals and tear out the still-pumping heart with the front teeth — as if the world had ever really worked in that guaranteed way; as if the world of living, prowling human beings had ever consistently honored, through all its stutterings, the need for absolute justice, even after death if necessary.

(But then with sons . . .)

Because, she had told him only two days ago, stroking his face with her smooth, broad, long-fingered hand as she had dared to speak the unthinkable, forcing him to face it. His wife, forcing him. It was then that, more sharply than ever before, he had understood without question what he understood now: that she, for all their lives together and before, had always been much, much braver than he had been; she, he saw all at once, had always, in her quiet way, possessed a kind of bravery so terrifying precisely because it did — could — face the unthinkable. The unthinkable as in *Because if I have to, I will,* she had told him in her quiet voice. *I'll do it as many times as I have to. Because I can,* she had said, gazing calmly — so calmly! — into his disbelieving face, *but* she *cannot. Not any of my children. Oh, no.* (She had rubbed his forehead then: briefly, softly.) *I can imagine what* that *would feel like. Yes, of course I've thought about it before. How couldn't I have, living here?* — *and I can again. Of course,* she had said, so quietly, *I can. But not her. Not any of them.* He had not asked her — he hadn't wanted to know — how she could possibly have imagined such things. (Although reports of such things happening, and far worse, came in constantly, sometimes from the very mouths that had been forced to do some of those things.) But she had told him: *It's just a question of leaving your body behind,* she had continued as softly as if speaking of the quality of salt. *Of appearing to surrender the way they need to believe you have. The way they always do. They like you to try to run from them and scream so that they can knock you down and, and* — (even she, perhaps thinking of their daughter or, more likely, of all three children, had not been able to complete that sentence, though he could hear in her voice how valiantly she had tried) — *but I,* she had said, gazing directly at him with that look — *I,* she had nearly whispered, all at once looking down at her hands, *I will never run, nor scream. Because,* she had continued, so quietly, *this time it's happening to everyone. To all of us.*

Then he had felt her looking at him. He had looked up from his stunned posture (head lowered, arms crossed at the wrist over his chest and fingers, right hand to left shoulder and left hand to right shoulder scratching busily at the base of his neck where the thick shoulders began — it was, he knew with the irony he had once reliably possessed, something of a penitent's posture) and confirmed it with a glance: yes, she was looking at him. She had continued to stand there before him, for the briefest moment having removed her hand from his face when he began his scratching habit that, as she had always known, signified deepest distress, even agony; and then, on the second go-around, returned her hand, that didn't feel quite so hard that time, to his face. All the while, in complete silence, she had continued gazing gravely, steadily, into his face — unfairly, he had thought, tacitly acknowledged between them as it had been that she, prepared to sacrifice herself in the most brutal ways imaginable for the safety of their children and prepared to kill if necessary whichever predator she divined as such, was the infinitely stronger: more immediately fierce than he, armored as he could assume she was prepared to be, had to be, in the ready determination she would soon need to marshal for her move with their sons and daughter, on the first leg of their retreat from news of still more hostile advancing forces, into the cataclysm out there, without the certain annihilation his hunted face would bring them. Armored (or successful in having convinced herself that, to whatever required degree, she was), yet externally matching him in vulnerability and in the perforce tamped-down desire she, a woman looking upon her drained, stunned, silently fearful husband, had just then felt for him. And he, in those moments before they all left him for who knew how long (or — the impossible thought — for always), preferring just then — in truth urgently needing — to conjure in his innermost eye what he had recently come to think of, correctly but also somewhat sentimentally (in partial character for him), as her aging loveliness, yet another thing she had to offer the world, apocalyptic or otherwise: her accruing wrinkles, more rapidly graying hair, and those sagging, flattened breasts between which, on more than one recent early morning, returning to the easier, uncomplicated play of their earlier years, he had enjoyed pressing his face — savoring once again, as he had in those earlier years, the feeling of her still-responsive nipples beneath his chin. (The consistent blasting of distant artillery on those mornings, one of the first warnings of the unrest that would herald the present invasion, had not lessened their ardor.) On the eve of her departure with all of them, it was in some ways more *manageable*, he'd thought, to cycle back to those images than to risk too soon the inevitability of looking directly into her face — into that watchful, grave face. The thought of all of them leaving him to flee in pursuit of some kind of "safety" . . . but what a ridiculous, insane thought! What had she and he been thinking earlier, to imagine that she, as a woman and refugee with their children, the small group of them having to traverse uncountable miles on foot, depending on possible rides from the few trustworthy faces they would encounter — the few trustworthy faces that *might* not try to rip open her or her daughter and sons, or worse — all that was more than enough; but then also having to look forward to fighting their way past all that desperation and rage out there — having to avoid even being *seen* at all in certain areas, day or night . . . for a middle-aged woman and three young people, what kind of "safety" was that?

But the only kind of "safety," he'd thought, as he and she had so unwillingly discussed. The only kind that remains in the face of no choice.

Thinking about all that and more in the hour of their parting, he had somehow managed to stand there before her. How had he managed it, he would ask himself afterward; how had his legs not given way beneath him, his knees not crumbled into bone dust? Not looking at her, but making sure to take one of her hands in his own (and even that small gesture, on the eve of her departure, had become nearly unbearable) and stand there with his chin on his chest, feeling in that impossible moment the return of his recurring desire for her — for all of her: for the wrinkles, graying hair, drooping breasts, and gone-heavier legs of the woman whose hand was touching his face; touching, stroking, as he kept his eyes tightly closed and smelled her and knew once again that she and only she was the only one ever about whom, for whom, he had always felt *that*: that and so much more. That fast, he is there again, completely; knowing that now, although he is not looking at her, he can see and feel her careful, caressing look on him: the look with which she discerns what, despite his best efforts at concealment, moves there. Taking in the stricken-ness just beneath his eyebrows and on either side of his nose, and the slouch of his shoulders that does not match the grip of his hand on hers, she moves fully into him — a move that only the two of them can fully understand, and that he, even while resisting his own vulnerability and her penetration of it, will welcome only from her. Looking into his face and squeez-ing back his hand, she communicates to him the truth that, to his subsequent shame, he and she both understand he had never truly wanted to know: the truth that every female in this country, and some of the more unfortunate males, had learned long ago. The truth, made harsher by invasion, war, and torture camps, learned by daughters, mothers, grandmothers, and, soon enough, fathers and grandfathers too. The truth about the body: that it can take this much, but often much more. The truth that, in the moments of "much more," the mind must be willing to depart the body: depart the flesh for another realm, as the legs are forced open, as the instruments or human flesh (or both) are forced in, as the fingernails are wrenched out, as the mouth and throat are forced to suck, swallow, and not spit out. As the face endures the slaps, punches, occasional kicks, from which, held in place sometimes by clamps, it cannot turn away. On that distant afternoon, imparting to him her solemn concern as she stroked his face and revealed to him the terrifying bravery no one, let alone his wife and the mother of his children, should ever know, she had spared him by not voicing the question that, on the gentlest of wings, had barely hovered between them: *What kind of world,* she had not asked. *Just what kind of world do you think we're living in?*

Feeling her hand on his face. His eyes closed. Aware of her scent.

Where, how, had she learned to stare like that?

Remembering that for all that time, neither of them had uttered a word.

Shortly after that silence between them, he hadn't been able to bear any more. Hadn't been able to listen to the questions she had not asked and the responses he had not been able to give, with her standing there before him that way, touching him like that: her hands still so smooth yet hard, so strong and confident as always, and so very assured in the guaranteed intimacy of their sojourns across his face and throat. He hadn't been able to stand there anymore with not only her eyes but her entire face looking at him, *looking* at him, like that.

So that now, here, in gathering darkness (although something had just detonated only buildings away, rattling the weary shelter in which he and that other man were crouching — the detonation sending up a fireball large enough to illuminate the other's eyelashes and the sharp, almost acquiline cast of his nose), in this place where she and his children are not (and for that he silently offers weary thanks to the god in which he will still insist he so passionately believes), he of course absolutely *will not* remember how he had looked back at her. Will not . . . but then he summons, quickly, the *No. Please.* Calls for it. Begging. *Please.*

And, praise god, it comes.

And helps him. Helps him, for a minute, not to remember the scent of her neck. Her hair.

For two and a half minutes, it pushes him away from the length and smoothness of her fingers gripped in his own.

For as long as two to three minutes, it shoves him away from his sons and daughter: from the feeling of their warm bodies grasped in his arms, pressing their faces against his chest before their rushed departure, and the way they all, on finally leaving, had looked back at him.

For as long as three to four entire minutes, it commands him not to pray for them. To banish them from his thoughts.

He forgets how many minutes have passed since he returned his inner eye to the last day he saw them. Standing now with eyes closed, registering little of the smoke- and flame-filled city out there, he lowers his head onto his chest in what might be taken as a posture of prayer, but which is in fact disobedience. Disobedience to those who would attempt to bend him to their commands after invading his country, but disobedience especially to the *No*.

The younger man standing beside him knows, in the way it is possible to divine impossible things, that here, with the stranger beside him beginning visibly, though still only slightly, to shake (he senses it; he can just see in the near-darkness an obvious trembling, although the other man remains silently standing with tightly closed eyes) — this younger man with many years of life presumably before him, facing this magnified level of absolute catastrophe for the first time in his life, knows that now he himself will think nothing of his mother, nor of his father. And will not think of his grandmother. He knows that here, now, he will no longer, not ever again, beseech the god in which, through each of these passing moments, he tells himself he so passionately still believes, to *keep them safe*, please, *on that farm, or by that river — the one where, so I learned when I was a child, the old ones always saw ghosts and demons, malcontents and heroes alike of the past century. Keep them safe there,* he will not think, *with all those others, even the blind ones and the mine-disfigured children, until they all, every single one of them, reach the mountains. The mountains —*

And he will not, right now — no, for why should he, he nearly asks himself outright, feeling the burn of his almost-fury at the thought: the fury his exhausted neck, chest, and arms cannot afford in these moments — he *will not* remember his mother's missing teeth, knocked out by a soldier's rifle butt hours earlier in the pre-invasion raid. But he will permit himself this: the fantasy of that soldier perhaps having later been captured by rebels. That soldier, impaled through the throat by shining bayonets, then, *that* soldier, eviscerated: his steaming guts strewn widely about for dogs' rabid pleasure. Suddenly aware of the slow heat beginning to creep just beneath his thin, gently arching brows, he feels it: the intense hatred-as-pleasure that lopes its way often enough through humans, and invariably begins in the mouth, with the unexpected souring of spittle and a tightening of the already constricted throat, just enough to corrupt and addle the outraged senses. It proceeds, that hatred, thickened by the blood it craves and without which it cannot long survive, onward to the narrowed eye — or, in his case, to the brow. For now, he will savor the pleasure and groan silently as it tightens its vise about his loins. Feeling the vise, he won't need to recall the enormous running sore at the base of his father's right leg, and how, for days, none of them had been able to find either fresh water or a doctor, or a nurse. His father, who, because of that sore and the infirmity it had produced, had not been able to run when the time to run had come. His father who, even up to the last minute, just before the sudden flames everywhere, had not screamed. He had merely insisted quietly, with the turtle's face that had remained his up to the end (or no, garden lizard's, friends had sometimes joked), that they all should go on before him. Without him. *Yes,* his father had tried to convince them all, *leave me here and go on — today, now, before they*

But all at once there had been too much fire. A noise loud enough to blow open his eardrums, that had sent things flying through the air suddenly filled with smoke, dust, fragments of houses; flames everywhere, and the smoke filled with that sudden rancid stink of cindering flesh; then all those unexpected limbs underfoot, cluttering the few paths of escape. Hands, broken-fingered and severed from wrists, curling into claws. Too much for him to remember fully now the rest of what his father had been trying, in those last moments, to say. Say before —

Then all the screaming *from everywhere*, he'd thought; the repeated blasts that he'd feared would rupture his eardrums, and the disorienting sensation of something like an earthquake: of many roofs caving in.

Legs and arms everywhere in the street, he'd thought that afternoon, remembering how, as he'd fled the immediate area with others, some of those running just ahead of him hadn't realized they themselves were on fire. They had swiftly become running torches and, utterly consumed, had dropped, twitching and flailing in agony, between all the other running people. Continuing to run, he had almost stepped onto a hand, intact but for its missing thumb and the entire human body, male or female, to which, up until only a few minutes ago, it had belonged. *One hand*, he'd thought, *with four blackened fingers, minus one.* He had heard the thinner, piercing screams of children, and had had enough time between explosions to notice the stink of entrails . . . and then somehow became aware, though it was ridiculous, of the shoes he was wearing, in which his feet continued to run. The shoes his grandmother had given him ages ago, that had been made neither for running nor for stepping on mostly burnt severed human hands.

Quietly stunned by his own utter stillness in the face of the entire world out there coming to an end — for this truly is the end of the world, he thinks as he pauses to note his astonishment at how the cliché, even in the actual minutes of its awful truth, still rings so hollowly even in the deepest, most vulnerable parts of his not-moving body — he watches a building explode in the distance: a fireball that really does roil, black smoke that really does billow. He watches, and confirms: the explosion demolished one of the city's oldest shrines, one dating back to a single-digit century, to which — so the holy paintings and ancient oral legends had attested — those accursed by sickness, vindictive ancestors, and the reliable sieges dire conditions could visit upon even the most strong-willed, had brought offerings to implore the beneficence of the beings in which, to their untimely ends, they had so passionately believed. He watches the fire and smoke and ash curl out of that once-holy place, and marvels, if only for a moment, at how easy it actually can be right now to pretend, with the slightest of sighs, that he is already dead. Easier to imagine himself already murdered. (Would it have been a bayonet, ripping downward toward the crotch, to disembowel? Or a mine, casually happened upon by his unwary stumbling heel at one o'clock in the afternoon?) More comforting to imagine himself slowly decomposing, withered and consumed by lowly organisms through all hours until flesh gave way to the slack-jawed skeleton, than to permit himself anywhere near the rage (but no, "rage" cannot fully describe *that* feeling — but let him have it, "rage") that, unchecked, granted the merest quarter for escape, could swirl up out of his pores and rip to shreds the purposeful sleepwalker's flesh that had made existence in that country possible, if not actual *life* — the sort of *life* those unfamiliar with that kind of existence took for granted. Rage: the sort that, behind a survivor's demented grin, had choked on itself for too long, and borne without a word the innumerable humiliations and assaults experienced at so many security checkpoints and border controls contrived to contain the targeted state and its suspect, to-be-corralled-at-all-costs citizens. Rage capable, quite on its own, of careening out into the world — into *that* world, now on its burning knees before him; *that* world, that, had the demented grin had its

way, would have known (but not discovered in time to save itself) the true, *truest* force of the destruction whose first name is
sometimes believed to be "insurrection" but whose final word is
always retribution. *Retribution*, he half-dreams, eyes still cast out
toward the fireball and the night looming above it; loving the
force and tremble of the word in his mouth and mind as he permits himself, though unaware of it, a few more minutes of the
dreamer's self-deluding gaze: the expression his face wears as he
briefly embarks now on a stroll, as had the man still standing
next to him, through the one place most dreamers know but can
never, in daytime's light, acknowledge: the place where all justice
is forever served, all wrongs forever righted, all grievances ever
salved; the country of dreams, etched in colors personal to each
sojourner but universally lambent for all. Watching him standing there that way with his long arms by his sides, his motionless
form only inches from the other man's and that half-dazed, half-
exhausted expression on his face, almost anyone would immediately apprehend his truth: that, though probably just approaching
his thirties, he is old enough to have lived through many years of
recurring occupations and invasions of which this latest will be
— already is — the most violent. Something in the rigid tension
of his shoulders, though he is exhausted, and in those brows, and
most of all in the dark centers of his eyes, betrays the fact that he
probably never, even as a toddler, knew a time when war hadn't
wracked the ground beneath him; yet, the barest suggestion of
softness — in his full, thick bottom lip, maybe — suggests that
this is the first catastrophe of its order that he has faced as an
adult. "Adult" merely in terms of official years, he knows; in that
country and others like it, children, while retaining their natural
love of mischief, reached adulthood far quicker than those in less
besieged nations. As a boy, he had sensed how early in life (and
especially, though not only, in the lives of boys) the demands
were soon presented, the lines drawn: lines mostly defining where

began and ended the volatile arena of a heightened intelligence, the thing actually closer to constantly edgy instinct, with which one knew and learned, fast, the essentials vital for survival: the awful prickling at the back of the neck that warned one, on an otherwise unremarkable morning, to avoid that central thoroughfare, because "they" — whoever "they" would turn out to be that day, that week — would probably bomb one of the buses that traversed it in the early afternoon. For the same reason, the pricklings might urge avoidance of the areas near certain embassies during the next month; as advisable as the eventual moving of a best friend's wife and children into a remote region with not even the slightest information slipped to anyone, no matter how trusted, about how she and her husband had always maintained connections to the captured guerrillas soon to face death sentences in the country's travesty of a national court. The pricklings tersely counseled common sense, such as knowing better than to harbor refugees who were seeking some way out of the country, unless one was already one of those "underground" rebels too committed to liberation and the thwarting of cruel alliances to care about death, torture, or the possible annihilation of family and friends: one of those dauntless people largely unseen and unknown as their actual selves, who laughed bitterly often enough at the joke of "safety" — a word that those initiated to rebellion had long ago learned possessed absolutely no meaning. (Of course he couldn't know that the very man standing next to him in silence, the man of whose body and breathing and even physical shape he was slowly becoming more aware, had been almost as completely radical and fearless as those people, but for his grave early mistake of making true love the rival to insurgency.) The pricklings had admonished him early enough never to utter the words "political asylum" or "amnesty" anywhere in public, to stay away from the city's congested central market on Wednesday afternoons and Thursday mornings, and never to be too sure that his grandfather's best friend or uncle's gardener didn't have an overly ambitious son in the secret police. It was true that he, unlike many others, had throughout his childhood played only the simple, occasionally raucous games children played in the streets and especially in poorer neighborhoods in the infrequent times when curfews had been relaxed. Later, he would both regret and feel relief over the fact that he had never — not at age ten, twelve, fourteen, or later — had the dubious fortune of having a rifle pressed into his hands by soldiers in need of fresh blood and impressionable eyes only too willing to believe that early violent death was a necessity for the attainment of true manhood and honor. The relief had been the later wisdom of the young adult who, to his credit, had quickly learned the critical importance of doing his very best to be always on the *right side* at the *right time*. Rather than the terrified running he had done that day through smoke and over scorched limbs, he prefers to recall that relief, and the wisdom, blessed spawn of shrewd instinct, that had kept him fortunately far from the ranks of enraged mercenaries with nothing, absolutely nothing at all, as their eyes had long ago told him, to lose: the young men who without fail provided the cannon fodder for ideologues' outrage, and almost never survived to witness the rare days, even months, of cease-fire in between occupations and the voluntary return of exiles.

But then without any warning, as he stands there so unmoving (though with a wary sidelong glance now at the other man, as if cautiously assessing his intimacy, past and present, with both risk and transgression), the relief of remembering his earlier years suddenly betrays him. All at once it shakes itself, lumbers with a heavy grunt, and transforms into his grandmother's fingers — or, rather, her not-fingers. The not-fingers that had been removed from her hand when a pro-invasion mercenary, only days before, upon hearing her plea for water as he stormed through their town in the company of five sturdy fellows drunk on the prospect of surely imminent victory, had brought a machete crashing down on her outstretched hand, leaving her with an outpouring of the fluid critical for life but useless for thirst. He conjures the five men as the kind he has seen before: all young enough to despise what hobbled every day around them as life, while scorning the possibility of the actual stench of their own deaths. He will imagine the assaulting man, though he never came close to glimpsing his face, in the hands of the secret police: imagine the blow-torch flame held just beneath his testicles by black-gloved hands, the thick boots slammed into the (oh *yes*) solar plexus, the electric shocks applied to his exposed gums — especially in the most sensitive place, above the two front teeth — and the ultimate, most sublime: the visit again, and again, and yet again to his tender unprepared asshole, of *that*. But not just any *that*: rather a *that* that would really, truly, *tear*. Rip apart. *Forced into him. Enough to shatter his insides.* A *that* that would not only sunder but completely —

(Exactly, he thinks. *Destroy.*)

He groans, quietly, with pleasure at the images. He prays to the god in which his grandmother had always so passionately believed that what he envisions *will* happen: the victim will be ripped apart, completely used, and finally end up decapitated — with an axe, better for the blade, or with a saw, better for the teeth — and will be dumped, with a heavy thud, in a roadside ditch. He lingers in that country of hatred inseparable, at least now, from more innocuous dreams, summoning just beyond his clenching hands the hated face of a man surely not much younger than himself. A man who, given the more-than-ever usefulness of masks, might have become anyone by now, but who, to this dreaming man now crushing beneath his feet every moving thing as he smashes his way through the hatred-country, remains what he has always been: the one who, laughing loudly and anticipating violent victory, had left his grandmother staggering, then fallen, with two fingers flung over *there*, rather far from her bewildered wrist, on the other side of a dusty road.

For all the time they have left to live, years or merely days, neither of them will ever speak of it: the impossible, improbable thing that begins to pull them closer, drawing strength and motivation first from the belly, from its deepest need that precedes even hunger. For now more than ever they see, not far off, the orange glows, flaring closer. Now they really do know that those volleys, echoing closer, will find their way soon enough into their hiding place. Utterly still and silent before the un-world outside, they will never be able to say out loud how this impossible thing now pulling at them has its origins in what they know: in the agonized yearning for a pair of eyes, and the parted lips that speak the familiar name. It simply cannot be possible to crave this kind of comfort — to feel anything in a place where feeling suddenly wears cruelty's flesh.

As the night stretches to its thinnest, it *can't* be possible, they each think, for the belly-need and the steady breaths it requires to insist without care, as it does now for each of them, that they are still alive: still, and cannot deny it, *alive*. The aliveness that, without any warning, all at once does *that*. Propels them. Propels them suddenly and in utter silence to reach for each other.

Touching each other. Impossible.

Holding. *Impossible.*

Breath on his neck. My breath on another man's neck. No, not possible.

Feeling his arms — but no —

The older man beginning to feel what is happening: the wetness on his face and the silent heaves that even her leaving with the girl and their boys, leaving him standing there watching them walk off without him, had not produced. Holding the other man's warm body in his thick arms and putting his face against it, feeling its breaths, he cannot forgive himself in this minute for the truth: that it is this embrace, this touch, that has made it clear to him now more than ever how much he really wants to live. Wants to live because *she* . . . because she.

(Because *they*.)

Because she, the other one thinks. Somewhere hopefully still breathing, and waiting for him. She, and all the others who know his belly-need, that is also theirs.

His mouth on mine. *But how*. But yes.

Nearer explosions now rattling their shelter.

For one of them it might be his first time so pressing this way against another man. For the other, drawing his mouth over the other's neck and face, perhaps (though still difficult to tell) his second. None of it, *this*, is possible, each of them knows. It is all as impossible as a grenade's melting a young girl from her collarbone down, yet somehow leaving intact her face and the sinews just beneath her neck. Impossible as months without rain, crawling amputees shouting praises to a god in which they still so passionately believe, and refugees who, though partly maimed, somehow make it to safety outside the country. As unthinkable as a wife's preparation to endure even *that* . . . and the radiant smile on a boy's face: a boy still young enough to gaze raptly at birds and secretly fancy himself someday becoming their soaring brother, his arms open to the sky, now working as a mercenary and smiling broadly as he aims a rifle nearly as long as he is tall directly at the face of a boy or girl younger than himself. With a slight widening of his smile, he pulls the trigger, laughing as the wavering target before him splatters into the dust. How, in such a world, to crave this touching, consume the breath and the embrace, as orange light advances and her face, *hers*, looms somewhere near. And how . . . oh yes, how to forswear silently, though the forswearing succeeds, any shame or disgust for this sort of thing that, for years, the religion in which they each still so impossibly believe had taught them was simply *forbidden*.

Disbelieving, believing, they have already begun to undress each other; the belly-need and the nearing orange impelling them to move at a speed greater than they have ever moved in their lives. Fumbling, pulling more frantically in the slowly lightening darkness, they know that now, especially now, they dare not look outside. Knowing that neither of them can afford, until the end, the fear in eyes and face that the merest glance out into that increasingly orange night would bring.

Doing all those things with his mouth and hands, with his entire body, the older man knows now that he absolutely *will not* think of her. Not think of her as he does all that to the man now beneath him as, shaking, they lower themselves to the floor. As he — one of them or the other — climbs on top of the one he so tightly holds.

Inhaling him. *Her*.

The other, taking in everything of the one now beneath him, now atop him, and disregarding unwashedness, rank body scents, refuses in these minutes to summon her face, still waiting for him. He had not wanted to think of her earlier. He will not think of her now. He cannot, dare not, while holding so close to him this man whom he does not know. Aware of the desert at which the body arrives after days without fresh water, he will not, as he might have done in pre-invasion weeks, imagine what, in spite of everything, may still be his eventual slow, husbandly descent into her softness that will feel exactly like this one, he struggles to convince himself, though not like it at all, he knows. Thrusting his face deeper into impossibility's odors and tastes, he nearly chokes on its lunge that, without warning but welcomed (but *how?*), charges between his front teeth to slide its fullness over his tongue and to the farthest edge of his throat. He refuses to envision her arms encircling his naked back in what would have surely been their conjoined triumph. He thrusts away, sharply, the sound of her imagined sighs, as he, to his own amazement and joy — *joy?* — sighs now; the same sigh that would have been released with her after . . . oh, *after*, he thinks. When.

He feels the older man's stomach. Feels its heavy softness in contrast to the muscular tautness of his own. Pushes his face into it, then into all that he cannot quite see beneath. It is precisely in this moment that he truly understands that he is, in spite of everything, young. If he survives to his wedding day, he will discover that her moans will remind him of his companion's moans just now. If he is not shot through the back of the head, incinerated, bayoneted, or otherwise ripped open before he finds her — for in the days to come he will, of course, find her alive, his belly-need tells him — he will, with mumbled thanks to the god in which he will tell himself it is still necessary to believe, take every part of her he can in his mouth, and do exactly what the other man just did to him: do to her in fact what he is still doing to me, he thinks. Do all of it and more, as with a great cry and shudder this stranger does what he does now so suddenly does it holding onto my hair and pressing my face into him throwing his head back with a gasp followed by an enormous tremor followed by another gasp and then another tremor as now I, I do this, am doing this to myself, one of his hands on me his exhausted face even now in this darkness looking at me as I as *I* my hand underneath   now on top   *oh now*

(And still they will not. Will not look up and out to see that orange light, ever nearer.)

The shudders now fewer. That smell. That taste on the other's face, and in his mouth. Throat. Especially in his throat. Then, despite the volleys echoing outside, between them only silence. Breath. Out, in. Their heads together. Now and then, their mouths. Faces cradled, and arms. It might even be possible, though difficult to discern in the dark, that they are (but impossible, they each think) holding hands.

Holding, and whatever else is possible as the night stretches to its very thinnest hour. The hour when one, pressing his face into the chest of the other, hopes that she and the girl and the boys did make it to the border. Hoping that she, in order to deter all those watching eyes focused on their daughter's breasts and the rounds of their sons' backsides, did not finally have to do *that*.

The other, before closing his eyes for what will be an abruptly interrupted nap, will, with the very last bit of energy he can summon, not quite pray but *pray* that they all will be safe: she, her parents, those remaining of his family. Safe if only for tonight and tomorrow, on that farm, or near the river where the older ones always envisioned ghosts. He will not quite pray that, with the blind ones and the lame children, they will reach the mountains, and that she of whom he just now half-dreamt, and her parents and family all of whom he had loved as they had loved him — *our future son-in-law, and how beautiful they look together, yes!* — will be, be —

Safe, he dares to think, *whatever that means now. Whatever it can . . .* he drifts. Slowly drowses toward what he hopes will be only (exactly: just that, with his eyes slightly closed, and nothing more). He nestles into the shape of what has become the two of them — the two of them in that way, in that abandoned place. Before falling off completely with his face in the neck of the man whose eyes will remain wide open until they are lulled by the apparition of unfamiliar shores, he does not offer up a final prayer to the god in whom, in spite of everything and also because of it, he still, like the man holding him and whom he holds, so passionately believes.

And so they manage it. Manage to convince the darkness and the night that they are sleeping. The night now thinned of stars and moon. Thinned of signs. Now, simply breathing, neither of them can be certain which one's finger belongs to which hand, which cheek to which eyelash, and which mouth to which lightest breath.

And so joined and simply breathing, possibly holding hands that might twitch as each breather drifts toward the shores of rapidly widening dreams, it is only minutes later that one of them feels it. The prickling. The prickling the younger man has known all his life, as, differently, has his companion. The prickling that now, without warning, raises every single hair at the back of his neck and wrenches him abruptly away from the almost-sleeper's uneasy drift. Aware of its sudden urgent heat as dreamers are known to discern, for their own sake, the encroachment of light, he feels it urging him to his unsteady feet, immediately steady in the darkness as, with nothing more hissed to the still dozing older man than a

Now. Get up. Come on. *Now —*

He pulls him to his feet.

Out of here, he hears himself hiss. *Out*

Get out: yes, for there is no time, they each instantly grasp. No time for the luxury of goodbyes, nor for the absurdity, in such a moment, of tenderness: a last impossible kiss, squeeze, or the face's final yielding to a caress — the face that, in that darkness, no one, even themselves, can see. No time for any of that. They run. Out into the night and the country no longer theirs.

And so running away from that place, increasing to the speed well known by survivors, they miss it. Miss, but hear, the bomb that, exactly now, sails directly into where they had just crouched. The crude bomb that completely incinerates it all. Obliterates. Still running, just beyond pursuing volleys, they will choose not to envision the blackened piles their half-drowsing forms would by now have become, had the prickling not attended them. Tonight and tomorrow and (depending on the success of incursions) the day after, they will run, hide, dodge. If they are lucky, they will neither fall to their knees in a prisoners' line, nor extend their wrists, palms upward, for the manacle's click that inevitably precedes the rifle's shot to the back of the head. For now, farther from what would have slowly curled into the air as the stench of their own roasted flesh, they will each try very hard amid detonations and dripping bayonets to jettison, though never forget, their own sighs and mouths joined in silence — the silence that may still precede the smiles that, though strained, just *might* widen their faces in an hour of peace or victory for their own; an hour when, if they manage to bribe scowling guards or otherwise inveigle their way into whichever refugee camp or internment center, they will find somewhere among all those fenced-in faces the familiar ones they had loved in that other life, the earlier one before the invasion — the faces that still, charged by belly-need, loved them. Faces remembered in the darkness-before-bright orange of an abandoned (or whatever it had been) place. Faces that will again summon for them joy once so unmistakable and still present somewhere: in a familiar chin, in an eye intimately acquainted with a brow's width, and in all the lovely teeth so agleam between parted lips that speak the familiar name — the lips that, like their own, will whisper once again into the darkness of some future night everything that the body and mind can never bear to remember, nor ever fully lay to rest.

SOUTH BEACH, 1992

A FTER THEY BOTH WERE SURE HE'D STOPPED BLEEDING, THEY walked quickly from their hotel toward the sea, reaching Ocean Drive soon enough, and settled on a café with straw-mat-topped tables laid out beneath a green canopy. They ordered club sandwiches and Cokes — no ice in his, he said. Even with the silence that had overtaken them on the heels of the fresh blood, it was easy enough now for them both to regard the laughing couples that surrounded them — mostly youngish like themselves, all deeply tanned and all so *healthy*-looking, he thought; like themselves, even now. They took in the bright t-shirts and loud Hawaiian prints, the slightly askew sun hats and baseball caps, the too-large, sometimes garish sunglasses (a popular film actor known more for his recent problems with drugs and drink hid, somewhat unsuccessfully, behind a pair), and the occasionally startling beauty in the face of a woman or man close by — one of the many models who worked locally, no doubt, in the company of another beauty here in the early lunch hour, pointedly focused on a crisp garden salad or spritzer with lime. Had they themselves thought of it, they would have described the general atmosphere as insouciant, decidedly vibrant, caressed by an ostensible élan and well-heeledness that was in no way part of their own regular days. Yes, well, this was *here*, after all, they both knew: right in the center of things, so to speak. The Miami that reminded them of home, far to the north — the city's ample-armed, weary-faced women, its steel-sided Metro and busy downtown stations, the noisier streets abustle with tense bodies in fervent search of green cards, and the deep pleasures of lilting and staccato tones in languages other than English — that Miami was way over *there*, across the water to the west; this particular stretch of the palm-lined, sea-flanking Ocean Drive was, they knew, where dramatically sculpted beauty could frequently be glimpsed, if not gawkingly admired: the municipality of well-nourished smooth cheekbones and narrow hips that spoke of First World comfort far removed from the assaults and twinges of urban anxiety. It was, they knew (and had accordingly, over months, saved their money for), a narrow land of shiny restaurants and cafés, up-market gift shops, "premier" dance clubs, smooth-thighed rollerbladers and joggers not much younger than themselves, and, on the other extreme, the elderly knock-kneed, bent-backed, die-hard couples, many of whom despite (or because of) the abiding weather of years still strolled the beachfront walks holding hands, and had journeyed to these shores from places like New York, Chicago, and other winter-harsh locales for the perceived blessedness of retirement beneath prehistoric sago palms and noon-drunk butterflies. With a slight movement as if resuscitating a habit they might once have enjoyed but knew they had never, in such a way, quite shared, they gazed briefly out at the beach on the other side of the Drive before the taller man automatically returned his eyes to that place on the other man's mouth where, only twenty minutes before, in a moment of shaving too closely, the blood had bloomed. The pelting noon shower that had blown in off the sea had departed just as suddenly, leaving behind an ambivalent sky slowly stretching back to its own previous distractions. Scudding clouds made way for the certainty of azure as the sun began again to burn down through the humid air onto the scattered puddles left by the rain. They'd been lucky to get a table right away; already the little café was quickly crowding up with those who had dashed in out of the rain and were still coming in droves off the beach to snack before heading back to hotels or home to doze off the sun's narcotic effects. The taller man shifted long legs under the table and watched as his companion began to suck his lower lip where the blood had been.

—*Don't* suck on it.—

—Why? You think I'm gonna get poisoned? It's a little late for that, isn't it?—

—Jule . . . —

—Don't worry.— The shorter man pulled back the left sleeve of his t-shirt to reveal the smooth plain of flesh which, the previous afternoon, the sun had slightly burned.

—Damn, I got tanned that fast in that little bit of time. Check this out. Look what your beautiful Miami Beach did to me.— He looked directly at the man across from him.

—Serious, Markie. I promise I won't ask you to share a glass with me tonight.—

—Aw, shit, now . . . so on top of everything else, you gonna start that 'Markie' shit? You only do that when shit gets nasty. Stop sucking on it, I said.—

—Shit *is* nasty. It's been nasty, hasn't it? Anyway, since when you got a problem with me sucking on shit? Relax.—

The taller man leaned slowly across the table, put his hand on the other's knee below it, and squeezed, hard. His companion raised his eyebrows.

—Yeah? So? Now what? Don't start on me with no lecture, Marcus. I don't feel like it.—

—Jule —

—Yeah, that's my name, sure enough.—

The other man paused and looked down at the table. He had sworn to himself that on this, their third day here, no matter what happened for the seven days they had in total, he wouldn't sigh. Neither sigh nor slump his shoulders in the anticipation of deep regret, or sadness, or beneath the weight of actual defeat, or whatever other lead-heavy feeling these recent days, even away from the tremulous space of home, had occasioned in them both. The waiter had just brought them tall sweating glasses of ice water. He closed his eyes for a moment and, for just those seconds, imagined the water streaming slowly — very slowly — down the back of Jule's neck. Envisioned once more, for whatever thousandth time, the slope and sheen of the neck right there, and the curls of the softest hairs right above where the night-meadow, familiar to all his senses and their attendant afterglows, stretched. They both knew: there was nothing — no, not anything at all — like pressing your face into the night-meadow even as you touched hands somewhere else in darkness and felt all of *that*, of course! — and moved on to all the other parts beneath. The byway made him smile, and (not for the first time that month or even that week, he consoled and reassured himself) directed him, partly in obeisance to a long-held, staunch modesty, to narrow the space between his legs as he felt stirring there again a few bumpings and proddings of the old-new emboldened surge. But neither the byway nor the surge, nor even a half-distant memory of the surge's hovering, in near-darkness, just above that part of his companion's pretend-sleeping face, erased or assuaged his thought that now, instead of the afterglow between them for which he'd hoped (and for which he'd believed Jule had hoped), it looked as though things were going to be like *this*, all because of a little . . . because of a little blood. (But no, not such a little thing, he thought, though trying desperately to push away the thought: not so little nor —) The man sitting across from him

was, he understood without looking back up at him, going to be
— going to be, yes, all right, a little *bitch* about it. (And so okay
then, he thought, be brutal, as long as Jule didn't see it in his
eyes or detect it in his voice.) A little bitch the way he so often
was and could be when shit got dicey, which, given recent dis-
closures, had been often enough, and which, he knew more than
ever now, was far from finished. Resistance to knowledge — to
everything — had proved useless. And — but well, all right, he
thought: even though we both know the same thing now, maybe
there really are some things he knows that I don't. That I can't
imagine.... He retreated quickly enough from the ellipsis. Too
much waiting there at its end, he knew. He did not quite permit
himself to think *Yeah, and shit that I don't* want *to imagine.* He
returned half-willingly to pondering safer, easier things, such as
the silk of Jule's neck and the night-meadow still brushing up
against his own face. Nowhere near the intention to dissemble
— not yet, anyway — he said:

—Jule, the situation —

—The situation?— The shorter man's slender eyebrows
leapt.

—. . . ain't all that. It doesn't even have to be like that. If you
could just —

—Just what? Say that everything's just hunky-dory, la-de-
da?—

—We came down here to have a good time, right? We're
gonna have a good time, right? Yesterday and the day before
were nice, weren't they?—

—Yesterday and the day before . . .—

—You know you don't have to worry about a damn thing.
Not a thing.— He stopped.

—Jule.—

—What?—

—Look at me.—

—. . .—

—I'm talking to you, boy. I said *look* at me, now.—

The other man looked at him; the faintest glimmer beneath his lush eyelashes hinting at the sultry charge that always did *that* between them and stroked along the emboldened surge whenever one assumed that stern tone with the other. In spite of everything, he couldn't help gently shifting his hips in his seat, imagining again the slow clench and release of muscles accustomed to both refusal and welcome. Yet that reverie did nothing to lift the sudden heaviness he felt in spite of their having awakened only a few hours ago; he wasn't at all sure he was up right now for handling the risks of directly meeting those other eyes, wherever they might lead this time . . . and he was pretty sure, wasn't he, still aware of Marcus's warm hand on his knee, where, the eyes so full of all that and more for him, they would lead?

But so much had changed already, he thought. Changed in such a short time.

—Marcus . . .—

—I got your back, Jule. No, just listen. You know what time it is. You know I wouldn't ever. . . . How the fuck could you think it would be any different now?—

—I didn't say I thought it would be different. But it is, Marcus.—

—How?—

—*How?* You're actually gonna sit up here and ask me . . .—
He lowered his voice as the waiter returned with their sandwiches and drinks. A few other eaters nearby glanced over at the thick-eyelashed man with the tense face; then, meeting the silver in the other's eyes, returned to their plates.

—I know you didn't just ask me *how,*— he finished.

Marcus looked down, sighed, leaned to one side in his chair and, still looking down, sucked his teeth.

—You heard what I said.— His voice very quiet.

—Boy, don't be simple. Or cute. I never would've thought you—

—Jule.—

—How d'you think it's changed? Now that — now that I know. Now that *we* know. I mean . . . Jesus, Marcus!—

—You see me going anyplace? I know that's what you're trying to show out about.—

—Showing . . . is that what you think I'm doing, Marcus? Showing out?—

—Aren't you?—

—You make it sound trifling. Talking about 'the situ*a*tion.' You make it sound like . . .— But what did it sound like? The rusty shavings in his mouth would not permit him even to consider that Marcus might be correct or anywhere close, but aside from the sun's increasingly oppressive advance just beyond the café's canopy, was that all at once the heat of shame, even embarrassment, that he felt now creeping up the long slope to his meadows?

A little more quietly:

—Marcus . . . goddamn. You should know that whether you stay or not isn't even the only thing I'm thinking about right now.— He stopped, hesitated; looked down at his left wrist. —No, it isn't,— he went on in a voice attempting firmness or steadiness, —and no, you're right: I don't see you going anyplace. Not yet.—

—You . . . you actually think I would?—

Jule put the sandwich he was holding down on the plate and stared at it. Please don't do this now, he thought. Please don't ask me to . . .

—They all do, don't they?— The shavings made his voice sound thin; brittle. —After a while.— He fiddled lightly with the sandwich's crust, white toast, he saw. He'd meant to order whole wheat toast.

—You know they do, Marcus. Remember?—

—Jule . . . *Jesus.*—

—Don't *Jesus* me, Marcus. I *know*.— Lowering his eyes again to the table.

—They all do, after a while,— he said again.

—Who's some *they*, Jule? This is *me* you talking to. Me. You got to know by now I wouldn't ever . . .— (Of course *I* wouldn't, he thought.) —Look at me. I'm telling you now, all right? You ain't never seen me act like somebody who would do some fucked-up . . . I ain't like none a them, whatever them you're talking about —

—Oh, so you want me to give you a list now? You already forgot?—

—Jule, I'm not thinking about anybody else who —

—Waymon and Acie. Charlie and Raj. Remember them? Charlie didn't even wait two minutes to get outa there after Raj told him. And I know you remember what happened with Bryn and Joaquín, or Jorge, or whatever the fuck his name was —

—I know you can't be comparing me to them, Jule.— He tightened his squeeze on the other man's knee. Conjured the night meadows again: their brush alongside his (yes, as always), as, in that most private recollected place and time, his palms, or Jule's, or both of theirs, pressed together once more toward formation of the sanctity he believed they'd both always envisioned as more steadfast than prayer. He regarded his left hand which, like that of the man across from him, bore no ring — something he and Jule had seriously considered three years ago — and thought, shuddering slightly, why, he really thinks I would. He actually believes I would just go. After all these years he still doesn't (uh huh: doesn't know me. *Me*. Shuddering once more, he absolutely refused to permit his own mind to form the word "trust"). Now comes the feeling that he will pretend really isn't there — that, he will insist, has never really been there: the looming of the stranger.

The stranger made so much more awful by the fact that apparently, as of today, nothing, not one thing even from the most daring, sometimes delirious moments assayed and vaulted during their five years together, had succeeded in banishing him. He felt the stranger's crouch deep within him, but said only:

—I know you can't be comparing me to those people. Don't even try.—

—No. You're right.— The eyelashes turned out toward the beach where a laughing man was pulling down another laughing man's swim trunks.

—You're right as usual, Marcus. I shouldn't even try.—

—Charlie didn't ever give a fuck about nobody. People tried to tell Raj to watch out for his ass, but he wouldn't listen—

—No.—

—And Waymon — shit. Half the time anybody saw Waymon he was sniffing up behind some blond bitch who didn't even want his ass. I— He stopped. —I can't believe you would even mention those fucked-up bitches in the same breath as me, Jule. I mean . . .—

The other man was silent.

—Jule.— He drew a deep breath; then said it, very softly: —Baby.—

Jule looked up at him.

—You know, don't you?—

—Know what, Marcus?—

—That I'm not like those trifling people.—

—No.—

—No what?—

—No, Marcus. You're not like them.—

—And you — you know . . . you know you could trust me, right? You know I'll — I'll always take care of everything, Jule.—

—Sure.—

—Just like always.—

—Uh huh.— Except that this ain't quite like taking care of the rent when I'm taking care of my sick mama, he thought. And won't be, neither, he thought; feeling just then a return, though slightly milder this time, of the chill and stomach-drop he'd first felt when he (or no, *they*) had received the news.

—Say it, then.—

—Say what? What you want me to keep on saying, Marcus?—

—That you could trust me. That's all.—

—No.—

—No what?—

—No you're not like them and yeah I can trust you. All right?—

The other man's mouth slowly formed something like a smile. —I just want you to feel good, Jule.—

—I feel good.—

—Okay. But I want you to feel *real* good.—

The other man said nothing.

—You starting to feel better?—

—Did I say I was feeling bad?—

—No . . . but last night —

—Forget about last night. Last night is over. Last night came and went. Okay? Forget about it.—

—Well . . . I was scared, Jule.—

—. . .—

—All that sweat. I mean, I just never saw no sweating like that before. The bed was soaked, and you —

—Yeah, I remember. I was there. Forget it, Marcus!—

They were silent for a few minutes. Then the taller man said:

—Aren't you gonna have your sandwich?—

—In a minute.—

—Do you want anything else?—

—I'm fine, Marcus.—

—Maybe if you just had some of the —

—I'm fine, Marcus!—

He leaned back in his chair and again turned his eyelashes seaward, toward the strolling couples and rollerbladers.

—This place is pretty, but . . . I don't know. Seems like snow queen city. I haven't seen one brother here yet who wasn't hanging onto some white boy.—

—Fuck them.—

—And most of these bitches wouldn't even look you in the eye except to spit on you. That's what I really can't stand. Just like Boston, or —

—San Francisco, you mean. We had a good time when we went there, though.—

—I guess.—

—You ain't glad we took this vacation, Jule?—

—That you brought me here, you mean? Yeah, I'm glad. I . . .— Then he himself heard the whatever it was in his voice that softened just enough to sidle shyly up to Marcus's, as it matched for a moment what had briefly relented beneath the lashes.

—I am, Marcus. It's just that —

—'Cause if you're really not having a good time, we could go back and —

—No . . .— He paused; then, before what registered as his own almost complete astonishment, he heard pass from his own lips the special affectionate word he used only in private, and then only very occasionally, with Marcus — that word which (all things considered, he thought) hadn't left his lips, even in reveries, in weeks. He'd actually said it, he thought; *wrenched* it out, it felt like. Said it even after what he had seen flicker, then flare, in Marcus's eyes when, that very morning, the bloom of blood had appeared as he had shaved; when, the previous night, the sweats had soaked the sheets; when, on a morning only three months ago, a morning that continued to rocket its shout throughout all his limbs, that officious voice had (so calmly! How could such information ever be shared so calmly, even by a professional?) disclosed to them *the news*: the cold intelligence that had confirmed, after weeks of out-of-the-blue wracking flus, congestions, stealthy rashes and pounding two-day-long headaches, that all at once, unlike Marcus, he was no longer (and would never be again) one of the many fortunate have-*nots*, but rather had metamorphosed in one dire instant into one of the *haves*. One of the *haves*, officially, as of three months ago. Three little months during which it seemed, felt like, hardly any time had passed at all. Or breath. Strange time and breath; weird hours and weeks filled with all kinds of odd shapes and disguises, during which intimacy, always a shy animal, became even more shrinking; during which willing surrenders of the self to the entry and steady lodging of the other became, without the impermeability of swiftly donned shields, a definite *not*. The intelligence alone had been enough — way more than enough for bouts with newly tainted dreams. Enough for frantic sink-or-swim thrashings just above the undertows, there and *there*, in all those spectrally shadowed fjords. But to sit here now, today, beneath the green canopy and the beaming sun in this place of happy laughing faces and schmoozing palms; to sit here across from that increasingly care-faced man who had always been Marcus and nothing more (that too had been enough); to sit here and know that even after Marcus's first bridling at the sweats and the blood, he himself could still utter, though with a wrench, the private word to the eyes that had, despite their growing worry and care, fleetingly betrayed . . . well, *that* was as unbearable as it was a prayer, sure enough; but it also meant — didn't it? — that —

Yes, he thought: that maybe it was still possible to say that

word and others, and feel: feel everything the words meant and
had meant even as you meant them. Meant them more than
ever, maybe.

*We sat there next to each other in the doctor's office and heard
together what he had to say all about blood. Body, blood, time, and
the passing of time. Years, months, hours. And I know you were sitting right next to me, right there (you were, out of my eye-corner I
could see you), but it was like I could hardly feel you. Your shoulder
wasn't pressing into me the way it usually does when we sit like that,
and you weren't . . . no, you weren't holding my hand. I'm sure I
reached out my hand for yours sometime, but I . . . no, I couldn't
find it. I wanted to comfort you even as I felt your hand so warm
in mine. I wanted to calm the trembling I knew your arms and legs
were doing (oh yes, I could sense it, of course), even as I wanted to
just fall against you and say, oh my God. Marcus. Oh. Yes, just please
hold me hold me and. But I could feel only my own hands, and the
doctor's eyes on me; warm enough, I remember, but sad, too.*

*After the sweats, after you woke up so scared next to me with
your eyes jumping right out of your head, you actually said to me
— said to me with your voice all shaking and sounding so full (so
full!) of rain, I thought — you said, Jule, you don't have to be scared.
You don't have to be scared, Jule, I swear. And I said, me? Scared of
what? (There was a river, not rain, in my voice.) Sitting up there
drenched and the sheets soaking like we had put a hose all over
me and them. I hadn't ever sweated like that in my life. I was, I
was. . . . You said what you said and I answered. —You don't have
to be scared.— But right then you weren't looking at me. Did you
know that? I wonder if you ever will know. . . . I saw it. Felt it. Felt
you not-looking at me in the dark.*

*You — you were looking at something else, Marcus, or maybe
somebody else (though it was just us two there), but not at me.*

*After all that, a long time after, it felt like, you touched me.
Put your long, pretty hand on my arm, then on the other arm, and*

squeezed both of them. You squeezed me, pulling me against your chest; then pulled me into you the other way until I could smell the strong sweatsmell under your arms. I put my face in there, deep into it, and breathed you in just the same way you used to breathe in what you always called my night-meadows. I felt your arms around me. I wanted you to touch me everywhere. I wanted you to squeeze me and grab me everywhere: look dead straight in my face and hold on and hold long and hard until I couldn't take it anymore, Marcus. I wanted to feel you in me and on me, pressing hard, I mean hard in me and on me all over me God until I cried out holding on so hard to you, but — but no. Not then. We didn't. You didn't. I . . . no. I could still feel you not-looking. And your arms . . . well, they felt like rain. Like they were full of rain. Like you were full of rain, I thought.

They were eating in silence. After a time Marcus said:

—Jule, I'm sorry.—

The other man looked at him.

—Serious, Jule, I'm . . . I'm really sorry. What else can I say?—

—You don't have to say anything. What're you apologizing for?—

—Well, I mean . . . this morning — back in the hotel . . . —

The other man lowered his head and closed his eyes.

—I'm sorry I backed off like that, Jule . . . —

The eyes shut tighter, almost imperceptibly, as a hand put down the sandwich it had been holding and moved beneath the table, where its knuckles clenched.

—I mean . . . you and me . . . I know . . . —

—It wasn't all that, Marcus.— The eyes opening, but still narrowed. The knuckles still clenched.

—What do you mean?—

—I cut my lip was all. The razor was sharp. Nothing more. Just a nick, that was all. I should've used more cream.— He licked his lower lip. Swallowed. Felt his knuckles beneath the table.

—It was just . . . Jule, when you started sucking on it —
The other man raised his head slightly to look at the table.

—I mean — you know what I'm saying —

—Marcus.—

—I'm trying to say, it wasn't like I was trying to back off when you wanted to . . .—

When I wanted to kiss you, he thought. Put my mouth on yours again, like always, and feel it, *feel* it. In mine. Part of mine, blood to blood and skin to. . . . You in me and me in you. (Feeling those knuckles so clenched. Were they white by now? Very, very clenched.)

—I mean — shit, Jule, you know what I'm trying to say. It's not like I was afraid of you, or —

—. . .—

—We're having a great time. I'm loving this, Jule-J, getting to spend this kinda time with you. This morning wasn't nothing. We just — we just have to be careful, that's all.—

—No.—

—No what? What you mean, no?—

—*We* don't have to be careful. *You* have to be.—

—We both do.—

—No. You do.— He did not add, Yeah, you do, mother-fucker, you sure do, because the whole time, every single one of those other times, I thought I *was*. That was just what I thought. Believing what other people told me. Believing their faces. Eyes. Until.

—What you mean, *I* do? Just because —

(All right, now, Jule thought: a deep breath.)

—Because, Marcus, I don't have to be careful about shit anymore. You understand? Not shit.—

—What's that supposed to mean?—

— Just what I said. I'm a — a *free* fucking man now. I can do whatever the fuck I wanna do.— And I just might, he thought, just like . . . but he turned sharply from the thought before its rage and vitriol were betrayed on his face.

Marcus sucked his teeth again: the mannerism that indicated his exasperation not yet congealed to full disgust or anger; then began saying something else to which Jule decided he would close his ears. Five years of on-and-off practice made that easy enough. And so now he won't take what I just said seriously, he thought, which is probably a good thing for him. I wouldn't want to take it seriously either if I was in his place. In a minute I know he'll start going on and on about how I have to begin taking better *care* of myself more than ever now and listen to everybody the doctors this one and that one yah yah yah and you know there're all kinds of new treatments every day baby he'll say on and on and now you don't need to start talking crazy shit Jule he'll say and look at me like that and baby you know we can do so many *things* to be careful and on and on and shit Jule you know I'll take *care* of you he'll say because I (but no please! I can't take hearing him say *that* word right now, please not right now please no no) and how we'll be able to go on and on in spite of but he just doesn't *get* the shit, does he? Even now. Doesn't have no clue that

—I just don't know if I want to be bothered, Marcus,— he heard himself say.

—Bothered . . . what do you —

—I *mean*. I mean I just don't know if I give a fuck anymore.—

—You don't give . . . about me?—

—I'm not talking about you.—

—Well what then?—

—You don't understand. You can't understand. You ain't the one that's got it!—

A few heads turned in their direction.

—Okay. You're right, I don't have it. Keep your voice down.—

—Please.—

—But what's me not having it got to do with you saying you don't care about —

—I don't know. Nothing. Everything.—

—You have to care, Jule.—

—Why do I *have* to? I don't *have* to do shit.— He raised a leg over one of the chair arms and began to scrutinize the skin on his left arm below the fine hairs; absently at first and then with a steadiness that gradually gave way to concern that moved quickly from his face to his neck and shoulders before pulling everything with it down into a slump of weariness.

—I'm just so sick of running, Marcus.— Very quietly, looking down. Thumb and fingers massaging his eyebrows.

—Run . . . who's running?—

—We are.—

—Running where? Why do you say that? Where you see us running to?—

—Right here. Everywhere.—

—What? Just cause we're taking a damn vac*a*tion for the first time in, in what, six months —

—I don't mean only this.—

—Jule-J, *this*— his hand swept out to indicate everybody and everything around them —this isn't hardly no kind of running. I don't know what you . . .—

The other man's eyelashes had already turned back out to the sea. When he spoke, his voice breathed as quiet as before.

—Maybe you're not.— Not yet anyway, he thought. —But I know I am. Just like the whole world now is filled with all these people running and running, trying to get away, and now it's like I'm one a them. But it's like now there's no place left to run to. And I'm ... Marcus, I'm *tired*.— He turned suddenly back from looking out at the sea, stared directly at the man across from him, and, without any warning, saw it: the gentle beauty that years ago had halted his own breath. He saw again the unstinting generosity in the smile he remembered, though Marcus was not smiling now; the frequent bravery in it, and *oh Marcus*, he thought as it all hit him again for the first time in so long: sometimes just looking at him was enough. Enough to draw out the tears never too far beneath the surface, and raise that slow trembling in his hands that he felt now as he thought Yes, that's it, I'm just so tired, but you can't understand that, can you? Can't and never could. Can't cause you were always the one to smile even when you didn't feel like smiling. The one who always had to say Aw baby we'll get through it, whatever *it* was, when most of the time we almost didn't get through it. But now—

—Tired,— he heard himself say again.

—Tired of . . .—

—I just don't wanna be fighting and ending up having to deal with this doctor and that one plus you and what your family says and what my mother thinks and on and on and carrying *on*. I never did want to. And now you and a whole bunch of other people are telling me I'm gonna have to fight and do this and do that and I . . . I *can't*. I don't want to.—

—Jule . . .—

—I just want some *quiet*.— Yeah, he thought, just that. A whole bunch of it. A whole bunch enough to change everything back to how it used to be, before. Enough to shush down forever all the loud noise of one morning in a doctor's office three months ago. Enough to shush down the sound of a long slow rain falling where pressing arms should have been and hadn't been, and where a face, instead of not-looking, should have *looked*. Well enough to shush down the cry that had ripped up after his own hand had reached for *his* hand to squeeze that morning in the doctor's office and found — for the first time? — only the empty space of someone there, sure enough, but not really *there*. Like the shoulder that hadn't been really there for the numbed face to turn to and rest. The same shoulder that later had, had (uh huh, there's a word for it, say it!) *recoiled*. All at once, with his next words, he heard his voice rising — rising, he thought, to something just two inches shy of a growl's easing its way toward a half-tethered scream.

—For once just some *fucking* quiet. And peace. Maybe even some time alone, just by myself. Without you, or . . . did you ever think of that? Me alone, without you *hovering* over me all the time, Marcus. Did you ever think what that might be like?—

He could only assume that the stricken look on Marcus's face was in response to the murderous one he felt on his own.

But I just want, he thought.

Yes, he thought, *really want. Just not to, not to get sick. Not to ever get sick, no, or have to go through all that. What the doctor talked about. What we've already seen. All those marks and rashes and scars like some a them got, or — God forbid. . . . No. Please, Jesus. No.*

That's all I want. Just to be, to be . . . all right. And you, Marcus. Holding. That's all.

Later, after the abrupt departure and the speed, Marcus will remember how, in this moment that has already begun to stretch itself toward what he can't yet know will be their flight, he cannot say anything, not anything at all, to the one across from him who has just begun, just like that, to cry. Cry quietly. Soft little sounds, more like slightly labored breathing than tears. Like grief and joy at the fleeting beauty of the day, it might appear to other people, or awe over all that gorgeous open water out there. Water and sky without end. And maybe, had they been home — someplace else, less exposed, safer and enclosed, not there so out in the open in the middle of all those laughing faces, I might have touched you just like before, Jule. Touched you with a real long squeeze, even if only under the table like before; even if (he does not think) trembling at the edge of recoiling. But not this time. Not so soon after the memory of blood glinting on a lower lip. Not so soon after the shock of waking up to soaked sheets. Not thinking about all that still might be ahead, still ahead oh God and unimaginable, unknown: what neither of them had ever bargained for and, outside of the sight of blood and sweat, hadn't wanted (like mostly everyone they knew) to think about. Then the hot shame floods his cheeks as he thinks No, and not here even in the presence of other men in the café who are clearly, like themselves, with each other. But these men were mostly white, they'd both seen early on, and so not, they'd thought, their most crucial brethren. He will comfort himself with that truth and not flinch before it — not this time — as an excuse. Because there are — aren't there? — too many reasons and more why he can't reach across the table now and take those hands in his own. Too many reasons now, right now, not to press that face so warmly into his palm . . . reasons having partly to do with those tears, he knows. Too many reasons and more he won't regard right now. Too many reasons for his hands to remain exactly where they are.

Right after we found out, he said to me, Marcus, it's like: it's like nothing's ever gonna be the same again. Not ever. Don't talk shit, I said, holding him (but that was hard). Nothing ain't changed, I said, except that . . . But a big motherfucking except, he said and looked at me. And I knew he knew I thought so too. He felt me not wanting to touch him and pulled away. I tried. I tried, but —

It's like things used to be one way and now they're a whole other way, he said. No, he said, looking at me like that, don't even try to say anything. I'm telling you now what I know. It's all gonna be different now. Oh, yes, it is. And you better remember that when the time comes, Marcus, cause that's some knowledge you gone need.

Don't tell me how much you'll take care of me and be here for me and all a that shit, he said. You can't hardly take care of yourself. That's the damn truth. But whyn't you give me a chance, I said, thinking . . . but I don't know what I was thinking. But he just looked into my face and said I'll be running from you, too. No, you won't, I said. Just wait and see, he said. Then he let me hold him in that way that felt almost real. Like almost the way it used to feel before we found out.

Neither of them glanced up immediately when two people brushed past them to sit down at the next table — two men. Neither immediately noted that one of the men held firmly onto the very thin arm of the extremely thin, mottled-faced man who shuffled alongside him. They presently looked up, as did some other lunchers, to see that the thin man might in fact have been fairly young, about their age, or slightly older, but for his face's betrayal, beneath a tattered sun hat, of its having collapsed further beneath the weight of impossible things: years of night fevers, perhaps, and rancorous bowels intent on fleshly cataclysm; the indignities of marauding spores indifferent to the low hum of machines hooked up to coax back careening organs, and prognostications of blindness and catalepsy. The eyes had clearly at last surrendered their protracted battle against becoming those of a desiccated lizard; the mouth had finally offered up its forlorn ledge to pustules. With everyone else who watched, they saw the dark purple marks, rather like an ample cigar's burns, on his exposed arms and neck. They noted how his merely shuffling to the table seemed to snatch from him the remaining breath he barely had. As, assisted by his companion, he sank with difficulty into his seat, they saw the bones edging up just beneath the mottled cheeks and everyplace else not shielded from the sun. Some of the other watching lunchers had already quickly returned to their salads and spritzers; a few, determinedly bent over menus or the sanctum of their own folded hands, began to converse in lower tones.

Much later, Jule would swear to himself that he had *not* glimpsed that look in Marcus's eyes, nor felt the sharp rise of his own gorge and the return of that familiar chill, but far colder, as they both stared (but, they believed, tried so hard not to) at the new arrivals. He would swear for as long as he could that he'd seen none of it: not those hideous blotches on the man's skin, nor those jutting bones. He would buck all memories that, leaving his unfinished sandwich on the gleaming white plate, he had risen out of his chair so abruptly and, with barely a glance at the man across from him, said

—Let's get out of here. Now. I could use a swim.—

in that voice that had *not* been so urgent, he would insist to himself, nor so connected to those sudden, unmistakable skips of his heart, he would think later, still beating. Pumping. Alive.

—A *swim?*— he heard the voice across from him ask. —After all that food? Are you —

—I'm fine.— He felt his mouth's resistance to the lopsided smile that, had it time, might have stretched itself into a full grimace and greeted the rising tightness in his chest.

—We have to pay. Is the waiter —

—*I don't know,* Marcus.— He tossed some bills down on the table — for the tip, he muttered — then turned around quickly, and with a light

—I'll wait for you out front. —

tossed over his shoulder, he set off between the tables without looking back, out to the sidewalk.

A strong breeze, similar to the one that had brought the earlier brief shower, had begun to blow in off the water; the sky looked as if it might cloud over again in a few minutes. Hurricane season, a woman in their hotel had said that morning, but God knows don't none of us need *that,* just say your prayers we don't get one before you all head back home.

Marcus soon joined him on the sidewalk, looking hot and irritated, but also as if he too would rather forget what he had just seen; forget it because it made him ill, nauseated him, confirmed everyone's worst fears about (but don't say the word, they both thought, please, *I can't stand to hear the word*). Jule heard the clumsy attempt at testiness, as if everything were perfectly regular and his own rapid exit had bordered on nothing more unusual than some "showing out" (again); nothing more than "Jule's flair," as some of their friends had always said, for the quixotic. —All right, now,— came the voice of the man standing beside him, just behind him, — what was all that about . . .— Something muttered about how they hadn't even been able to enjoy . . . enjoy what? Then, from a place that all at once sounded both terribly close and far away (though less testy) floated words about how they couldn't swim right this minute, Jule, they'd left their trunks and other things back in the hotel . . . and then a pat — a pat! — to the back of his head, which gesture made his knees tremble, following the shudder his spine just then insisted on. He did not turn back to regard the face of the man who'd patted him. *But I know . . . yes, I know I'd know that face anywhere*, he thought, *voice and eyes. His mouth. But his hands. . . .*

He was barely aware in the next minutes of Marcus's voice shouting at his side, then again behind him, then Marcus's footsteps pounding after him, in part because he was barely aware that he was running. Car horns blared and a few brakes screeched, followed by loud swears, as he dashed across the Drive toward the beach, but none of that, he knew, meant anything. He was truly in flight this time, he thought: toward the sea, the sky. The rain, and maybe. . . . What did it matter if Marcus was racing after him, shouting out his name in the street, calling for him to stop? In a minute he knew he would feel that other hand's press on his elbow or shoulder, doing its best to thwart his flight, but soon enough none of that would matter either. He ran. Flew. Actually felt himself rising into the air. *Freedom*, he thought, *free . . . but whatever it is, might be, feels real heavy, like something else*, he thought. *Like something pretending to be light —*

WOMAN   IMPOSSIBLE TASK

.

I MPOSSIBLE, YES. BUT HOW CAN SHE NOT DO IT?
After all, someone must. At least that is what she thinks. That is what she tells herself.

Someone must make the bread. Knead it. Roll it. Dust it with flour. (Although now there is no flour.) Someone must . . . — but she will not pay attention. No, of course not. Not pay attention to those sounds outside. (Yes, screaming again. But not screaming now. Not like before. In the time of the light, all that *light*, and the noise. So much noise.) Those sounds . . . yes, more rifle shots. In the distance. The grenades — will the grenades come later?

(*The grenades always come later,* she will not think.)

(*Someone must go on making the bread,* she thinks)

(How empty the house. *How still the light*, she thinks)

(And all the holes, holes, holes everywhere, where the walls exploded —)

Time: the time now, which she cannot know — perhaps it is better that she not know: three o'clock in the afternoon.

Her fingers. Dusty. *From flour*, she thinks. *That is flour on my hands, the flour no one can find now. It is not dust or dirt from the roadside. It is not evidence that I was digging in the roadside yesterday and the day before, looking for —*

Oh but no. No, no. Why think of that now? She is making bread. You are making bread. Bread without flour. The kind of bread that he always loved.

But he is gone now —

Yes, along with everyone else in the house —

Yes, along with everyone else in the street —

Soon it will be dark, absolutely dark, with no lights on anywhere around here —

The flour no one can find now. One cannot find flour or children.

They warned us two weeks ago, two months ago, to keep our lights turned off after dusk. They said, will be dangerous. They said, might be bombs. If the raids come, if the invasions come . . . They said, And keep your children inside. Inside, they said. But now all the children are gone. Now everyone is gone, except me, except this woman standing here who is me, except this woman standing here in what was once her kitchen, trying, trying. Trying to make bread without flour.

She; she does not; she does not, as she stands there; she does not, as she stands there in this moment; she does not, as she stands there in this moment so perfectly still — she does not (no, I *will not*) vomit. Vomit, vomit blood, vomit liquid, all over the floor.

No, nor make a sound.

She. She-I. Does *not.* Does not *make.* Does not make a —

There are sounds, there are sounds; there are smells, always smells; please wipe off that rock, a voice that sounds like her own says; the rock is sticky, you must wipe it off, says the voice again — yes, it is hers; I don't like the way it shines, she/her voice says; a part of his face is still shining on the rock, she whispers; now give me your hand, someone tells her, bending over her; no, I promise I won't hurt you, he says, but (so she will believe later she glimpsed in his face) afraid to move her; but who, who are you, I don't know your name, she says, feeling the hard ground beneath her; Oh, was he your husband, he says, waving his hand for some of the others, also in uniform, to come over; was he your husband, he repeats, and did you see when the explosion; Oh, she says, moans, as another of them bends over her; please wipe off that rock, she is trying to tell them, part of his face is still on it; all right now, just quiet, try to stay calm, we're try- ing to help you; where, one of them said; yes, he said, asking again, your child, where; Oh my God, oh my God, please wipe off that rock, she hears herself scream, although she is not screaming; what is this on your face, the other one, younger, says to her, it's blood, isn't it; if you would just let me; no, I'm a soldier; yes, one of our own army, I'm here to help you; yes, he says, yes, I speak your language, of course, aren't you understanding me; she's in terrible shape, the first

*one says, looking down at her like that; noise, so much noise; smells,
so many smells; is that the smell of someone's insides, left on a rock to
dry in the sun; and* She, *oh* She *lying there on the hard* hard *ground
covered with sticky rocks,* She *does not make, no, not make a sound;*
She *does not* make; *there are sounds, there are sounds, and smells,
whose insides are those drying on the rock; part of his face was left on
that rock; no, her child, no, no idea, no, no one has seen the girl; the
girl who could not possibly have been the one she had seen standing
next to him just before the bright light had flashed; no, well, it appears that almost no one from that village, her village, is still alive;
yes, part of his face was left on that rock; she feels the rocks of the
hard hard ground beneath her back; whose insides are those burning
in the sun; and look at her smiling,* She *feels herself smiling beneath
them looking down at her, all of them so afraid, she thinks; so afraid,
she thinks, to move her (and oh isn't the younger one in the cleaner
uniform handsome — how can they send these young boys out to
do this kind of work, there are so many flies, so many bad smells);*
She *feels herself smiling, looking up at the so blue sky; looking up,*
She *does not vomit,* She *does not stare back at the faces staring at
her,* She *does not make a sound,* She *does* not; *yes, obviously shock,
saying something about her husband's hand and a charred girl, can
you get her to sit up straight; let us help you, please, let us help you
(but voices, so many voices, now not the first time nor the last); will
you give me your hand, I promise I won't hurt you; his hand, she remembers, had come flying through the kitchen window — of course
it had been his hand, she would know his hands anywhere; and still*
She, *that* She *lying there who is somehow she, does not throw up;
please wipe off this rock; well, because it is too red, too bright; too red
and too bright and too; yes, his face; yes,* She *had seen the look on
his face just before the flash of bright light and the noise, just before
his hand came flying in at her — just before all the dogs in the street
and the people began to scream; yes, his face looking at her like that
before his head had hurled off toward the rock; grenades had made*

*the smell and the hands; where are my hands; where is his face; I
have no face; now* She *has no face; HerMy face is on the rock (but he
had not screamed); please excuse this smell; all the rocks are melting,
just like the hands and my; may I please scream,* She *does not ask;
please allow me to melt; I speak your language, one of them says, but
who is speaking? but I will not* She *says I will not throw up*

No, She *knows.* She *knows that it could not possibly have been their
girl standing in the street next to him when the light and the noise
— the light and the hands —*

But quiet. Quiet then.

Bandages. Yes. And water. Quiet.

A hospital? How could there have been one? It had been flaming.
Had it not been flaming when all those hands had carried her to
the hospital? Or had that been some other building?

Whitenotquiethospital with hands, hands everywhere. Hands
reaching out. Stretching.

Stretching in the hospital. Stretching out of the rubble. Stretching from underneath —

A hospital, or a camp. They had taken her to one. *No, she's in
terrible shape. We need this. Yes, and some more of that. Tinctures.
Swabs. No, clean. All clean.* (Soldiers? Doctors? Nurses? But voices.
Always too many voices.) *She's in horrible shape. Oh all these people
here,* she had thought, gazing around at all the burned and the
melted, the maimed and the half-armed. The no-longer-handed,
the blinded, half-legged. *They are all taking so long to die,* she had
thought: whereas he and the charred girl, the girl who could not

possibly (no, of course not!) have been their daughter, had died so quickly. One, two, one-two-three. *Here is a head, there are some fingers. Here is my daughter, there is her skin.* Gone. Quickly, she had thought. Ashes. In the sky. The charred parts. All gone.

The charred girl caught out in the street by the blinding light, standing as she remembered seeing her stand so still and open-mouthed in the street by his side, could not possibly have been (no, of course not!) their child. Her daughter. Their child. No, no. A great resemblance in the face of that girl to their daughter, an impossible resemblance — but no. And she *had* seen the girl, before the light, turn her head up to him and put her hand on his arm and say something quietly like *Daddy*, as their own daughter would have done. "Daddy." But no. Of course not.

Where is her daughter? She must be wandering the streets again. Always such a bad girl. She never listens when we tell her, when he told her, when she told her: Stay home. *The streets are not safe. They are dangerous, in fact. Do you understand.* Stay home. *Stay close to home in the village. Stay inside home. She does not listen. Children often do not listen. Even in times of war, bombs, flashing lights and melted skin, they choose not to listen. Young girls who do not listen end up charred. End up as smoky, blackened things. Where is her daughter? But how incredibly that other girl, the one who had stood out in the street next to him when the light had flashed and the noise came, had looked just like her. How she had put her hand on his arm just like her: had, for whatever reason just then — who can tell why children play these games? — called him "Daddy." Looked up at him that way with her hand on his arm. Bad girl. Bad wandering girl. Bad notlistening wandering girl. Girl who will wind up blackened and charred one day: spread across those fields and fields of ashes.*

But quiet. Quiet now. A hand, once, perhaps twice, on her forehead.

Then blackness. Stench. *I am dead,* she had thought, *and glad to be.*

Here, where there is no bread, she had thought while dead. *Impossible task.*

Not a sound, except those screams —

And then. Then somehow. Somehow one week later, or two. (Who could keep time? It was/It is so much harder to keep time when you are dead.) However much time, but too soon: up out of there. Her body, walking. Impossibly. Told to walk. And walking. *She will have to leave now.* (One of the many voices.) *Yes, now. We have absolutely no more room.* Out of the stench-hospital, the whitenotquiet hospital. *You will have to leave now,* one of them said to her while she was dead, *we need the cot. Yes, yes, other bombings.* Of course. And so. And so still dead. And so still dead she had risen from the cot. Risen and. Had folded her — her *hands,* that was what they were, across her chest. Felt the places, all those places, where their hands had fastened thick bandages. And felt the scars . . . the stitches. The veryhurting places. And then, somehow, impossibly, had . . . walked. Walked out past the dead and the crying-out and the outstretched hands. Out into light and noise. She. Alone. *Woman,* she had thought, *alone. With hands.* She has/I have two hands. Her eyes unseeing. Deadwoman notseeing and walking. Walking slowly so unseeing slowly. But walking very quickly past fields of ashes. Ashes quiet. Past fields of hands with twisted fingers. Twisted fingers reaching. Reaching up out of the ground.

Back to the village of everything dead and quiet, her bandaged feet had commanded. But of course. Where else? Where else was there to go?

In the village, she had thought, *it would be possible to make bread. Bread,* she had thought. *For someone will always need it. Children —*

Her bandaged feet, propelling her there. Onward over the dusty roads littered with ashes and . . . all the hard white parts. Grinning. Deadchildren. Deadpeople grinning. The verywhite hard parts sometimes partly exposed underneath where everything else had been torn. Through clouds. Clouds of flies. Dogs everywhere. Bloated deadanimals. The smell of burnt feathers where cocks, only a short time ago, had strutted. Crowed.

Past all the soldiers. The soldiers sometimes sick. Very sick. Bleeding. Bleedvomiting.

She *had never vomited.*

But then well. And so. And so finally. And so finally reaching. And so finally reaching the village. (The village: more than a day's walk — and well, no food — almost no water — the water, contaminated? — contaminated, in that river? — But anyway too late. Too late for her and for those. For those she had seen on the way. Those she had seen on the way who had been eating dirt. Clawing it up with their hands. And she, joining them. Dirt was good to eat. Good, good! Dirt, clawed with the hands, and some kind of yellow vegetable snatched by all of them off a deadman's bloated chest.) *But how quiet,* she had thought upon arriving back in the village; *how quiet the village with no one in it; village of deadpeople crushed beneath the toppled houses. The houses the people burned in the middle of the night. Underneath all the noise. How difficult will it be,* she had wondered, *to make bread with dead hands.*

The house, that house, their house: a ruin. Completely ruined though not entirely burned. No, because part of the kitchen still standing. The little metal table on which she had always made bread (but how, *how?*) still standing. Covered with dust. Dust that was "Ashes," she thought. Ashes, and more.

The smell of smoke still inside what remained of the house.

No voices. No voices anywhere. No birds. No trees.

Quiet. Very quiet.

No water.
No flour.
Nothing but the hands.

And watching. Watching herself. Watching herself walk in. Walk in over the rubble. *Watching her body, watching my body, watching my body her body as I walk in.* Then seeing: Yes, that had been the front door, over there had been a window — she had recognized it! Then stopping. Listening. Turning neither to the left nor to the right. Holding her head, for just a moment, that way. Listening — listening for —

But no voices. Not from anywhere. Nowhere.

No sounds except —

That is the sound of my hands against my sides. Pat, pat-pat. That is the sound of my breathing: in out, in out.

Moving over the rubble, over all the stones, to behind what remains of the little metal table. Seeing nothing but the view of nothing at all out there beyond the gaping space where her kitchen window should have been.

The bread: her hands: *pat, pat-pat*: preparing:

Add a little water. (And do not think, she thinks.) *Now, press it down.* (No, nor remember.) *Roll it out a little more, it's too thick.* (It had been his hand.) *Press down those edges.* (Yes, his hand, of course. Who else's?) *Oh, you'll need some more water, it's too dry.* (His hand that, minus the rest of him, had come —) *Hurry, knead it, punch it, quickly!* (— had come sailing, sailing, sailing into her kitchen window, at three o'clock
    three o'clock
    three o'clock
    in the afternoon)

How quiet it is without the children. The children's shouts outside in the streets. The children who had been everyone's, and there. One of whom had called me — why, called me Mother. But now switch to something else. Quickly. (The bread dough: feeling soggy beneath her hands. She needs flour, but who can get flour now? She needs dust, dirt . . . the things found these days in roadside dust and dirt. She needs —)

A breeze, blowing through what had been her kitchen window, eases its way in to where she now stands perfectly still behind the used-to-be wall that had once formed part of her kitchen. Part of their house. Eases its way in, carrying no scent, thank God, of burned things. Easing its way in, to tell her, quietly, gently: *Perhaps now that you are dead, back here in the everything-dead quiet village, you will no longer dream. For deadwomen — no, they do not. They do not dream.*
    How she hopes, squeezing as hard as she can the impos-

sible bread, that deadwomen do not dream. How she hopes, even dares now to pray, that they do not dream of blinding light and noise — and that her exhausted eyes, when they finally are permitted to close for an hour or two, will never permit behind their twitching lids visions of charred girls. Reaching hands.

Feeling, as she had walked back over the dusty roads on her way back to the village, proud of herself. Proud that she had not vomited when one of the voices in the hospital had said something to her about the girl. Said something (we are speaking your language, can you hear us, understand us? — and that one had shaken her, looked long into her face) — said something about one of the soldiers having found the girl. (No, not the entire girl. Parts of her. They had not meant for her to hear that. They had not meant for her to know.) Said something about how she must have been with her father when the light had flashed, the fire licked out, the noise knocked apart the houses. The girl had just turned fourteen. Had had long legs, one with a deep scar from childhood games. Had had wide eyes — yes, shaped like almonds, everyone had always said. Eyes —

Everything had blurred even more after that: light, noise, and hands reaching out in the white notquiet hospital. Blurred, then completely fallen apart. Fingers, and the skin nearest the elbows. You will have to leave now, we have no more room. All had fallen apart. Fallen off. Melted. The smell. She had not vomited. There had been no warning before the light, noise. No warning before his hand had come flying. His hand with his ring on it. The ring that he had, that they had . . . — She had not vomited. No, nor screamed. No other women had been present when the voices had — who had they been? — when they had told her about the girl. When another one, the cruelest voice of all, had talked as if she had not been there, as if she had been unable to hear (can you hear us?) about the charred thing found not far from her father. Someone from the village who must

have recognized . . . Fingers had touched her then, lying there on the
cot, but fingers had also fallen off. His ring . . . whoever it was who
had picked up the girl and put her someplace, the place they put all
those things, must have looked down to find his hands blackened. It
is never easy to hold charred things, especially when they fall apart in
the hands. Fingers, so many fingers touching her as she had lain on
the cot. But please hold on to your fingers, she had thought, feeling
herself becoming dead. Hold onto them, keep them attached to your
hands, so that I will not vomit.

Now if only she had a spoon. And salt. Just a little. If only she
had a larger spoon. And some sugar. Yes, just a little. And a knife.
And just a little warm water. Impossible task, but how can she
not do it? How can she not do it, she asks the lingering breeze,
confident now that, looking out at the rubble that remains
just below where her kitchen window should be, she will not
vomit. Loving the feeling of herself not vomiting. And so the
dough will be a bit lumpy, her fingers tell her. Her fingers still so
strangely attached to her hand. Lumpy, but I, she, will press it.
Roll it, I-she will. Praying that tonight no dreams, no dreams.
Nor smells.

Feeling her ring. The ring that cannot possibly still be there, but
is there.

Tight on her finger. There.

The hour feeling somehow like three o'clock,
three o'clock,
now three o'clock in the afternoon —

but much later.

The sky, darkening. But still some light —

She must make the bread. *Melt the dough. Stretch the skin.*

The dough must not be charred. It must not end up in a field of ashes.

Is it three o'clock here? It will always be three o'clock here. There will never come a time when it will be any other time than three o'clock, she-I thinks. If he had been wearing his watch on that wrist, it would have shown three o'clock exactly when his hand came flying in. I would have recognized it, the watch, and said, oh, well! I see the time.

Darkness, soon coming.

— *but must make the bread. Dough, even without flour.*

Impossible task —

Young girls who walk out into the street in the middle of the after-noon and say "Daddy" and put a hand on his shoulder the way that one had might end up in parts. Charred.

But now busy. Busy, busy, in the growing darkness. Bread. Dough. Hands. Flour. And now only a few sounds. Sounds like *rifle shots again in the distance,* she thinks. *Like grenades.* But now knead. *Knead. But no light. So dark now everywhere. No light that will burn. No fire on my hands. Only darkness —*

(*Yes,* no one tells her, *the village is empty. Empty —*)

(Will there be fire in the dreams?)

— and darkness. And so many smells. And bright flames. She sees (but darkness everywhere now). She sees —

A pile of shoulders — there was a —

And legs —

Legs, yes. And then, out of the darkness —

Always. *Every time —*

Those reaching hands.

HE WHO WOULD HAVE BECOME "JOSHUA,"
1791

SOON, AFTER IT ALL IS OVER — AFTER MANY MORE HERE have ceased breathing and also have risen and flown — we will remember how, immediately after she clamped her jaw shut forever and stiffened, she began once again to tell it: the oldest woman on board, telling us all again how fiercely that jealous river of our memory, before it destroyed every living thing in its path, had once flashed through a solemn pair of eyes, even as two boys, their legs caressed by slinking weeds, remained hidden beneath those waters for seven uninterrupted secret days. We will remember how, with her mouth perpetually closed and her form rigid and unbreathing, she told us how so long ago, in that village, a young girl fought with all her strength (but at last to no avail) to escape the coming horrors foretold by whispering trees, and how, not long afterward, the ground all about became soaked with the salt water from three days of a woman's agonized tears. We will remember how she recalled what some of us, even in this darkness, witnessed for ourselves: how only a few nights ago those two, including the one who, like her, always spoke without opening his mouth, did not sprout wings yet arose out of their rigid forms among us all and flew: *flew up out of here and out over the water and then into it,* her voice told us, *to reawaken back there. Back there,* she reminded us, *in the oldest water of our longing, so very far from here.* She who should never have been taken with the rest of us: an error committed by someone back there who was not, unlike us, of there. Someone — surely one of *them,* the ghosts so fond of forcing open our jaws each night, as they bend over us and leave behind that bitter taste in our throats and on our tongues — who did not look carefully enough into her withered face, at her sunken shoulders, and at those useless, sagging breasts. Someone who surely knew that she would be no longer useful for breeding — of use to whom, with those drooping breasts, that slack, hanging jaw, that sour old woman's smell? — but who thought *ancient, yes, but perhaps a few years of harvesting left in her. The hands like claws,* that someone must have thought, *all the more useful for grasping the grain. So load her, then,* that someone thought; and so she came. Came but, fortunately for her, ceased all breath only a short time ago.

For all this time, none of us except her have been able to tell how long we have been out here. But "Forty-seven days," she groaned, whispered, late one night — sick in her stomach, we thought, from the constant rockings and heavings beneath us, unlike anything any of us have ever known, especially in this way. In this way bound here on our backs, every single man and woman and child, staring up into this darkness that is always blackness, that is never anything but hotness. Stench. And the cries. *So hot,* a child nearby us moans, writhing but bound far from her mother no longer here, *and filled with the stench of what we all are becoming: what we are becoming,* groans another in another corner, way over there on the far side, who also would have flown, had he been able, like the others, to clamp his jaw shut forever and close his eyes. *What* they *are making us into,* another cries out in his dreams when he is able to sleep, when small things, and sometimes bigger things, do not move beneath where he lies and reach up to scurry over his exposed flesh.

She who would soon stop breathing also knew, in the way she has always known these things, how those two managed to fly.

"Forty-seven days and nights," she said, not opening her mouth, "because the star of wanting has gone over *there*, and the golden star of remembering is now directly overhead. Oh yes."

How can you know, mother, a young boy all the way across, on the other side, lying next to his older brother who had already stopped breathing, asked — asked also, immediately after she spoke, without opening his mouth.

She did not answer. She did not have to. We all heard her silent claim, and believed her. Already well on her way to flight, she was one of those, the very few, who could see entirely through the thick wood above us, all the way up to where *they* walked and paced, wrapped in their anxiety and sometimes fear about us; all the way up to the blackness, the openness, the star-filledness, of the sky above all that open black water.

"'Charleston,'" she said one night, her lips never moving. "'Charleston' is the name of the place. The place where we are going.

"Or no, 'Cartagena de Indias,' she said a few moments later. "And for some, a place called 'Paramaribo.' Those are the places. The place where *they* will do all those things."

What things, a small voice asked. From a girl as small as her voice, her hands bound at her side. Her entire form clenched like a fragile heart, beating.

"The place," she said, "where they, and many others who resemble them, all of them with filthy hands, will pry you apart. The place where they will pry apart your buttocks, weigh your breasts in their hands as if fondling stones, examine with one hand or two your private parts, move their dirty fingers over your teeth — but quiet, child," she said to a young boy beginning to whimper — quiet, now." She did not look at him. Preparing to leave us, she looked at no one in the darkness; only up, in the blackness, toward the sounds of them walking above. "Quiet," she continued, "for you must know, if you have not learned already, that they are capable of anything. Anything," she said, very quietly, "and more. More, yes," she continued, "and still more. But perhaps you will be fortunate enough not to live to know. Perhaps you too, on a night like this one to come, will fly as those two did. Fly so that you, like they, will finally know nothing of those places," she continued, quietly, "where so many of them will attempt with their eyes and noses to assess your age. Your age," she said, looking out at no one, "and the ultimate strength in your back, hands, and loins. The strength they will assess that will determine everything. Everything that they will then tell others of themselves. Others who, wanting to know, will shout 'How much?'"

The boy whimpered still. And still she refused to look at him.

How much? another voice asked. But do you mean — ?

She remained silent, then said:

"You will know more when this — this *thing* arrives in 'Charleston,'" she said, "a place unlike anything you have ever known. A place of — of fetid swamps. Swamps filled with those who have the dry not-skin of ghosts. Like the ones who walk up there and come — come down *here* each day and each night." We felt her eyes close tightly then. Felt her fingers curl toward the tightened palms. *Mother,* someone did not dare ask, *why are your eyes shut so tightly? She is dreaming of reaching fingers and that bitter taste on the tongue,* someone else whispered, before her eyes opened again and she said:

"Or when it arrives in 'Cartagena de Indias,' a place fortified by what *they* call 'cannons.' A place where, as in the place called 'Paramaribo,' they will dump the last of those who stopped breathing here into the sea, and curse their luck. Women, men, and children. Enough not-breathing to choke the sea.

"But I am not going to speak of any of that now," she said — barely moving just then where she lay, we all sensed; closing her eyes once again so as not to see what she refused to speak of any more, we knew — "for in only a short time I will be gone. I am going to remember, for the last time, the two who flew. Remember them," she said, "with the hope that I will see them, in flight or already back there, when I am gone. Remember, when I am gone." It was then that we all heard, yes, *heard* her draw her last breath. Her form, stretched out beneath the metal that held her as it held each of us, stiffened. In the light of the following day, when *they* descended to do what they always did — gazed upon us briefly to see if we still breathed, tossed that foul water over us to barely moisten our lips, and smeared over our mouths that sickening mash that none of us would have fed even to lizards — they would see that she had gone. With lips curled in disgust and words snarled in that gibberish none of us could understand, they would release her stiffened form from the metal and carry her up there where, as we each would see clearly in abiding dreams, they would dump her rigid form over the side. Over into the water that spread out there so very far, all around. Everywhere. The water, we thought, that was the key. The key to flight.

"Flight, yes." So rose her voice out through the blackness and over us, into us: into our deepest dreams when we managed to sleep (but who could sleep unless the sleep crept toward flight?), only a short while after she stopped breathing. "Flight was his destiny, as, on this night, it has become mine. As it will be for many of you before this — this *thing* arrives in the other place.

I always knew that some night he would fly. You know who I mean. He whom I and some others often called the beautiful one. The one with those lips that were never meant for speaking, but for other things. Secret things. The one who, in my village, the same village from which many of you also were wrenched, held in his eyes from his very youngest days the secrets of trees and all their sorrows. The one who, as a child and later as a young man, even up to the time he joined the warriors for training, descended into our great jealous river for days at a time, worrying his parents to frenzy. 'But where is he?' they would always ask anyone in the village whom they believed knew. 'What has happened to him now?' But hush, I would tell them. Hush. 'He hasn't gone far,' I would tell his mother, who often worked alongside the rest of us, his youngest brother strapped securely to her back, in the crop rows. 'He's probably in the river again. At the bottom of the river,' I made sure to tell her.

"'At the *bottom*?' she would cry out, looking at me with that gaze of agony only a mother can know. 'But he — he can't —'

"'Daughter, hush,' I would tell her. 'Have you forgotten that you brought him to life on those very banks, as the river listened and watched?'

"And this was true. How even a mother can forget! You would not think it possible, but so it was. He was the fourth of her fourteen children. Her husband was a sturdy man, with the legs of a baobab and the arms of an ambitious palm reaching for the sun. The two of them, like many in our village, had been fruitful. But among their fourteen, twelve of whom survived to the time of their special brother's coming of age, he was the only one among them capable of breathing water, river water, and of descending into its depths for days at a time to scour and seek out all the mysteries that the world, the world of water and light and silence, was beginning to reveal to him.

"'It's your own fault that he loves the water as he does,' I told his mother severely one time. 'For remember that on the afternoon of his birth, you felt weary and stopped to rest your body on the banks of the river and feel the warmth of the sun on your outstretched legs, as everyone in the village knows you did, foolishly far in that moment from the women who would have assisted you in crouching and dropping him into the world. And so when you suddenly felt the heat of your own water rushing out toward your legs, you should have moved back farther from the water so that its swirls would not enter his birthing blood and captivate him from birth. It *mesmerized* him,' I told her, frowning and folding my arms in disapproval before her; for in truth, though a good woman and more generous than almost any other of her age in the village — and she was at that time, of course, still young — she had from the seedling days of her youth been a willful girl, bent on doing everything her way, come what may, learning to fear neither the disciplining wrath of her parents nor even that of her husband, who anyway adored her and the willfulness that makes a powerful woman and wife. I now believe that even those who had gone on before us, before whose presences we bowed our heads on moon-filled nights and in seasons of drought, would not have daunted her, even if their voices had spoken to her from the moon and stars themselves, or from the morning sky. She deserved that scolding, even though the women who would have helped her deliver him had also scolded her, as had her husband. 'If you gave birth to him on the banks of our jealous river that, as you well know, has always had a mind of its own more than equal to yours, to say nothing of its greed, how could you not expect him to grow up partly as its child? But one thing is certain,' I added, seeking to comfort her creeping shame and dismay, 'your lovely one will never drown. For the river, loving him as it does and knowing that he is partly its child, will fiercely protect him — and in its doing so, he, your beautiful one, will protect others.'

"I could not know then how far my words would walk to prophecy, as you all saw when, clutching so tightly the hand of that other who had lain beside him here where you all continue to lie, barely a hand's length from my shoulder, he flew out of here only a few nights ago. Some of you in here from my village asked me back there how I could possibly have known all these things at the time, and more. And I say to you again now, not breathing, as I said to you then, 'The trees told me.' And some of you heeded me, and some of you never believed. Those of you who doubted would not believe — and in this sense you were cruel — how my girlhood dreams had always been thick with the murmurings of trees. 'So-and-so will die after the season's first rainfall,' a soughing palm would warn me when I was only a child, when all I wanted to do, in that stretching hour of sleep, was rest and press my cheek into my mat and think about the stars plummeting before the moon, sometimes watching them do so as, listening to the soft sounds of my parents' and grand-parents' and elder sisters' and brothers' voices outside, I thought about the calls of night frogs and slapped away mosquitoes: my parents and grandparents talking so softly about the day's work and the exhausting tasks to come, or about whose daughter had just given birth to a fretful or blissful child, or about ferocious raids on a distant village, the flaming calamity of which they prayed, with shortened breaths, would not happen to us; my sisters speaking very softly as they toiled on some evening work, curling their lovely toes into the dusty earth, I imagined, as they perhaps dreamt of the elegant necklaces and bracelets they would acquire on the day of their marriage; and my long-armed broth-ers joking, quietly, and tensing to alertness whenever, as they sat on the ground nearby the adults, one of the elders, usually my father or grandfather, sharply called to one of them to go get something from someone or go carry something — a calabash, a pile of rice or grain — to someone else. As a girl, I wanted to hear only those things, and even — especially — the words of all their dreams, if I could; words that I imagined would be the deepest blue color you could ever imagine: blue like the dyes my mother and aunts used for the clothes they made out of — why, out of nothing, it seemed to me at the time; out of the magic of their hands that wove with the skill my sisters had already learned, and that I, soon enough, in that early time of my romances with the moon and stars and night frogs, would learn. I didn't want to hear from the trees that murmured to me at all hours about people dying and becoming ill and sleeping with each other's wives and living with men whom they despised but whom their fathers had told them they would, without question, marry. I didn't want to look into the faces of girls and women working in the crops and hear the trees tell me that the unhappiness in some of their faces was caused in this one or that one because she had not wanted the last baby she had borne, or because her husband viciously beat her out of the sight of her parents and brothers who refused to attend to her pleas, or because she was a subordinate wife who was treated as a noxious insect by the primary wife her husband preferred. Nor did I wish to hear from the trees about the joy, although that was easier to take, over that year's harvest being the most plentiful ever, or about the river yielding more fish and other edible creatures than had happened in who could remember how long, or about the election of a truly just chief, *finally*, who would ensure, even if it meant that he himself (though not his wives and children) starved, that everyone in the two villages over which he presided had enough to eat for months to come. I was a girl, remember? A girl in love with butterflies and the mystery of the sun's shimmer across spreading fields in the hottest hours. But the trees would not leave me in peace, and so . . . yes, that was how I came to know things. But it is only now, after I am nearly gone, that I understand that it was in all likelihood the trees, with their constant murmurings, that somehow kept me from being suspected, with this gift of seeing, of witchcraft. Miraculously, I was spared the torments of that suspicion that were too often visited so unsparingly on others. But it grew exhausting, I tell you. And even now, I have no knowledge as to why the trees never warned me about *them* — those who pace above us all now, who one day with no warning whatsoever would arrive out of nowhere in our village, helped in some cases by our enemies, to wrench us out of there with their snarls and lock us into this darkness.

"I didn't know about any of that, but I did know about him. The beautiful one with those lips. I have not talked about his eyes yet, because I simply cannot think, even now after so long of having known them, of how to describe them. If I told you that they were filled with the river, on some days even possessed by it, and reflected its sheen and glow and restlessness, would that be enough? Enough to summon for you the way the river danced and bellied itself to the sky in his eyes during the sun's hottest hours, and veiled his eyes from any attempts by others to scrutinize his soul as the river veiled itself at dusk? Enough if I told you again, as I have before, that fish did not swim in his eyes, as they did in the river, but other living things? (Those among you who knew him will know what I mean by this, and what I have always meant.) Enough if I told you that, as he grew and leapt into the river in those searing hours, seeking escape from the sun as some of us sought to escape it in brief afternoon respite beneath trees and in the cool darkness of our homes, when he descended to the river's very bottom and spent hours there breathing that green water he emerged with a knowledge in his eyes of the world's oldest secrets that the murmuring trees, in their insistence in telling me about everyone else but almost never about myself, had never told me? Now you know why I cannot fully describe his eyes that glanced in that way above his beautiful lips and set off the utter comeliness of his face that was like . . . like one of our masks used only for the observation of death or marriage. But you must also know this: that it was most definitely the river, not the rain or any other water, that inhabited his eyes, and later his voice, when he actually did speak.

"When he actually spoke, yes — for the stubbornly silent child he had grown into from the infant he had been, the infant who never cried and hardly ever laughed but only gazed so intently, always turning his infant's neck toward the river, clearly did not care for words. He lived for years without anyone, even his mother suckling him at her breast, knowing the sound of his voice, or even if he could speak. When he misbehaved, which was rare, except for his extended forays to the bottom of the river, he never screamed. The relentless teasings of his brothers and sisters produced in him nary a sputter. His mother's pleadings, coaxings, cajolings, and tears, and even his father's formidable threatening stare and the resounding smacks to the child's backside that invariably followed, also failed to move him.

"'This child is a stone,' his mother wept. 'Is he spiritually affected?'

"'No,' I told her. 'Affected or bewitched, no. He simply has no need to speak. Anything that you need to hear from him, you will hear in the laughter of the river. Listen to it, and you will hear.'

"She stared at me as if I were a wild creature that had ventured into the village, jaws stretched and teeth bared, ready to snatch a child from its mother's arms.

"'I'm telling you,' I said. 'Go to the river and listen now. You will hear your son's voice.'

"How did I know this? Ah, but I think that you already know. Of course: from the trees.

"And go to the river she did, willful one that she was — trudged there, her lips curled in scorn, with the excuse that she was in need of more fresh water, although her fifth daughter had fetched many bowls of it for her only that morning. Her son, edging nearer to the age when children tirelessly seek out mischief, remained in the village under the watchful eye of one of his elder sisters.

"And so it was that, that very afternoon, kneeling on the riverbank, while craning her neck toward those swirling waters, his mother heard her son's voice echoing directly out of those depths.

"'Mama,' it said, 'I wish you would stop worrying. I'm fine, Mama,' it said. 'I simply will not speak.'

"'But — but *why?*' she cried out, dropping her handsome bowl on the bank and breaking it in her distraction.

"'You ask so many questions, Mama. So many for a woman of your age. But I have no answers to give you,' it responded.

"Shocked at the boldness, even impertinence, of the reply ('Whatever else might be happening,' she thought, 'the river is clearly spoiling him, and indulging him to no good end in a disrespectful tongue'), she returned to their home and, with tears of rage streaking her face, beat the mute child for the disrespectfulness with which his voice, carried through the river, had assailed her. His face remained expressionless throughout her blows. Poor creature, I thought, watching her later. What sort of woman was she, to have grown into the world with such a savage need for explanation of everything? Who had so trained her not to accept and live with what simply was? Do you see more clearly now what I mean when I speak of her willfulness? But as some of you know, she was eventually forced to accept not only the strangeness of her son's silence and the river's claim of what her own body had produced, but also the unimaginable . . . but I will get to that.

"And so every day, just before the sun sank its feverish head into the forests beyond and while her special son sat quietly by himself back in the village, contenting himself in his solitude with some little boy's game — a fascinated contemplation of orderly ants, or his own silent nonsense-naming of everything from pincered beetles to sluggish snails — she journeyed to the river, sometimes with a large bowl on her head, to pray to the river to keep her child safe, and to hear his voice.

"And the river . . . but then some of you must remember. It took pity on her, and offered her son's voice to her every single day. Some of you were there, and witnessed her ordeal. For while her husband and sons were out busy hunting, stalking, and working with the warriors and sometimes with some of the neighboring chiefs, and her daughters busy with weaving and helping others in the village with each day's innumerable tasks, it was she alone who bore the burden of communicating with her child by way of that grave water. A few of you women who went to wash there regularly saw her, as I, in turn, saw you there. 'My son, how are you feeling today?' she would ask the river, kneeling on the bank before it — asking the river for her son's voice because the child's face perpetually revealed nothing except its unyielding determination to remain silent — as the boy's voice came forth, telling her, depending on the day, 'Oh, Mama, I feel fine today. I love you, Mama,' or 'I have a little stomach pain today, Mama, will you boil me some tea?' or 'Mama, please tell eldest brother to stop pinching me at night when we go to sleep. He always holds me down and pinches and tickles me, Mama, and then laughs at me. I hate it, Mama.' (That bullying would soon come to an end, on the day the younger child walked in utter silence with his offending brother to the river, pulled him in with a shocking strength provided him in the instant (but never again) by that strange parent, and held him under the water, in the deepest depths, until the bully panicked and mutely, with bulging, terrified eyes, begged for mercy. His solemn younger brother released him among the water's thick man-length weeds that eagerly clutched at him, the river spewed him forth onto the bank with a great splash, and in that exact instant six waterfowl darted overhead and dropped foul drops of green and white shit on his cowering head. The ticklings and pinchings ceased forever that night.)

"And so she, a generous woman willing to walk the additional distance each day to communicate with her most beautiful child in privacy, far from the titterings or stares of women washing in the water, learned to accept that her life was and would be from that time onward like no one else's.

"Concerning his future — the future that would also be yours and mine, up to the moment I stopped breathing — the trees sent me only one dream, part of which I shared with him. By that time I was already an unmarried woman approaching middle age, condemned to childlessness and solitary nights in part because of those dire dreams that, throughout the years, had never stopped whispering . . . calling. If any of you wonder now why I never married, imagine which man among you, or any man you knew, who could possibly have lived with such restlessness and never-ending anxiety. What child could have withstood life with a mother so wracked every night by visions of other people's sorrow? I ask you, but even now none of you, whether still breathing or not, can tell me.

"In this dream I saw, clearly, his face. He was at the time of the vision just entering the age when boys begin to become men and soon prepare for warrior training: when the curling hairs sprout in their armpits and private parts, their bones thicken, their voices (if, unlike him, they actually speak) deepen, and their hidden manhood becomes a stirring force with a mind of its own and the unpredictable surges that (if the boy has any sense of decency and values his family's reputation) make him blush — the same surges that will one day make his bride gasp and cry out as she receives him. In the dream, I saw him in a future time, grown to full adulthood and standing out in the hot sun in a place I could not recognize — standing with his legs bent and quivering, his head bowed, and his entire self completely naked in the sort of nakedness that indicates neither pride nor humility nor expected desire, but rather utter shame; indeed, complete humiliation. 'He is almost completely — almost completely *broken*,' was all I could think within the dream; shattered, it seemed, beyond anything any of us could imagine, as if he were a depraved criminal discovered among us and made to atone publicly, in disgrace, for the evil and betrayal of his crime. Then I saw that there were a great many — well, at the time I did not know what to call them, although I know now, having gazed upon them, at first in disbelief, with my own eyes — a great many of *them*" — falling silent for a moment — "whatever *they* are, with their dry skin like that of ghosts. A great many of them standing about him. And his hands . . . they were — were —

"Oh yes. They were bound. Can you imagine? Now, indeed, you can. Bound at the wrists, his hands, with a great metal ring about his neck. His aspect beneath that blazing sun, as all of *them* shouted and pointed at him and called out things in a gibberish I could not understand and which the trees seemed unable to translate, but which I divined somehow had to do with the shape and look of his private parts and his entire body — his aspect before all that and more was of utter misery. Complete degradation. He attempted to bow his head more deeply to avoid looking out at them all shouting in his direction, but sharp, pointed things on the metal ring about his neck prevented him from doing so.

"Did I mention that his legs, already bent, also were manacled? They were. Joined by chains, heavy chains, at the ankles.

"At one point one of *them*, shouting like all the others, jumped up onto the place where he stood. It was a kind of raised flat place that had been fashioned, it seemed, out of some kind of wood. Three others of us stood not far from him, their hands and legs also locked and their necks similarly surrounded by the metal ring with sharp points. One of *them* stood nearby, as if guarding them, a long metal thing held tightly in his hand. His eyes alone told you that whatever that thing was that his hand gripped so tightly contained the power to, to . . . but I cannot bear to remember that particular vision anymore. You will have to imagine the rest.

"I wanted to forget this part as well, but this moment of the dream has persisted in my deepest memory even up to now. Persisted in reminding me that one of us who stood there among those three nearby him was a, was — was a *woman*. A woman, her private parts exposed in the blazing sun as if she were no more than a lizard hung by its tail from a tree branch by a cruel child intent on killing for sport. A woman, so disgraced in front of all of those — in front of *them*, with her brethren beside her, themselves disgraced, yet evidently not entirely broken, in that they steadfastly refused to gaze upon either her or each other, so as not to acknowledge in any way their shared humiliation. 'I will not look upon my brothers now or my sister,' the men thought, as she thought similarly about them. So the trees disclosed in the dream, and so it was, had been for others, and will be, I know now, for an untold number to come.

"The one who jumped up onto that place actually then took *into his hands* the beautiful one's private parts, and . . . *pulled* them. Pulled them forward as if to display their form and weight to all those watching and shouting below. He then roughly turned him around so that his backside faced all of them, and (you need not imagine this part, for you have recently seen it with your own unbelieving eyes, and felt it in your own unbelieving flesh) pulled open his buttocks — yes, his buttocks! — as if to say to those . . . I don't know what *they* were; but as if to say to them, 'Ah, now, look. Look at him, take a lasting look. You will see for yourselves!' — after which some of them began to shout even louder, and raise their hands in the air, with something

— I could not determine what it was — grasped in their hands. Something that some of them seemed to be counting, a few of them pulling whatever it was out of the fabrics they wore.

"This all seemed to go on forever. But at last it appeared to come to an end, at least for the beautiful one, after which the one of *them* who had jumped up there pulled him roughly down off that place, with his hands still bound and neck yet constrained behind that metal ring. He pushed him in the direction of another one of *them*: this one covered in dark fabrics and with a dark sort of covering on his head, who said to still another one that word that I did not understand, uttered in reference to him, and which the trees hammered into my brain on repeated nights afterward: that word that, in such a short breath, would blot out for all time all of who the beautiful one had been. The word that would make him someone else. The word that I did not understand until, frantic, terrified and not quite in my right mind for the first and last time in my life, what the word signified became clear: clear as the inevitability of death. I ran the very next day to the beautiful one's mother and told her about the dream. Begged her to safeguard the boy-nearly-a-man from evil spirits, to pray for him and do a chant, with some of the other women and the healers, for him; perhaps, I urged, she ought even to take him to the river and push him into it and charge him to stay immersed there for the rest of his days — for at least there, in those depths, he would remain alive, caressed by his powerful other parent's wavering weeds; he had stayed down there before for as long as four days without once surfacing for breath, and when he did, inhaled that humid air above the river for only a few beats of a rapid bird's wing before descending again. For surely, I tried to convince her, nearly pulling out my own hair with fear, some sort of disaster would befall him, as the dream had suggested, if she didn't. 'You must,' I begged her, 'you must!'

"Though frightened by my terror, she did not understand it.

Like me — like all of us — she had always been one to believe in dreams, for like all of us, she had always understood the power of the terrible and beneficent presences that, with an eye toward evil and the fragility of life, sent them; but as the boy walked slowly into our presence, unseen by us both beneath that morning's already furious sun, she could not comprehend the magnitude of the horror I had witnessed in the dream. And indeed, I could not blame her. Blame her, no — for what had she in her village-bound life ever seen that could possibly have helped her understand what that dream portended? The raids on our village and on those only a drum's beat away, that had occurred since the earliest time of our awakening, had always been conducted by those who, though they hated us and wished us accursed and dead and would burn our homes to the ground to achieve that aim, nonetheless resembled us. In their enraged, violence-drunk faces we saw merely the difference of an earlobe, or an eyebrow's wing, or the length of a leg from backside to foot. Who among us, raised and formed entirely in our village or in one of yours, could ever understand the horror of suddenly seeing ghosts with dry skin, like *them* who continue now to walk and prowl above, binding us and affixing those terrifying metal rings about our necks, as they shouted and pointed at us and fondled our most private parts? Which of us here can possibly imagine it, even though it is exactly toward all of that and more that — so I know now, having ceased breathing — we move right now? And so his mother could not. Standing there with his youngest brother strapped to her back and already late for her tasks in the crop rows, she could not comprehend any of it; and besides, as I could not fully understand then but know better now, she was of course fearful of surrendering her child, her most beautiful child, to his more powerful parent: to the river through which, up until only the evening before, the boy continued to speak to her and confide in her all manner of things that she cherished:

his hatred of mosquitoes (which he regularly captured, with his bare hands, for the darting fish he adored, and who brought him in their gaping mouths all manner of peculiar items in return), his childish fear of golden-throated lizards, his obscene delight taken in the kisses, along his innermost smooth thighs, of the river's eager weeds during the afternoons he lay at rest among them for hours, and the shock and then slow pleasure he had felt only two nights before when a fish, curious about his lingering presence down there, nibbled gently at his tender private part, instantly causing it to stir and stiffen, for the very first time, before the weeds' ever-rapt caresses.

"I tried my best to get her to understand. It was only then, with great reluctance and still heedless of the boy himself watching us with his usual solemnity just beyond our backs, that I told her the word the dream had disclosed — the word that the whispering trees would not permit my brain to forget until I told her.

"'*Josh*-u-a,' I told her, trembling.

"'What?' she asked, staring at me as if I had completely taken leave of my mind. (And who could have blamed her?)

"'*Josh*-u-a,' I repeated. 'It is — it is a name. A name that *they* will give him.'

"'They — but who is — Josh-*u* —' She tried to repeat the name, but her tongue would not embrace it, accept it.

"'What sort of a name is that?' she asked, her face contorting into utter bewilderment. 'What kind of — of *name*? — what kind of name can Josh-*u*- . . . what kind of name for a child, for any man or woman, can that possibly be?

"'Who would give their child such a name?' she wanted to know.

"I had no opportunity to respond, for it was then that we were startled out of our confusion by the sound of — but can you imagine? — wild laughter behind us.

"If you guessed who it was, you are probably correct. Yes, it was him. Her lovely son, laughing out loud just behind us and clutching his belly as he laughed as if its smooth flesh might burst open right there before us. He who since his birth had never breathed one word with his mouth open aside from what the river carried from its depths to her anxious ears; he, that shining boy with his mouth so wide open then in laughter that revealed his glorious teeth, the bright healthy pink of his tongue, and the unmistakable sound of mischief in his gales that stunned us who had never known his voice; who, in the case of his mother, had surely dreamed of what that voice would sound like in the heat of the stretching day and in dusk's cooler hours.

"I stared at him, unable to move. She stared. A few others, passing by, stopped where they moved, as stunned as we. I wonder now how his sisters and brothers, and especially the elder brother who had once taken such fiendish delight in tickling and pinching him, would have reacted to that shock, had they been there.

"'*Josh*-u-a!' he cried out, gasping through his laughter. '*Josh*-u-a. What kind of name is that? I, *I* would never have such a name. I would chew snakes' eggs first, crunching between my teeth even the bitter shells, and then fling my head back to the sky so that the sun would know what a foolish boy I am. "And oh Sun," I would shout, "now finish me off with the midday madness brought by your vengeful birds!" I would swallow whole first the fish who make me happy, *happy*, at the bottom of the river,' he shouted — yes, he, that boy, raised his melodious voice! — 'before I would hear anyone call me a name as, as — as *not*-a-name as that. I would fly up to the clouds first!' he shouted, leaping into the air then with his eyes closed and his arms stretched out to the sky. '*Josh*-u-a!' he shouted, laughing, the very air all about suffused with the ringing mockery in his voice.

"'I know my name, Mama,' he cried to that hapless woman

still standing perfectly still, her youngest securely wrapped on her back. 'I know my name,' he shouted, 'and it is —'

"And yes, I tell you. Absolutely. It was then, before our unbelieving eyes, that he spoke in that voice of birds and birds' wings his name: the true-true name his parents, in consultation with the elders, had bestowed on him in the hours after his slide out into the world from between his mother's legs. He spoke it once, shouted it once after, and then ran up to his not-moving mother and, with tightly closed eyes, wrapped his reaching arms around her. He squeezed her, pressed his glistening face against the belly that had carried him in her inner waters that had preceded his first taste of the river, and then looked up at her. A look . . . but to all of you, I need not describe it. You will understand when I say that in that look exchanged between them, begun in his river-filled eyes always so veiled beneath his thick lashes, everything transpired. All things in that look, I tell you, and more.

"And she — she was able to wrap her arms about him for only the breath of a leaf's plummet to earth before he wriggled out of her embrace and was gone — returned to the river for the day and that night; returned to the water that simply could not bear too many hours without him. That jealous, jealous river. He dashed away in joy and laughter, shouting one time more as he ran, but both she and I saw his mouth clamp shut as he gained distance from where we stood — and as I pause here among you now, unbreathing and gazing down upon the rigid body that only a short while ago was mine, I assure you that from that day onward, although he spoke from time to time, he never again opened his mouth to utter a single word.

"And so it was from thence onward, until the hour of the river's enormous wrath, that our village became known as the village of the tall salt trees. For upon the spot, and for the following three days and nights, that overjoyed yet forlorn woman still bearing on her back her beautiful son's youngest brother walked on heavy-to-light feet out to the crop rows, weeping. She wept from joy, she wept in silence from deepest sorrow, and her tears penetrated the ever-watchful earth that saw fit beneath all those tears to drink them in as they cascaded down her face, down over her sloping shoulders and then down the length of her entire body, beneath the clothes she wore through those following days and nights: down over her dusty feet and through the dry spaces between her toes to the earth itself, where, by the beginning of the next harvest, a race of tall trees, though given to alarming bending at their greatest heights — trees encrusted with salt about their sturdy trunks and tasting of salt along their broad, beckoning leaves — sprouted out of the thirsting earth, vaulting within only one planting season to impossible height: the eldest brethren of any palm or baobab. They were the tall salty bending trees that all in our village quickly learned never to eat nor even to touch; for to touch or taste of them in those times, as now, would produce in one the most unbearable sadness: a longing-unto-grief filled with an aching awareness of the fleetingness, brevity, of this thing we continue to call daily life. The earth receives and it gives back, but the heart of sorrow, like silence itself, is never far from its core. And so it was, and so we know it shall be always.

"I did not at first know it, but in that very moment I too, still stunned and seeing again before me the child leaping and calling out his own name, began to weep the tears to which so many years of the trees tormenting my nights and days with their dire predictions had never moved me. I wept in happiness for his mother and for him, and that was the first and last time in life or death I ever wept, even in the hour of my father's, and not long after my mother's, departure. But the earth, unlike in the case of the beautiful boy's mother, refused to accept my tears. Refused perhaps because it knew that those tears, core and heart of the memories that would one day be recalled through my voice that would speak in spite of my mouth clamped perpetually closed, and even after the final ceasing of my breath, would be so sorely needed here.

"And, well . . . some of you know how the story ends, having seen it for yourselves even through all this darkness. You know that he flew out of here only a few nights ago, although you may not know why exactly he held so tightly onto the hand of that other who flew with him — indeed, you may not even know who that one was whose hand in flight he grasped so tightly, impossibly, in the moments just before they flew, in the exact same way he had grasped it the entire time they both lay bound here among us all. It was the same hand the beautiful one had grasped in his deepest soul, and that had grasped his in return, even in the time when, seized in nets like the rest of us and thrown with us into those — those *caves* at the edge of the enormous water that spreads out there and beyond, they could not possibly have held hands. Caves at the edge of the sprawling, vacant water. Suffocating caves of stone into which we all were thrown after that first — that first journey. Moving away from our homes, those nets about us, on that journey of filth and dust and nothing-to-eat and all of us piled one on top of the other in those things that carried us farther and farther and that took days, you remember, nights and days . . . until the place of the fetid stone caves beside which that spreading water began, where *they* fastened those metal things so tightly about our necks and wrists and legs, and threw us into the caves until, some of us barely able to stand and barely breathing, we departed them for here. . . . All of you remember. It was not possible to hold anyone's hand then. To grasp the fingers and the palm and try so hard, gripping that flesh, to remember. If, throughout those nights and days of hunger and heat and the stench of excrement everywhere (for we simply had no place, in the caves, to do anything; we simply had no choice but to pass everything onto the form of the person, man, woman, child standing beside us, behind us), the beautiful one could not grasp that other's hand in the flesh, I know that he grasped it in his deepest soul as the both of them wept with the rest of us and trembled, trying so hard even then to stop, *stop* breathing, with the rest of us. So it was, wasn't it? The beautiful one never let him go. He managed to hold onto him and keep him close, whether in the stench of a stifling stone cave or in this suffocating darkness.

"And it is true that I have been calling the one I knew first 'the beautiful one,' but the fact is that — as some of you may have noticed at the caves, between your tears and trembling — they both were lovely. For remember the other one for a moment, those of you who knew him. The one who somehow reminded you of the beautiful one but for his eyes, which held nothing of a river, not anything at all of water, but rather of fields: dozing fields beneath the sun in its most impatient, unforgiving hours. His eyebrows perpetually arched as if halted on a journey ever upward toward his crown, and his mouth wider than the other's — quicker always to move to laughter, or a broad smile, or even to gentleness. It loved jokes and even bawdiness sometimes, that mouth; and of course, it loved receiving the beautiful one's kisses — the kisses of he who, during all those evenings out of sight of the village, upon the somnolent riverbank, in view of that powerful swirling parent who approved, lay on top of his beloved, holding his face so gently as he moved against him. Their love, that, for the both of them, and the beautiful one especially, began to our astonishment not on water, but on land.

"Love, yes: up to the time of the descending nets and the river's vengeful rage, that was certainly part of the story. And so for this recounting let the one with the arching eyebrows become known to us all now as 'the laughing one.' For in this accursed place I wish to call none of our true-true names — our most sacred names bestowed on us by our elders, our parents, and by time.

"We all saw them, of course. None of us, not even their parents, were especially surprised. Since the sun had first scorched its way across the earth and birds had discovered the use of their wings, it was hardly the first time such things had been known, whether with men, women, or all those somewhere in between. We saw them on so many afternoons exchanging glances, and walking together whenever, away from their varying tasks, they each could find the time to seek out each other's company. Once, at dusk, on the banks of the river, one of us espied them lying down there — simply holding hands, the two of them, as the beautiful one, in between caresses given to and received from his beloved, communicated quietly with his powerful swirling parent. It was clear that that age, for them, had arrived: the age when one or the other, all at once caught unawares beneath the sun, bathing his own soft flesh on the river's shore or arching his neck to receive the sun's ardor on his chin, suddenly notices the hint of promise in the smile of the other not far off, also bathing and watching him. Watching, in silence, the way the water glistens on his back; a boy his own age, with the same reaching arms and thick legs so fond of wrapping about trees. A boy like him, with that mouth. Yes, that one, and those hands now stroking, so slowly, his glistening-wet belly. Watching, each of them, when not even a possessive river-parent can thwart the heart's startled movement in those faces suddenly aware that their forms are standing utterly still, aware of each other. The other boy's parents and sisters and brothers worked in the days with everyone else, and demanded that he too, of course, work with everyone — yet the two of them, already wrapped in the stealth of a curling dream, found time to meet each other. The whispering trees, inquisitive and prying still as they had always been, revealed the beginnings of their love to me, and for once, fascinated both by those visions of beauty and by love's insistence, I did not resist.

"'Meet me at the river,' he murmured without opening his mouth one morning to the laughing one, quickly clutching the laughing one's hand as they walked out from the village to the fields. 'When the sun is highest,' he murmured, finishing the sentence again not with an open mouth but in thoughts the laughing one immediately heard: 'when I will be waiting for you,' he thought. The thoughts were entirely heard by his companion, who did not laugh just then, so full of longing was his heart, but also fear of what awaited them both.

"And so when the irascible sun had reached its most furious, the beautiful one stood gravely on the banks of his powerful parent awaiting the boy he loved — aware of his own heart's increasing jump as he saw the laughing boy approaching him from the distance, running toward him in spite of the intolerable heat. The one who might have become 'Josh-u-a' took his beloved's hand right there, as the river watched. Took his hand and pressed himself against the other boy who did not laugh then — could not, for his mouth all at once surrendered to the other's mouth pressing against his. Surrendered to that other's belly pressing unclothed against his. Surrendered to every part of that form pressing against his. Pressing, stiffening, as, their mouths joined and their arms holding round, holding, the one who might have become 'Josh-u-a' led him by the hand into the river: in farther, deeper, until they stood together up to their shoulders in water. It was then that the boy who had so suddenly transformed to a man looked at his love and saw, in his gleaming eyes, just how afraid he was. *Because I have never done anything such as this*, the laughing one (though not laughing just then) communicated without opening his mouth, *and I do not know if I —*

"*But hush*, the other told him without words. *Hush.* And immediately pulled him down — yes, *down*, I tell you, as those of you who lived in that village will know it: deeper into those waters they descended together, and deeper still, until they reached the place where, for seven uninterrupted days and nights, without once rising to the surface, they remained. Remained unseen by everyone except that jealous, possessive river-parent and all the slinking weeds that, in both affection and desire, swirled themselves around and through the legs of the brother they had long known and the one they had just acquired. And so it was that, in the caressing arms of his brother and beloved, the laughing one learned to breathe deeply of water, light. Darkness. And time. Darkness and light in the river moving in time through his mouth and lungs, and so much more.

"And so down there, obviously, they soon enough became part of one another. The laughing one, in keeping with his destiny, breathed in, in addition to water, his first and only love — losing for that time nearly all memory of who he previously had been. Pressing his mouth so tightly to the beautiful one's as he pressed his face everywhere else, he looked into that face and saw, more than once, his own eyes staring directly back at him. The same happened to the one who had brought him down there: in those depths, opening his eyes to look down at his own hand holding the laughing one's hand, he felt his companion's body pushing against him, holding him as the weeds swirled between their legs and lingered over their thighs, and thought, 'Is that my hand, or his? Is this my arm, or his?' Believe me now when I tell you that he could not summon an answer, nor did he ever summon one, to calm his pounding heart. Protected and soothed by those waters, they became each other, moved through each other . . . and perhaps that is why, when they emerged back onto land unclothed and dripping on the seventh day after their descent, many of us also suddenly, to our shock, could no longer quite tell them apart: the beautiful one — but no, the laughing one, we stammered — which one was which? Even their parents, to their consternation, could not tell which was which; nor could they undo the bond of those hands that gripped each other so tightly and would not, even in this darkness and that of the stone caves, be undone.

"And that time of their bliss? — for it was bliss, far more than happiness. It continued, until the day when *they*, without any warning, without even a neighboring village's alarm of a drum signaling ruin or complete disaster, arrived at the edge of the village. Arrived with their torches and strange metal objects that burned our homes, set fire to the entire village, and killed everyone whom they did not take away to this darkness that now carries you to the place many of you soon will know. *They* came, shouting, bellowing and screaming, and shackled, man-acled, netted: aided, we now know, by some in other villages who resembled not *them*, but us. And even now, though I speak to you from this place of not-breathing, I have no idea what ever happened to the beautiful one's mother and father, or to his sisters and brothers. Some of them might have perished in the river's terrifying wrath that obliterated the village and several of the neighboring villages, already despoiled, that evening. The laughing one's parents were cut down almost immediately, for they dared to resist. And his sisters, brothers? I think . . . I think that they might be out there" — turning the sound of her voice for a moment upward and out toward what we all knew was, out there, water, nothing but water — "and the better for them, I say, for it. But we cannot know that now. We cannot know that as we cannot be certain about the two who flew, although I suspect that, shortly after leaving you all forever, I will meet them and see them, each still grasping the other's hand. All we can know at this time is that that very night, the river of our village, the river that since the earliest days beyond all memory had given us water to drink and fed and bathed us even while providing two boys with a place in its depths for seven secret days and nights of their beginning love, overflowed its banks. Rose up with a roar, that oldest water of all time, enraged at what had befallen us whom it had always loved; enraged at the devastation of our village and the all-at-once taking of our lives — and enraged most at the theft of its most cherished child whose limbs, from his youngest moments, had felt the caressing of those weeds so far down beneath the surface . . . those weeds that in their desire for his most secret parts and for him had wrapped themselves about him and whispered, in that language only one like him could understand, *Stay. Now, breathe in.* So the enraged jealous river swept up with a crash over its banks and *inundated*, that was what it did, *overcame* all the land around with the fury of vengeful water: charging crashing water that spared no mercy for trees, plants, animals, nor the lowliest insects and creeping things, nor the crops our hands had loved and tended, nor the salt trees that had without fail wept their own miserable tears. The river swept out over the land and obliterated it all from the remembrance of those, ourselves, who had trodden that earth and reaped from it the breath and food of life since the first curl of time. It leveled the primordial forests in search of us and its beautiful one and his desire, having no idea that those two, like us, had disappeared, vanished: all of us, snatched from that world out onto the great broad back of the river's mightier ancestor that is this water across which we now move: this great water over which untold numbers of us will yet rise, aiming to awaken back there, our hands and necks free at last and our legs unclamped. Our river crashed through the earth of our beginning and ending and roared its agony over our departure into every inch of the shuddering earth, until, exhausted over what had become, beneath its fury, a landscape of utter death, it soaked its final force into every particle of that drowned land — over all those leveled fields and forests where, for all time to come until the explosion-unto-flame of the sun above and even the stars, the source and agony of that oldest water of our memory would be seen no more.

"And so even the river died upon our departure. Died, pulling deep into the earth all living memory and life within it.

"And now? Ah, but you all heard it. You saw. After we all were thrown into here, those two, bound like the rest of us but still, within this darkness, reaching for each other's flesh in their deepest souls, decided. Decided that they would fly. They were not the first among us to decide so, but even now they remain among the most determined. Fortuitously shackled beside his beloved over in that corner, the one who might have become 'Josh-u-a' opened his mouth in this darkness only once, to say to me as you all heard him, 'Mother. Mother, we're going to fly,' he said. 'Mother, it will not happen to me again. *That*. No, nor to him.' Pressing, in his deepest soul, against the flesh of the one beside him. 'We will not remain here,' he said (still calling me 'Mother,' for I might have been his mother by that time through all my tears shed with the rest of you). He then fell into a silence that, even now, though I am no longer breathing, whispers throughout every bone of the body I no longer possess.

"What was he referring to in saying that 'it' would not happen to him again? Well . . . but now close your eyes. Children and women, grown men and boys, close your eyes tightly, and keep them so. For you know, as surely as it happened to him on only the second day of this journey, it happened to many of you as well, and will yet happen to more. That which began with a step. A footstep signaling the descent down here of one of *them*. A movement in this darkness slightly illuminated by the fire that one of *them* carried that betrayed in his ghost's face the crime that would soon occur. A movement by the flame-bearing ghost toward the one espied perhaps only by chance, or with complete cruel intention, as the one lying there with that face, that mouth: the beautiful one. A movement of the ghost toward him.

Then a bending over him. The ghost standing directly in front of, above, that face. (No, keep your eyes closed now, children.) The beautiful one lying there, unable to speak, or choosing not to, no matter what happened. His beloved reaching for some part of him in the darkness barely illuminated by that small fire held by the ghost above, but unable to feel, just then, his stiffened hand. The ghost who descended suddenly, extinguishing the fire he carried; then, in the dark, doing that to the beautiful one. And again. Yes, in his mouth. Gripping with those ghostly hands his face. Forcing it upward. Gripping it tighter still. Muttering down to him words none of us could understand in language but which we all received in tone. For women, you . . . you *know*. Know well by now the peculiarity of that grip and the prying of the jaw. As you, too, men and children, know, and will soon know more. That ghost who descended, one of *them*, in him. Pushing in past the lovely teeth. Pushing more, gripping, and the only sounds those of the beautiful one choking as the ghost above him rocked, grunted. Groaned. The beloved next to them taut. Rigid. Feeling just then the crackling of his own flesh. Hearing his love next to him choking. Keeping his eyes tightly closed the entire time, then opening them to see, in that dimness, his love, also with tightly closed eyes, gasping for air, for freedom of the tongue trapped beneath, with the ghost still moving that way above him. Then the ghost suddenly grunting, moaning, then shuddering, tensing, as the beautiful one all at once became aware of a bitter warmth on the back of his own tongue. He opened his eyes to look once, only once, at the ghost standing above him, staring down at him like that. The ghost who grunted again as he had grunted only shortly before; who then touched once, twice, that part of himself. The ghost turning then to stumble back through the darkness, between all of us, to ascend. Gone but not completely gone, having left that much of himself behind, and so much more.

"That would not be the only time, of course. It happened three times more to him. As it happened to those among you who, though the bitter taste rests still on your tongues and on the most parched flesh in your throats, refuse to remember it. When it happened, some of you, if you did not first think of the power of your teeth to rip and tear in order to draw both blood and screams, you thought, wildly, of flying. Some of you did fly, in silence, with not even a whisper of farewell to those trembling and lying so close alongside you. And so on what would have been the fourth night of the ghost's visit he, knowing that the ghost would soon come again to bend over him with that wan flickering fire, decided to think about not any of that but rather what it would feel like to be at last out of all this stifling darkness, away from this heat and stench and the constant cries of that suffering child in the far corner, those children in the other corner, those three girls and that coming-of-age boy who just, who only just . . . close your eyes, children. Away from the sound and feel of those things scurrying about on the floor and sometimes over our flesh. What would it be like, he wondered, to *hold* firmly once again his beloved's hand — and in that moment he decided: 'We will fly,' he thought to the other, as the other heard him, understood, and in that instant clamped shut his jaw for all living time.

"All living time, yes. For now you will remember that, over the next few days, neither one of them accepted either water or the morsels of filth *they* gave each morning, from their filthy hands, to keep us here. The mouths of those two remained steadfastly clamped shut, their eyes firmly closed, as, touching fingers whenever they could in darkness and throughout the light that edged increasingly closer to them, they began to dream of the long journey that would soon take them out over all that spreading water out there and then into it, deeper, farther, until, their skins soaked unto even the blood beneath as the river had wrapped them in its belly for those seven days and nights, their breath stopped completely. 'Not again,' they each thought, 'not ever. Not ever again on the tongue,' they each thought, 'nor in the throat, leaving that bitter heat and taste behind. Not in the mouth, nor anywhere else,' they thought. Their eyes closed, the light that the promise of flight brings creeping closer to their silent, slowly departing forms, they did not see what was done in that way to the rest of us, but heard it. Heard the chokes, the muffled cries and gasps from those of us selected, women, men, and children, and remembered them. 'We will not ever forget,' they each thought, mingling their thoughts and dreams of breathing water once again, as their forms grew lighter still. As they wept for all of us and for themselves and the many who had gone before and all those yet to come . . . wept without ceasing, their eyes never once opening through those hours even as their breaths gradually slowed.

"And so it was," she finished. The oldest woman on board, remembering this. "On the sixth night after the last time his mouth was forced open, their bodies stiffened for the last time. Stiffened in the hour of noises uttered at the edge of death, when so many of us, groaning with a bitter taste on our tongues and metal tainting the blood blooming on our wrists and legs, dreamt in fever and fire of leaving our forms behind. Without a word, without even a whisper to anyone (for they, like all of us, could not bear farewells, but they, like us, also knew that this departure would in no way be a true farewell), they arose at the same time from their rigid flesh, their hands and legs slipping through the metal; arose, their hands joined in that clasp that could not and would not ever again be parted. Arose with only two words to me from the both of them, uttered from their tightly clamped mouths — *Mother*, they both said to me, opening their eyes only then to gaze on me that way in the dark — and then *Good-bye*, they both said. But I . . . I could not answer them for the bitter taste in my mouth. *Good-bye, children,* I could not, would not say; for I, sooner perhaps than any of you, knew just then in my deepest soul that I would regard them soon again.

"Out. Up out of this darkness. Up out over that moon-bright endless water. Their faces gleaming, their eyes once more closed. Holding hands. Moving their closed mouths toward each other's. Flying out over the water, then down into it, into those waves. Never — no, not ever — releasing the clasp.

"Breathing water, the two of them, and — for all any of us can know — soon wetting their newly opened mouths in the vanished river now deep beneath the earth. The river of their longing and ours.

"And he will never be called 'Josh-u-a,' I thought after they left, barely making out the shape of their rigid forms still lying there, completely unmoving, in that corner. 'Nor will the one he loved ever be called such a name by one of *them* when this — this *thing* arrives in the place of which the whispering trees foretold so long ago.

"And one more thing that you all must know, though some of you will never live to see it. In that place, whichever of those places toward which this thing is moving, there will arise from between your thighs and others' many Josh-u-as: Joshuas seeded by *them* in you women, to be one day nourished by the milk that, no matter how much you will pray for it, will *not* flow with deadly poison from your breasts. Many Joshuas, then Daniels; and Jacobs, and Samuels. Innumerable Ruths and — and *Abi*-gails, and Naomis. I cannot know, even now, all the names. All the names so unimaginable, the like of which none of us has ever heard. All the names bestowed on those brought into the world by weeping women and by some of you men whose tears will salt that earth upon which you and those after you will toil until the blessedness, soon or distant, of ceased breathing. Those tears will salt that earth that for an immeasurable time will know no end of sorrow: blighted earth that will produce not a race of tall salty trees but rather a race of tall ghost-skinned creatures who will curse your memory, ours, with still more unthinkable names as their ghostly hands and other parts, in darkness and light, pry apart. Mark that you understand that none of them will remember, nor ever wish to remember, what they have done here and will do again as they continue to leave that bitter heat within you. On you. They will choose to forget as their lands spread before and beneath them embittered by the salt of tears — so that it will be up to you, to each one of you, whether living or dead, breathing or not-breathing, to recall. No matter what name is bestowed, forgetting will be an execration upon the oldest water of your memory and on your children and each of their children still to come. Remember this even as, in one of those places, the force of your dreams and desire salt the earth. Your dreams and desire, that will always also be mine.

"Also mine, as now I too am — now I am gone —" And in that moment her voice ceased. She did not need to say *Good-bye*, for *Good-bye* it would not be.

Out and up, the oldest woman on board. In pursuit of those now breathing water.

And I —

Lying here, remembering her words from that mouth forever clamped shut, I know that I too will soon fly. I too, holding fast to the memory of my mouth and other parts forced open and that bitter heat left in my throat and on my tongue, will soon clamp shut my jaw and close my eyes. My eyes seeing nothing yet hearing it all as, in my deepest soul, I reach for a hand nearby me; for another hand, then still another. In my deepest soul I hold them, and do not let go. I will never let go.

As now, on the third day after her departure, my form is stiffening, as stiffen some of those nearby me.

And last night, the darkness is whispering to me again, *a dream filled with the murmurs of sighing trees came yet again to you, is that not so?*

Yes, I whisper without opening my mouth, *a dream. I-*sai-*ah, the trees in it were murmuring. I-*sai-*ah is who you would have become, the trees' ghosts are telling me. Soon one of* them *will come to clamp upon your neck a curling hand that, without care, will burn into your flesh with blazing metal some design of meaning and use to* them. *I-*sai-*ah, in this place of one hundred or more Isaiahs and Josh-u-as, Re-*becc-*as, where, during so many moments of so many days and nights,* they *will lash you ever closer to not-breathing. To blood. Closer, but not before, on many nights and even during some days,* they *will attempt to hold you down, pinion you, and leave in your mouth and throat and any other possible place the bitter heat that always follows their grunts and sighs above your rigid form. For you too, with all those others, one morning stood naked and exposed in that hot place where the oldest woman on board dreamed the beautiful one who might have been called by* them *'Josh-u-a' also stood. You stood there, like him refusing to shame by looking at them the women standing next to you, as all of* them *shouted and pointed at each of you, wanting to know. Wanting to know how much.*

But no, I tell the trees again, not opening my mouth. *Oh no.*

Tonight, one of *them* will descend once again to pry my jaw and speak those unintelligible words to me before he lowers and bends. But tonight — now, before his footstep — I am already gone. We are. Hands reaching —

Rising out of that darkness. Hot darkness. Up-out over the black water. So much water. Then down. Down into it. Feeling — hands —

Now breathing water.

Awakening. For this is —

Yes, it is. The oldest water of our longing.

Here. Back there.

OUT THERE

EXCEPT FOR THE STINK OF INCINERATED FLESH WHICH presently permeates most of it, it has always been a small, unremarkable enough country town like many others in Jamaica. Located in the parish of St. Catherine, it has a main street (really just a dusty two-lane road, now paved) that features what one sees nearly everyplace else in such towns across the island: a Chinese-owned dry goods and general shop, dark and cool inside, that smells of carbolic soap and bleaching detergent (and whose owner is, like many like him across the island, referred to by locals as "Missa Chin," although "Chin" is not his surname); an (incongruously imposing, for a town of this size) Anglican church, painted completely white, up the hill from the main road a bit; a Seventh-Day Adventist church in matching white not far from it, on the same side of the road, shaded by a very old, gnarl-trunked guango tree; a Kingdom Hall of Jehovah's Witnesses slightly farther along, partly shaded by its own massive lignum vitae tree — beloved by butterflies — and surrounded on three sides by sternly clipped low hedges; and, on the way out of town, a modest, white wooden Pentecostalist church. A small primary school stands on a hill just above the Chinese shop where, during the daytime, children run about or stand to attention in colorful uniforms (the town does not have its own high school); and, just a bit farther down the main road, a bar with a Guinness Stout sign over the front door, a Red Stripe sign in the street-facing dark window under the corrugated zinc overhang, and a card table set up just to the left of the front door, surrounded by a few chairs, usually occupied in the late afternoons and evenings by loud-voiced, loud-laughing men bent on marathon games of dominoes. The police station — small enough to fit a desk, a few filing cabinets, three big-bellied, narrow-hipped policemen, and a few bottles of white rum — sits two towns over. The drive from the station to this town is not far, and the police, especially in situations that ignite their genuine interest, are known to make the trip in reasonable time.

On the night of the exorcism, the services of the fire brigade — located in the same, larger, nearby town as the police station — will be more urgently needed.

But in fact, people who had gathered in front of where the torched house had been began to talk about it exactly as Jamaicans would: a what a way the fire did hot-hot-hot. So he would hear some of those gathered around and still watching saying later, only a short time after it all was over. As far as he knew (for these were not, finally, truly his people; this was a town in the parish of St. Catherine, and he was and had always been from Kingston), none among them had seen a blaze like that in the area for years. Much worse than anything anyone had ever seen when the cane was burning — but out here, they would all be accustomed to that. Far worse than the fires in the hills during the weeks in the dry season when not even one drop of rain fell. He would learn later from various sources, some of them enraged and others joyful, that the fire had licked out from the walls of the house, had ultimately exploded nearly all of the windows, and then proceeded to unleash its rage into the nearby breadfruit and star-apple trees on the neighboring property — the trees which, like those in the house's front garden and like the sad former dwelling itself, of course did not survive. It did hot-hot, *you see, one woman had been shouting to her friends when he had arrived, and when de window dem did bust out mi did* frighten, *you see?* Glass, *she had been shouting, waving her arms about and turning this way and that, glass just a fly,* fly *out all over de place. But what had truly terrified another woman — a woman in her early sixties, he had guessed, with iron-gray hair tied back in two taut braids that met at the base of her neck; one of those women with the grim unyielding lines on either side of her mouth that revealed or suggested the devout church elder who feared neither death nor the temptations and unyielding fretwork of Satan — that woman who, he had believed merely from looking at her and meeting her horrified yet steady gaze, had not, unlike almost everyone else in that crowd, had any part in setting the fire — what had truly terrified even a woman like that, a woman staunch even in the face of Lucifer and all his earthly and other minions, had been the screams, until the smoke or flames engulfed him, of the person whom all in the crowd had wanted to kill, trapped by them inside the house. — Him did cry out, you see?— she had whispered to him as if she had known him, a stranger in the town — as if she had known everything about him all her life, he, a stranger to all those gathered but perhaps recognized by some in the crowd even in their wild hysteria as a sometime frequent visitor to the suddenly deceased; he, freshly arrived from the city in his shining Pajero and business suit and city man's shoes, straight from his office, wearing the navy and cream-striped tie Carole had bought for him last Father's Day, as, in the paralyzed daze that had struck him upon apprehending what had befallen the person he had been going to visit, he had somehow made his way along the edge of the still-roiling crowd, having left his car*

*far behind, closer up to the scene where the fire brigade men were,
though too late, doing their work as a few policemen watched and
talked amongst themselves. Moving back with the crowd from the
still fearsome heat emanating from what remained of the house, he
remembered thinking, How could* they *not have known about this
sooner and not gotten here sooner? Had they had a hand in* helping
*those who . . . nothing, of course, would surprise him or anyone with
common sense about Jamaican policemen. But speculation, he realized then, unexpectedly lucid, would serve no purpose whatsoever:
the demon had been exorcised, many people in the town who were in
the crowd clearly believed; all else (unless another undetected demon
walked among them and also needed to be purged) was, at least for
the moment, immaterial.*

*And the woman who had looked at him as if (so he thought)
she had known him all her life and even everything about him had
gone on to say, quietly:*

*— Him did cry out and bawl and try fi escape, but every time
him did try to get out the front door de man dem standing up there,
five of dem, did chop him back with dem machete. So him could
never leave de house. Him did* scream, *you see?—*

Scream, she had said.

Carlton, he had thought. On fire. Screaming.

Screaming, sentenced and condemned: finally judged guilty
by some in the town of the worst possible crime in Jamaica, sur-
passed only by carnal abuse of children, and often not even by
that, provided no one ever found out about it, and provided that
abuser and victim were not both males. Carlton sentenced after
a few years of living in the town as an undeclared but obvious to
everyone battyman: an execration ultimately not to be borne in-
definitely by the town's most righteous and vindictive, and not to
be borne in particular because Carlton had not been raised there.
It would have been more difficult to incinerate unto ashes one
who had grown up among them, who as a restless, mischievous

boy had stoned mangoes out of trees with them and shared grater cakes and someone's godmother's cornmeal pudding; harder to burn alive, assisted by kerosene and paint thinner, someone whose grandmother, as a helpful Christian neighbor, had offered to wash out their mother's linens on her washboard and mind the younger woman's pickney for a few hours, and whose uncles had shared with their parents thick yellow yams, a roasted breadfruit, a fresh bunch of callaloo, a bit of ginger root. It would have been much harder, if not impossible, for the men who had blocked his egress as the fire had roared; more difficult for them to threaten to eviscerate him with machetes if he dared to step even one foot outside the inferno in which they all had condemned themselves to watch and listen to him die — *Yes, come outside now, battyman, and face you judgment,* several of them had shouted: harder to do all that to one who would have grown up beside them day by day as *their* battyman, one whose face they would have known and, needing neither closer investigation, reason, nor nuance, about whom, casting narrow glances at the swinging of his hips or dangerous flick of his wrists, they would have divined his future unspeakable (despicable) predilections. Yet still, even against their silent disgust at imaginings of what he and his kind *did,* massa God, behind closed doors, some of them would have felt they had to care for him somehow, *their* battyman, even if often at arm's length; cared for him, the developing nastyman, even if, as children and later teen-agers, they all stoned him with large rocks for his girl-ish ways, his mama-man womanishness . . . *that* battyman, whose face and hands they would have had to grapple with deep in their deepest souls before killing him (for the horror in his eyes, facing their ultimate betrayal and cruelty, would have reminded them of too much in their own eyes), would have been much, much harder to obliterate in fire as a heinous demon, as opposed to the brown big-belly battyman arrived among them only a few years ago. Some of the more ambitious in the town in the matter of exorcising demons surely hissed among themselves the fear-burdened words that would have preceded the exorcism: *All battyman* mus *fi dead. Dem* mus *fi dead, becau' oonu know seh dem* cyaan *bring dat deh nastiness round ya so.*

In the context of Jamaican country towns, of course, he knew, as Carlton had known, that there had been nothing unusual in all *that*: like everyplace else on the island, this behind-God's-back place had its share of whisperers and rumormongers, malingerers, hategatherers, and fundamentalist Christian fanatics, the Jehovah's Witnesses and the Adventists being the most intolerable and intolerant — the "narrowest of the narrow" as Carlton had once sharply remarked; those who remained committed to the thundering, apocalyptically draconian pronouncements of their mostly unforgiving god. And so, having decided to live among them, ever vulnerable to the rages they believed their god delivered to them on earth via His prophets and representatives, Carlton had, finally, been exorcised — eradicated by fire from the plain of normalcy, decency, and upstanding Christian virtue.

It had been in the moment of those thoughts, or immediately afterward, that, his nostrils filled with the stench and smoke of he who had been successfully destroyed inside that house, he had collapsed — *for the first time in my life*, he thought as it happened, *Jesus have mercy* -- and fallen forward into the warmhot darkness of that early evening and the noisy, excited crowd surging and shoving about him, all of them still driven back by the dying fire's heat. Fallen to awaken, inconceivably, in the lap of that same woman only minutes (hours?) later. That woman whose name he still would not know when he returned the following day, but whose face, looking down at him like that as he'd lain in her lap, he had not forgotten, nor her words: *Tek care now, never mind*, she had whispered far beneath the crowd's din

— and hadn't some people of course been looking down at them, astonished at the sight of the tall brown man from town so dress up-dress up just a drop down pon de ground so? *Just tek care now*, she had whispered, moving and pressing her hand over his wet, hot forehead as if bestowing upon him a tacit benediction. But she *knows*, he had thought. She knows everything, he had thought, about Carlton, me . . . and then true terror, warmed by the dying conflagration, shot through his limbs in the form of utter rigidity . . . for had that *Tek care* been a warning? *Tek care*, he imagined her saying in that softer-than-soft voice, the voice of the unwavering disciple. He wondered if a woman like that would ever actually say something like *Mek sure seh dem neva find out about* you *and come fi bu'n you too*. But then, in those fleeting seconds as he lay with his head in her lap, the only thing he had been able to think clearly was *She knows. She sees who I am and what I am and she is looking. She is looking at me.*

All of that had taken place the night before last, just up the road from where he now sits in his car. *Mur*derously hot today, someone in the office had said before he left work and town early that afternoon with some excuse already forgotten: hot to rahtid, the person had muttered, and worse tomorrow.

But now, out here, still inside his car where he hopes, for at least a little while, he will be safe, he will not think about Carlton's arms.

Sitting here with his eyes closed, barely taking in the noise of some boys down the road playing some game — stickball, pretend-cricket, or, more likely, football — and taking in the sweat-smell of his hands on the steering wheel, smelling to him like the scent of identifiable agony, he screws his eyes shut even tighter to keep at greater distance the vision of the arms that, in those last moments, must have flailed. The hands that must have clutched desperately at whatever might have —

(*But the machetes waiting outside*, he refuses to think. So many gleaming machetes brandished just outside the heat-buckling door, as close to the entry as those who held them could withstand as the racing flames built to a roar and devoured the dry wooden house and the live flesh within it. The live flesh that, so cooked, must surely soon have lost its shape, although the bones, discovered in the after-rubble by the fire brigade and police, had kept theirs. So he had heard. So some people, people who had been there and seen the entire thing, who had watched it — some with their children beside them, he'd noticed — the children gazing in fear and fascination at the blazing house as their parents, uncles, elder brothers and sisters had hurled stones into the conflagration and screamed *All battyman fi dead Bu'n to bomborassclaat now, battyman, and* nyam *up you bloodclaat judgment* . . . so many had taken part in the screaming and shouting to merciful Jesus for final justice against the depraved. So many machetes waiting. Raised in clenched fists. Raised and ready to slice apart the limbs of the condemned one the moment they had appeared at a window. *Appeared through the crack of the flame-engulfed front door*, he will not think.)

The arms that, as everything had grown hotter, as the flames had moved closer, must have begun to crackle   *Oh yes*, he absolutely refuses to think, *and   bubbled*

So hot. Very hothot. The front door barred. Blocked. And then the acid, waiting out there in bottles gripped by those others. Waiting, while all those faces had shouted and screamed for the hands and face of the condemned to dare to emerge from the flame-consumed house.

Carlton, he thinks but refuses to think.

A what a way de fire did hot-hot-hot, so many had said only the night before last.

Sitting there in his car with his head on his hands on the steering wheel, parked in what he hopes is an unobtrusive place at the edge of the town, he will not now think anymore about the arms, *those* arms, with the machete marks, *those* marks on them — on what had remained of them.

Carlton's arms, his mind insists.

And, well, it had been an astonishing moment: when, this afternoon, aware of the day-busy town about him (though slightly slowed in the heat; it had just been going on one-forty-five when he'd arrived), aware of its looming star-apple trees so dark and thick above the main road in the heat-stilled afternoon and, farther down the road, breadfruit-laden trees stretching their wide green fingers in the faintest breeze-stirrings above him, he had actually managed, though eyed by unseen people no doubt watching the stranger in town from behind their dark, burglar-grilled windows — windows grilled against thieves and, more critically, gunmen, even in a small country town like that one (yes, he had often thought on so many past visits to Carlton, as they both had discussed, Jamaica had indeed changed that much over the years and into the new century, to the point that even in the most back-of-the-beyond country towns people were rightfully fearful of pitiless gunmen slamming through foolishly unbarricaded windows and doors into their humble homes) — he had actually managed, in spite of so many hidden or inscrutable or frankly hostile faces watching him, certain that they had seen his face, *him*, in Carlton's company on numerous occasions before, though he had often taken as much care as possible to visit Carlton only after dark — he had managed to walk only a few minutes ago up to the smoking, smoldering ruin that, up until two days ago, had been Carlton's house: had managed, incredibly, to confront it: his knees not betraying him as ruthlessly as they had the night before last, but not keeping absolutely steady counsel for him either. Aware of his shuddering knees and the demonic churning in his stomach that later that afternoon, on the drive back to Kingston, will come very close to producing a ferocious spewing of vomit as bitter as the cerasse tonic that his grand-mother had always forced down him as a child and that, like most children, he had always loathed, he had looked at those still-smoking remains, making sure to remain standing back at first in the more manageable distance of the road that went past the house and its (miraculously unburnt) neighbors. He had seen, impossibly, everything that was no longer there but which his memory, in that agonized minute colluding with the powerful need for illusion, had refused to relinquish: the house as it had been throughout his time of so many visits. Looking through wide-open eyes that had in that minute conjured the past, he had seen, in the first gaze, anyway, not a house and garden ravaged by fire and rage, but once again Carlton's hedge-bordered small garden that had flanked the often-parched lawn edged on two sides by scarlet and yellow hibiscus trees; then the few small callaloo beds, and the always-dusty, fairly neur-asthenic-looking almond tree (Carlton had always insisted that it needed more sun, but the two damnblasted star-apple trees nearby, he had frequently good-naturedly complained, did *tief* all de light fi dem, dammit); and finally the two young Julie mango trees, now fatally blackened. Clinging to that mercy, he saw again in recollection the awning-shaded front verandah on which Carlton had loved to sit in the early mornings, on one of his straw chairs, especially on Sundays, sipping hot mint tea ac-companied by a piece or two of hardo bread reliably dipped ev-ery few minutes in a tin of condensed milk. (In spite of caveats from his doctor to cut back on sugar, coming more frequently as he'd entered his early fifties, Carlton, like many of his coun-trymen also running to plump and large-potbellied, had from childhood never been able to get enough of condensed milk. It had been one of his most supreme food passions, and sometimes, with nothing more than a playfully surly "Chuh! Mi *cyaan* live without mi condensed milk, man," he had been known to eat it directly, lovingly, from the tin with a favorite bent spoon.) Sunday mornings were free for him, having long ago abandoned the church habit himself — a fact that surely had not endeared him to particular factions in the town, especially given what people soon began to suspect about him, the still unmarried, mildly effeminate man well into his fifties: a born and bred Kingstonian who had made the unlikely move there from town three years ago into that house that had belonged for over seventy years to the elderly woman whom many in the town had revered: Carlton's centenarian Aunt Violette, who had been known by all and sundry locally for decades, since her husband's death thirty years before, as Miss Vie, and who, upon her death four years earlier, had bequeathed the house to him, her most beloved close relative still living in Jamaica who had faithfully taken the time to visit her at least once a week during her last few declining years remaining after Jesus-have-His-mercy had blessed her to see one hundred and three. Perhaps recollecting the many childhood and teen-aged weekend evenings he had spent sitting on that same verandah in the company of his parents with Miss Vie and her husband his Uncle Hubert, straining to listen undetected from a farther corner of the verandah to the grown-ups' intricately plotted stories and without-mercy judgments of what they invariably and without qualification termed other people's backsliding and slackness, he would sit as the grown man he had become on one of the straw chairs and watch on Sunday mornings what he had been fond of calling, in both affection and mild contempt, "the parade" of people marching past to church in their white and black, even the poorest women without fail in hats and their very best for-the-Lord shoes, pulling along children in shiny black shoes, the girls usually in stiff white, blue, or pink cotton dresses and with similarly colored ribbons or fastenings in their hair, the boys and men more often than not wearing short-sleeved white cotton shirts punctuated by long, thin black ties, and nearly everyone clutching firmly beneath their elbows or in determined fists Bibles and prayer books.

There was nothing romantic about any of that, Carlton had known; no matter what ministers thundered or their flocks moaned in response, there was nothing paradisaical or blessed about it. While always loving the devoutness and determination of the (usually) large-buttocked women in their hats and the men and boys in their narrow ties and cheap, shiny-seated trousers pressed to greater shininess for the Lord, he had comprehended the parade for what it was: merely the routine weekly march of fundamentalism, through the boredom and anger of poverty, to its place of most efficient coalescence and buttressing in prayer, chant, and song. It was the same fundamentalism that, though he couldn't entirely have known it then, would shortly make possible the apocalyptic fire that would consume his own flesh and, for those responsible for the flames, obliterate the degenerate whom they all had somehow managed to tolerate, tight-lipped, for three years: he who had dared to come from the city and live among them with his nasty ways and defile dear Miss Vie's house (although no one in the town, even those who had actively watched, had ever caught Carlton *in flagrante delicto* with one of the good-looking young men who had occasionally visited him from someplace else — never one of their own young men, of course — nor with the older, always worried-looking man, perhaps just slightly younger than Carlton and also a brown man like him; the man now watching, now a witness). Aston, now himself a watcher, though in mid-afternoon as opposed to during a flame-brightened night, he is amazed that he can actually look in the direction of the house and, without feeling any nausea or trembling this time, remember what had been the living room: the place from which Carlton's burnt remains had been removed by the fire brigade, or the police, or whoever had been charged with the task of dealing with the crime and its leavings without recourse to the excuse of repulsion at having to handle the remains of the loathsome thing that, to so many in the town, Carlton had ultimately been. Too soon after that minute-long respite in the recollection of Carlton's boisterous laughter and a vision of him licking condensed milk off his thumb, his own eyes had charged forward to the unbearable present, to face the once-house and all that he remembered of it. It was then that he'd unmistakably felt, as he feels now, just beneath his twitching eyelids, his own eyes' pulsing incredulity: utter disbelief that he'd actually managed to view the still-smoking ruin without violently retching right there, or remembering how much "the deceased"'s incinerated flesh stank throughout the entire town and then must have wafted out over the hilly dark green fields just beyond the town's farthest houses and the white wooden Pentecostalist church — the fields where, walking past them on similarly heat-struck afternoons or cooling evenings in earlier years, he had sometimes glimpsed (and, in Carlton's smiling company, occasionally gazed raptly at) the slim-waisted, smooth-muscled Rastafarian men and their undreadlocked brethren, toiling steadily with machetes during the days' hottest hours; those hard-working men utterly unaware of the admiration their laboring forms received from the two strollers; unaware of the sheen that glistening sweat and sunshine brought to their dark, V-shaped backs, as it had done to their enslaved ancestors in centuries before.

The men who, as his and Carlton's (he'd believed inscrutable) eyes had lingered over and hungrily partaken of their straining forms, their taut arms swinging the machetes sometimes in unison as some of them sang — singing so heartfully unto the Lord or their revered Jah, in all that heat! — and others worked in utter silence, their backsides hard and rounded as the large, sea-smoothed beach rocks found on parts of the dark-sanded

south coast, had always immediately charged his quickening
blood back to images of Solomon, he'd thought. Solomon about
whom he had told only Carlton, of course, and no one else. No
one else because there had never been anyone else to tell. For
Carlton, while never a lover (although Carlton would not have
minded that, he had always known; the older man had passed
him enough sidelong glances of barely concealed desire over the
years), had been truly a friend. Unlike some of his and Carole's
more ardent Catholic friends, he had never believed in "confession" as some of them claimed they did, usually when white
rum-drunk, during the spirited evenings at the house in Stony
Hill (the "better" part of Stony Hill, of course, above its square)
that he and Carole had bought together twelve years ago, sixteen
months after their marriage, invariably filled with friends on a
Friday or Saturday evening and their typical laughter, flirting
enabled and emboldened by drink, and off-color joking that led
to passionate but good-natured arguments about absolutely everything, from the prime minister's most recent stupidity to the
fuckery so-and-so's nephew had gotten involved in with some
land-development scheme in, of all places, Trelawny, to rass. *Yes,
man, a whole heap of money invested in de rassclaat ting and not
a damn cent seen in return.* There never had been anyone else to
confess his sins to, and the heaviness they had unfailingly levied
on his soul except Carlton: no one at all in the entire world, he'd
believed and still believed, no one anything like Carlton . . . and
now, after the ashes and the stench that he himself had inhaled,
there never would be again . . . he was certain of that.

And Solomon, about whom he had told Carlton almost
everything? Solomon who, soon after their first fortuitous meeting, had, in spite of the potential obstacles of his own high-
brownness versus Solomon's deep blackness, insisted that Aston
call him, so intimately, "Brattie": what the St. Thomas fisherman (a Baptist, but one who had been intrigued by, curious

about, and not at all suspicious of Anglicans, even a city brown Anglican like him — so he liked to think, remembering Solomon's good-Christian forbearing smile for nearly everything fit for decent discussion) had made clear was how he preferred to be addressed, not long after they had first encountered one another on the winding south coast road out in the dry parish somewhere either just east or just west of Lyssons (to whose beach the city man remembered having made day trips with his family as a child), though Solomon was more commonly found sooner on the road, closer to White Horses than to Morant Bay. That had been a blazing Saturday early afternoon, when the staunch Adventists were at worship and those in the area who fished and knew and competed with each other stood in that particular place by the side of the road with their day's catch in the hope of selling all before the sun's vindictiveness ravaged their bounty. Driving by slowly as he had been, half-dreaming about something peculiar Carole had mentioned to him that morning (he had been on his way up to the Manchioneal area to retrieve their youngest daughter from the country house of one of their friends with whose daughter she was great friends), he had seen the fishermen standing by the side of the road, and *that* one. (And he did buy some snapper from the man; the fish was remarkably fresh, and he could only hope that the men had traveled far enough out on the sea to catch it safely away from the more polluted waters closer to the island; he would give it to their friends, why not? — and Manchioneal was by that time close enough so that the fish would not, in his air-conditioned car, start to smell.) That one who after only a few minutes of conversation had told the high-brown city man, as if he were a true bredren, that "Brattie," not Solomon, was his preferred name: one of those at first on the face of it ridiculous, but still charming, Jamaican pet names originated sometime in childhood: *Yes, sah, is mi uncle did name me so, a true,* Solomon had told him early on in his deep eastern St. Thomas-inflected patois during one of their subsequent brief meetings by the side of the road . . . the city man always *happening* to drive past in his Pajero and the country man standing exactly there, or in a tree-shaded spot nearby, holding up for drivers' inspection a ring of snapper or sometimes a few brilliant azure-finned parrot; sometimes chatting quietly with his cronies or with a large woman who stood perpetually nearby selling sodas, cookies, cakes, fruits, and sundry other small items from a bright yellow cart — or on some days, out nearer to Morant Bay, she only cooked for the fishing men, it seemed, and left her cart elsewhere. Solomon to his eyes on all those passings-by always so utterly beautiful; probably in his mid-forties (you could never precisely tell the ages of the very poor as you could more accurately with others: a faceful of wrinkles and a mouth of missing teeth — none of which, astonishingly, marred Solomon's sculpted beauty — could belong to a person still only in his mid-thirties); the fisherman not at all self-conscious or uneasily poised in a poorer man's cupidity before the upper-middle-class city man. "Brattie," with a fisherman's rough hands made tough by harsh hours under the unforgiving sun out on the sea, from the very first completely unabashed about speaking full patois to the English-speaking city man whose nasal middle-class patois consistently betrayed its upper St. Andrew origins. He had been struck by the fact that, in speaking with him, Solomon never struggled in self-conscious English as his kind tended so often to do, ashamed as many of them had been taught to be of patois yet stumbling through all the typical mispronunciations and embarrassing malapropisms glaringly present in their unguaranteed English: "Missa *Si*-mitt" for "Mr. Smith," "cer*fiti*-cate" for birth "certificate," "extinguished" for "distinguished." Yet, with his shrewdly attentive eyes, Solomon seemed to take in a great deal during the few brief conversations they had had, even (especially?) conversing with a city brown man like him (about the weather, the sea's bounty or lack of it — what else could they really talk about?). He himself had wondered more than once if his own kind was occasionally held in contempt by Solomon's cohort, all of them black and obviously poor, because of the privilege *they* knew his light brown skin conferred in a country still deeply ambivalent about each of its many colors — and, of course, because he possessed a flashy enough car, a Pajero of all things, far beyond their most far-reaching impoverished dreams. *Mi uncle,* Solomon had told him early on, *dat was mi modda brodda, him did all de while tell mi moddah seh dat me would grow to be one spoil-up pickney becau' she did never one day cane me, even when mi did run up and down de road wid all de odda bwoy dem round de place so. Him did always tell her seh 'You a go spoil dat deh bwoy deh,' him did seh to her. So him did stay, always vex-up,* Solomon had said, laughing not entirely lightly, *him did always act kinda fenke-fenke. But trust me, mi did know seh him was a good man, a good Christian. So now one Sunday morning when we did mek weself ready to go a church him did start to call mi 'Brattie.' 'Brattie,' him did seh to mi, seh, 'you is one liccle Brattie-Brattie-bwoy,' him did seh to me pon de road. So de name kinda stick, eh? And from that time all de bwoy dem in town did follow him up and start from then to call me Brattie. Is so dem call me til now, but mi true-true name mi moddah gimme is Solomon, fi true.*

He had listened enraptured to the tale of naming originated in vexation and a poor country man's exasperation, endeavoring to imagine the high-spirited, mischievous young Solomon. He imagined the uncle's unpredictable wrath in a country that in those years had been powerfully convinced of the absolute correctness of *very* corporal punishment: *Eh-eh!* he imagined the wrathful uncle scolding, *but what kind of hardhead-bwoy dis? Mind mi don'* bruk *you forehead, brattie-bwoy!* The reverie caused him to smile, and did not demand that he acknowledge the rippling feelings of protection toward that younger Solomon-Brattie who, as he himself as a boy had dutifully attended Sunday service at St. Jude's in Stony Hill in the company of so many other well-heeled upper St. Andrewers (and he and Solomon were roughly about the same age, he'd guessed — such different Jamaicas, such extremely different youths), Brattie had no doubt scampered with other surely shoeless boys through the dry St. Thomas brush on Sunday afternoons after service in search of mongoose, duppy soursop, and mangoes pregnantly ripe-to-bursting and ready to be stoned out of trees, as the heat-weary adults who beat, fed, prayed over and raised the boys with equal care gave over their bodies to the one day of rest granted them by Jesus Christ their Savior and the others who actually owned their lives. His face, carefully smiling in measured response to Solomon's recounting of that childhood time, had not dared, then or ever, to betray its utter surrender, before that face, to the rich patois he adored in spite of his class's frequent disdain for it (or at least disdain for those who could not speak anything else). He dared not betray his surrender to the storyteller's stone-hard body inured to hardship and the spreading sea where it had all begun. Nor could he reveal the final giving over of himself, in deeply guarded dreams, to Solomon's mouth and (rahtid, man, there was no getting away from it) his eyes — his *eyelashes* — that suggested something and more of the sea, and thus made perfect sense, he'd thought, as a fisherman's.

"But if you could ever *see* this man," he had told Carlton shortly after his first encounter with Solomon. (Carlton had greeted the rapture on more than one occasion with a wry though generous smile.) "And his *body*, you see? Jesus have mercy. Look here, nuh? When I tell you 'bout *body* —"

"You gwaan," his friend had responded, the shadow of a deeper, more profane laugh in his thick throat. They had been in Carlton's living room one Saturday evening, spending a few hours lyming over rum and, of all things, codfish dumplings, another thing Carlton loved, even in the evening; he joining the older man in looking incredulously and with a desire so vaulting it had actually pained his crotch at some "rude" photographs of Jamaican and Cuban young men someone had provided at cost; how the *rassclaat* had Carlton always managed to get such things in Jamaica, not even using the internet? He had had a couple of hours before having to drive back to Kingston and some party he and Carole had been expected to attend somewhere in Norbrook. "You is one rassclaat whore," the older man continued, unable to resist the tease. "You know seh you just a look him becau' you tink seh him hood *big*, sah!"

"Old dutty sport!" he had nearly shouted in laughter, calling Carlton the word men like themselves called each other in affection and wrath. "I shoulda lick you inna you rass!"

And they had laughed and laughed, making some bawdy comments over the photographs, Carlton especially — *Lord Jesus, but watch the hood on* this *one, eh?* — while sharing some more rum between them. But, with his typical reticence (reticence, yes: for what kind of friend had he been, really, to Carlton, so unwilling always, though Carlton had not always known or sensed it, to speak what he really felt? But there was so much safety in silence and withholding, wasn't there? Hadn't he found that to be so with Carole, and she with him, though neither would ever dare admit that to the other?), he had secretly taken deep offense to Carlton's thinking, and worse, *saying*, even in affectionate jest, that his only interest in Solomon had been because he'd believed the fisherman to have a huge hood. *It is so much* more *than that*, he had thought just then, actually infuriated in the moment and slightly shocked to find himself suddenly so unexpectedly angry . . . in fact all at once literally hot beneath the collar of his polo shirt, with each passing minute becoming quietly more furious at his dear friend whom, he admitted just then but only very briefly, he sometimes despised: despised him, he'd thought, sitting there with his year by year increasing paunch and sweating in his old-fashioned bush jacket; going to bald and jowly as would a man in his fifties who drank and loved too much his stew pork, rice and peas, oxtail, yam and dumpling, and potato pudding; a man who in his fifties still growled and mewled like a teenager over "big hood" and "suck-ready batty" and laughingly called his own battyhole a "pussy." How could it not be difficult to despise all that in the running-to-fat, even froglike (if he were to speak the truth) Carlton, even as he loved him?

But not so easy now to continue despising all that, nor to acknowledge the envy he had always felt for Carlton's always-startling zest for life even in the midst of so much disapproval and scorn — in fact hatred — for the perceived degenerate. Not so easy to deal with all that when one you had once so secretly frequently despised even as you loved him was now only a smoldering pile of ashes, with some bone fragments intact among the embers.

Darting away from that image as he feels the vomit rising again in his throat, his head still on his steering wheel, he remembers that on that particular day when Carlton had laughingly accused him of feeling more lust for Solomon than he himself would ever dare admit, he had also been angry with himself; because what exactly had he meant in thinking *It is so much more than that* — what was the "it," what was the "so much more"? And for *whom*? Something "more" for a blasted Christian-to-rass fisherman who had probably never in his narrow life given thought to anything like *that*, and couldn't possibly ever have seen — as it was best he never did see — the look in the city man's eyes directed toward him? That look? The look that said, *You*, that (so he often feared) practically begged when he saw Solomon each time *Please* and *Will you* and *If I could just once*?

What had he meant when he'd thought *But it's so much more?* — ah, but he had known exactly what he'd meant. The very thing that *no* man in Jamaica was ever allowed to feel for another.

And so what Carlton had immediately divined, and what he had hated him for divining, had been part of the "it," though not so clearly understood at the time by himself: he *had* felt that yearning, the vulgar yearning (as he preferred to think of it, which also excited him), to kiss that — that *hood*, dearest Father Divine; to wrap his mouth around the hood as Carole, sometimes in distaste and other times in weariness, though they had produced two children together, had wrapped her mouth around his. ("But chuh, Aston, man," she had complained on several more recent occasions — perhaps her jaw had ached? Perhaps she had she been bored or agonized or simply disgusted at the prospect, even though he had often delighted in burying his face deeply between her legs, barely coming up for air until with several shudders and spasms she had cried out and pulled his hair and hissed his name, knowing that in tasting everything of her he had in fact possessed her as she had him? "Not *again*, man? I tired, you see? Get some rest tonight, nuh, man? Next time, all right? Yeah, man, I promise.")

And so of course he had never told Carlton that yes, believe it, he had always wanted really and truly above all else to *curl* his fingers around Solomon's (surely) ginnep-sized black balls and *squeeze* his hand around the (surely) plaintain-thick uncircumcised black hood — uncircumcised, of course, he thought, especially with country people — and rub it, rub, after which he would raise his hand to his face in order to sniff and lick, suck, what he knew would be the strong roadside sweat-crotch smell, pure *hood*: then pull that hood that was not brown like his own but black as the ace of rassclaat spades, he thought (stiffening more at the thought — how much stiffer could his own hood get before it tore a path through his zipper?) . . . pull it, the fisherman's road-sweaty sea-salty rancid cock, into his mouth, *inna* it, in order to taste and suck sweat and strong hood smell and ultimately Brattie's charging heat that would have jetted so powerfully, *power*, out of that engorged blackman hood. The hood that he had not yet seen and only in his most locked-away thoughts dared to imagine in dreams enabled by surreptitious glances at Brattie's crotch whenever he stopped to chat briefly and buy fish from him. The hood that, on nights lying next to Carole in their air-conditioned bedroom, back from some party or get-together or yet another excruciating visit to her parents in Jack's Hill (they had always tolerated him; he was socially a product of Meadowbrook, not Jack's Hill; he had attended merely Calabar and the University of the West Indies, not Campion and Cornell as Carole had; with gimlet eyes that grudgingly granted him quarter because of his complexion that perfectly matched Carole's and had helped to produce even lighter grandchildren with wonderfully pliable hair, and because he was, finally, a true *professional* with his own *corner* office and secretary, as she was, they tolerated him), he had imagined Solomon-Brattie filling his throat, and then (yes, of course) taking him from behind: Solomon's hood deep inna what he too would have liked, as daringly and rebelliously as Carlton had done, to have called his *pussy* — shouting out in his most dangerous, utterly unspeakable imagination words like *Brattie, come breed me, Brattie-bredren come fuck me, come now, Brattie and grind-grind you cocky hot-hot inna mi pussy* . . . Solomon's blackman hood *filling* up his pussy, he imagined, and *roughing* it in a way nothing Carole (nor any woman) could ever have done or would ever be able to do. He had never told Carlton how many times he had imagined all that, the more violent parts, and then the kiss, kiss*es*, that Brattie-bredren would have bestowed upon him . . . kisses bestowed mouth to mouth as the other man threw his fisherman's arms around him and *held* him and

(But even if anything like that had been possible with Brattie, *where* . . . in Jamaica? he thought. Where the *claat*hole, you rass, would you have met with him, the fisherman, *where?*)

— then to feel all at once the deep-set revulsion but also the onrushing joy and liberation surging upward and out through him and into what would surely be a darkened bedroom as he realized that after so many years of hiding and choking down these feelings yes Jesus this was indeed the *faggot* in him   it was the big, unrestrained *battyman* in him in that moment at last free completely unrestrained it was, dear God, the *cocksucker* in him, wasn't that the word they used in America? — his legs just then flung up to that high ceiling in his mind, prepared for any new adventure, like the kisses that would fill his own mouth with the taste of that black St. Thomas fisherman smelling of ripe sweat and the sea as Brattie, his Brattie, kissed him *everywhere* and he, Aston, the respectable man lately from the *best* part of Stony Hill who could not possibly be dreaming such things, tasted and smelled himself, his own flesh and fluids, on Brattie's balls, on that belly, and in his kisses, as Brattie tasted him. That beautiful fisherman in the mouth of a brown man condemned to that life in upper St. Andrew with a woman whom he did . . . whom he *did* love. Carole. (Loved her? Even now, after all these years? But yes, of course.)

(But then there was also the fact that . . . a woman's tongue *was* so completely different from a man's, wasn't it? It had none of the power, none of the thrust and the force, of a man's tongue forced in, *shoved* in, between the teeth — at least Carole's did not. Had it ever? Had his own? he wondered, and could not remember. And a wife's tongue, especially that of the mother of his children — well, that was more known, *familiar*, than anyone else's. In such knowing there could be none of the danger that brought such a rush to the loins and all the senses, starting with that unmistakable quickening of the blood; in the familiarity there was, for him, increasingly less pleasure in what he experienced as the safety that simply was not . . . was not life on the *edge*. It was not that place on the edge where a man could have a pussy, a pussy*hole*, a *bomborassclaat* pussyhole, in fact, and his wife could fuck him in it, fuck him hard and deep without questions or revulsion precisely because she would already know: know the things that kind of woman and wife knew.)

But then what fuckery, he thought. (And now, inappropriately and inconveniently, his hood was harder than a rassclaat mashstone.) What *complete* fuckery, he thought. Carlton deader than dead just down the road and me sitting here not moving, cyaan move, just mash-up. *Mash-up.*

Fuckery, yes, because Brattie, he thought, would never have done what he himself had done two days earlier upon apprehending just what exactly had happened out there. If Brattie had driven out to Carlton's house from Kingston as he had two nights ago (thanking God that Carole had a late appointment with a client in Manor Park, and had arranged for her sister to come over and stay with the girls after school), expecting as always to find his friend moving about heavily in his front garden at dusk, perhaps scowling encouragingly up into a recalcitrant hibiscus ("Dem want some rain, you know," he was fond of saying when they didn't perform to his expectations), Brattie would not, he thought, upon actually reaching the burned-down house, have fallen forward as he himself had: behavior that he, raised among Kingston's privileged as a straight-backed, tight-lipped Anglican, had always found most distasteful at other denominations' funerals, especially those of poorer people: yet another person felled by cancer, the cruelty of guns, diabetes, heart failure, or one of the many other scourges that took out the poor quicker than anyone else, and mourned with the most unseemly cowbawling, breast-beating, stamping and screams of *Lawd, Lawd* and *Mi cyaan tek no more, Jesus*. He was certain that, had Brattie witnessed what he had — the stench of Carlton's freshly roasted flesh still floating in that evening's cooling air, competing with jasmine for supremacy, but also the post-execution crowd's hysterical furor — the fisherman would not have lurched forward as Aston had done in the way of all those people at the mawkish funerals, his hands grasping fistfuls of air where there was none and his mouth shrieking undignified pleas to Jesus and His Heavenly Father on learning what had transpired that evening; summoning in his shattered imagination what must have been Carlton's agonized screams in his last surviving minutes.

Minutes in which the scars must have happened. Scars on the mostly completely scorched hands that the police had later verified had been those of *the resident*, as they had officially referred to Carlton, in the strange toneless way Jamaican officials and especially the less educated, painfully self-conscious in their use of English, employed when working in "difficult" situations. Scars that had been caused by machete blows, evidently wielded by people in the crowd outside when "the resident," in agony, had attempted more than once to flee his burning house. One woman in the crowd, someone who (she herself had said) had witnessed the entire event from beginning to end, had murmured to someone standing beside her that yes, man, the battyman had indeed tried to escape the house after a few of the younger men in the crowd had set fire to it, but as soon as he had showed his blasted face at the front door, begging the roaring crowd to let him out of the house, the fire practically tearing up his backside, several of the men both younger and old had rushed forward, braving the heat, smoke, and reaching flames, and chopped furiously at the faggot's hands, face, and body with the machetes and pickaxes they had brought to the event specifically for that purpose. *Yes, battyman, come out now and face you judgment.* The battyman had had no choice but to lurch back directly into the inferno, by that time some of its beams and ceilings already collapsing around him. Some of the crowd had, of course, brought containers of acid with them to dash upon his flesh if he managed to gain even so much as five inches out of the house; as she remembered, about twelve men, maybe thirteen, maybe more, had stood guard around the house's few remaining windows that had not exploded, right up until the minute the structure finally shuddered and toppled in a swirl of flame, smoke, and sparks. Another small country house gone to ultimate ruin, and what would Miss Vie have said and thought, some in the crowd wondered aloud, to live and see her house bu'n-up so — but *eh-eh, no bodda ask dat,* a sharp voice sounded out of the crowd, *you shoulda ask instead what did mek her go and put a bomborassclaat battyman up inna her house fi live.* But don't blood always thicker than water, someone else had muttered. . . .

No one in the town, of course, would ever tell the police who had planned the execution — many in the town, or only a few — and so meticulously drenched the faggot's house with gasoline on every side. Nor would anyone disclose how the executioners had managed to do it in the early evening, although the sun had already set, without Carlton catching a glimpse of them, or even sensing, just beyond his windows, their temporarily muted rage. Outside of those who played dominoes and drank beers or stout or rum with the police when they were off duty (or on), no one would ever know what exactly they thought of the whole thing; the fire would be designated "suspicious" by them, and the case closed at that. Carlton had not come from a family of any significance with connections to an important M.P. or hotelier or developer. He was certainly not white, nor "Syrian." Whoever had been responsible, whether only a few or many in the town (including those who attended the Adventist or Anglican church, or the Pentecostalist or the Kingdom Hall, or those few who called Jah their god), had managed without too much expense or toll on their time to send the filthy-dutty nastyman in a storm of ashes back to the hell from which his unfortunate mother, wherever *she* lived, had not been able to save him. As common as similar violence for different or the exact same reasons was in Jamaica now, the story would barely make a forward page in the *Gleaner* nor even in the sensationalist *Star*, especially since the journalists who heard in time of the case would not learn until some time afterward, and then only by hearsay, that it had been a fucking nastyman, not a regular everyday respectable person, who had been incinerated alive in his house.

He had not even had time to call up Desmond, the nine-teen-year-old originally from one of the Kingston ghettoes — it had been Riverton City, hadn't it? That sounded right — whom he had met a few times at Carlton's, now living in Toronto, whom Carlton had "mentored" in recent years, to find out if he had heard the news . . . although of course Desmond must have heard by now; news of another murdered battyman trav-eled quickly and sometimes eagerly through Jamaica's clandes-tine homosexual channels, and invariably rapidly made its way into those northern cities: Miami, Atlanta, New York, Boston, London, Birmingham, Toronto, and every other damn place jampacked with the migratory population. He could not imag-ine Desmond's reaction to the news any more than he could assess the truest depths of emotion that, in utmost privacy, must, he thought, have passed between Desmond and Carlton; the dead man had been unusually reticent in regard to his re-lationship with the younger man, and, unlike his more casu-al past encounters and adventures, had never once referred in conversation with Aston to the size or shape or even existence of Desmond's hood . . . none of his usual ecstasy unto a fever pitch about how it did *taste*, Lord Jesus, and how it did *feel*, and dear God how it did grind-grind up inside me *so*. . . . *Desmond*, he himself had thought, his own hood stiffening whenever he had been in the beauty's presence or, lying next to or on top of Carole, had thought about him, though he could of course never have betrayed any sign of such an amorous reaction to Carlton for whom Desmond had so clearly been the universe's center, alpha and omega. Whether or not the lithe, long-legged, long-eyelashed, full-mouthed dark vision (Carlton had always preferred dark men) had at first fully reciprocated Carlton's passion — the vision who may or may not have been the demurest of whores, whom Carlton may or may not have been paying for visits to the house that each time may or may not have involved sex — remained, after the ashes, unknown; in recent months he had cynically, almost bitterly thought Who but a whore would be able to summon the performance of passion for Carlton's unmistakably middle-aged face, his sagging, flabby chest, his protuberant belly, and his flip-floppy, distinctly *un*firm, uninviting buttocks? (Like mine in a few years, soon enough, he had not enjoyed thinking; because yes, youth was that fleeting.) For men, unlike women, could not fake *that*, the evidence of actual desire, no matter which sexual positions they preferred or said they preferred. Yet Desmond had, at Carlton's urging and perhaps with his financial assistance, applied for a visa to Canada and amazingly (for people with ghetto community addresses were not always so fortunate) been granted one; he had not much money in the bank, according to Carlton, which the Canadian High Commission interviewers would have no doubt found problematic, though he had many family members still in Jamaica, which would have eased some of their *Will-this-one-run-away-and-disappear-into-Canada-or-not?* suspicions. Maybe it had really been requited love, he thought, smiling again at the idea of Carlton so happy when he spoke about Desmond, while knowing that the younger man, though fearful of leaving behind all that he had ever known in Jamaica, even if "all" had been mostly downtown west Kingston's stench and squalor and the violent political factionalism that plagued those ghettoes, had ultimately really wanted to go someplace where "Nobody don't know me," Desmond had said once, "and me don't know no one. Especially not any of de nasty dutty sport dem." (At the time, Aston had thought but not voiced the opinion that he knew Carlton would not have welcomed: Toronto might not be the best place, then, if you wanted to avoid all the dutty-nasty Jamaican sketel sports. Why not try Montreal or a less Jamaicanized place like . . . Dallas?)

"And look at this, nuh?" Carlton had nearly shouted in triumph only a few weeks before the burning — only weeks ago, when he had still been daydreaming about visiting Desmond up there — "the bwoy write *back* to me, you see?" And it was true. In spite of the anxieties Carlton had expressed almost from the afternoon of Desmond's departure about all the possible "distractions up there" that would soon lure him into another world entirely (and of course there were enough stunning black men in Toronto to keep a Caribbean man who gravitated toward black men happy, to say nothing of men of other colors), there had arrived regularly from Desmond almost since his first week in Toronto a sequence of frequent enough emails, postcards, and even brief but convincingly passionate letters scrawled in his nearly unintelligible script: the eager but erratic handwriting of one not quite fully literate detailing the nearly-lurid passions and writings of a young man possibly believing himself in "love" — a word that Desmond, at least, had been fond of using in writing — yet adrift in a world thick with temptations, bewilderments, disappointments and, God knew, tragedies; the younger man apparently actually still missing Jamaica in spite of everything, and especially his beloved granny in town, but also Carlton who had so cared for him and who, with the younger man's granny, had been more of a parent to him than had ever been his philandering, rum-besotted father and cowering mother back in the stench and ordure of Riverton City.

And so, he thought, amazed at the simple yet startling truth, it *had* finally been Carlton's love, its force and raw determination to protect, at all costs, the beloved, that had not only insisted but demanded that Desmond emigrate, as soon as possible, from the country which, as Carlton must have known better than most, having lost other male friends to stabbings and machete-opened throats, might one day kill him. Carlton in his fifties had obviously known what Desmond had not yet wanted to admit: that Jamaica would not, for long, look favorably upon a young, gorgeous, large-eyed, mildly effeminate enough to be suspect man from the ghetto so clearly not interested in women neither as actual people nor as mere pussy. The key was to remember the phrase *not for long*, and to know without doubt when that tenuous time had finished and the more threatening time had begun. Most people surely knew, even if they steadfastly refused to admit or even entertain that they possessed any such knowledge or instinct, that to be a beautiful, effeminate, young sexually suspect male in Jamaica, but a *well-off* one, was one thing; the *well-off* part the principal saving grace, aside from the great luck of having a fiercely watchful grandmother or miraculously open-minded big brother who moonlighted or worked full-time as a gunman or, even better, as a don. To be beautiful (as opposed to handsome) *and* poor *and* girlish and ultimately suspected of being that way . . . but no. The green-mountained island would not, without the eventual warning swipe of a machete's kiss, put up with all *that*, especially in the case of someone like Desmond: someone assuredly not to the manor born and unable to protect himself with their money and education, their frequent enough trips to Miami, Fort Lauderdale, Atlanta, and New York, their tinted-window SUVs (like Aston's Pajero and Carole's Land Rover), their (usually) highly professional jobs, and their well-barred, gated, substantial homes in Mandeville and in the suburbs of upper St. Andrew and Montego Bay. (The homes of course progressed from substantial to palatial the higher up along certain roads, toward particular hills, one traveled; a fact some of his and Carole's non-Jamaican friends, especially those from the States and Europe, often found difficult to grasp: all that wealth in a *third world* country? their bewildered faces invariably expressed.) But in spite of Carlton's having known all that and what it would eventually portend for the likes of himself, Carlton, he thought with a rush of anger at the dead man, had decided to stay — to remain in Jamaica because he had finally always loved it and perhaps because he was, in the end, a bit of a fool. The thought made Aston angrier. It had not been necessary to have been that much of a fool, he thought, no matter how much you loved your country that did not at all love you. Yes, Carlton had wanted to stay in Jamaica, in complete denial yet fully aware of what might happen to him and especially what might happen living as such an obvious battyman in a back-of-the-beyond backwater town like that one that had not produced him as its own. He had come to love, and had wanted to keep, what he had fondly described in recent months as "mi liccle country life"; he had long ago wearied and despaired of the often mean-spirited, youth-and-beauty- (and money-) obsessed circuits and clandestine weekend battyman (and sometimes battyman and sodomite, when enough women appeared) parties in the farther, wealthier and more hidden parts of upper St. Andrew, although, like many of the men who attended those gatherings, he had worshiped and continued to worship feverishly, even remorselessly, at the sacrosanct altars of youth and beauty. All of those were, and had been, compelling enough reasons, in Carlton's universe, to remain. But but he had also wanted to remain in Jamaica and not "jump ship" because even when faced with the reality of vicious crime in every parish across the island and gunmen who would as easily spit on sand as shoot a four-month-old infant through the head, then laugh about it over a rowdy game of dominoes edged by white rum, he had never ceased to love things like the sudden and completely unexpected appearance of a doctor bird at six-thirty on a still-misty morning, its wings blur-beating as, hovering and darting, it dipped its needle beak into one of his hibiscuses; in spite of all the crime, he had never stopped loving, and participating in, the easy laughter still common to many Jamaicans, that he knew North Americans and certainly English people could not equal — "de no-soul people dem" was his favorite term for the English, who, these days, were anyway completely irrelevant to him and most of Jamaica; but the term, for him, had become applicable to the Americans as well. Those people didn't know what laughter *was*, he had once said, unless it was at someone else's expense. And they didn't know how to live, either.

"Besides," he had once said with a completely straight face, until the punchline, "can you see *me* trying to suck on some white man liccle-liccle hood? Some fenke-fenke bakra massa!" — to which they both had broken up.

But Carlton had also never stopped loving his yam and curry goat and plaintain and sweetsop and condensed milk, and *how*, he had often voiced in an irritable tone to Aston, could consuming such things in "foreign," in Toronto, New York, Manchester, Miami or Brixton — Finsbury Park! — possibly compare to enjoying them at home? And then, in spite of sensing the increasing hostility building over time just beyond his windows especially after dark, he absolutely could not retire for the night each night without sitting either on his verandah in the darkness, or in his living room with the overhead fan going, listening either to the TV or the radio (preferring either Irie FM or the BBC) or the reliable peepers, or perhaps even to the shouts and laughter of the boys still playing pretend-cricket or stickball, or more likely football, not far up the road, as he thought about Desmond, perhaps, or someone else whom, in one of the well-hidden corridors of his labyrinthine and mostly lonely past, he had loved or tried, against vaulting odds, against the intense need for supreme masculinity from one or the other, to love. He had telephoned Aston often enough on his cell during those evenings, perhaps in loneliness or simply the generosity and love of friendship, or both, sitting in his place on the verandah and telling him in the quiet voice he reserved for that state of mind in the just-after-dusk time about what lovely tough-*tough*-man he had noticed walking up the road that day, or how the fields nearby were dry-dry like matchsticks after suffering the bitterness of no rainfall for more than five days . . . in fact exactly the kind of weather that, less than three weeks after that last conversation, would enable the flames that, fed on the drought-dry wood of his house and the dessert of gasoline, would consume his flesh. Carlton had not wanted to give up any of the things he had loved about Jamaica — and who, knowing how incredibly beautiful Jamaica could be in spite of all its problems, especially if one had at least a little money, could blame him? Who could blame him, the damnblasted idiot romantic (because yes, Aston thought; he was *very* angry at Carlton for letting what had happened to him happen) . . . at his age still so foolishly in love with how the sun, before finally surrendering to dusk, always blazed its protest over the hills in the west each early evening . . . what a *beau*tiful sunset dem must have in Negril, eh? Carlton had once rhetorically asked him about that part of the island the older man had never seen *and never will now*, the survivor thought just then, thinking, *I am a survivor, yes, I have survived my friend . . .* only to be violently startled out of his reverie, jerking his head up off the car's steering wheel from which he had not moved since his entry into the town that afternoon, by a man's face unexpectedly at the driver's window: an elderly-looking slouch-shouldered man, very thin the way his sort often was, Aston thought, with deeply black skin and white hair, etched facial furrows on either side of his nose down to his mouth and below his ears down to his chin, missing teeth and those remaining gone long ago to deep yellow, and a curled, cracked hand outstretched to Aston's churning face: *I beg you a twenty dollah, sah?* the man asked; he was chewing on what looked like a piece of orange peel. Twenty dollars, what was that now in the exchange rate, about thirty U.S. cents?

But he could not. Normally, acting on one of the motivations commonly felt among those of his station and higher — mild fear, guilt, annoyance, or the desire to chase from his view the visual and olfactory affronts of rank poverty — he might have given a little something, he thought, even if stopped by some of the truly annoying, aggressive car windscreen-washers on Waterloo Road or Trafalgar Road in town — but not today. Not here. Not looking at this man whose deeply black face reminded him somehow of Solomon's. Was it the poverty in it as well as the blackness? Was that how Brattie would look in twenty years' time? But this man, he thought, even though clearly elderly and in a somewhat infirm state, might very well have been one of the men in the murderous crowd who, with their machetes and acid, had barred Carlton from leaving the burning house. *Come out now, battyman, and face you bloodclaat judgment.* Had this wrinkled, stoop-shouldered begging man been one of them? This man who might have been a grandfather, a great-grandfather? Who might also have been an ardent Christian, the Bible and assorted prayer- and songbooks being the only books he had ever read in his life, if he were able to read? Had he had been inhibited on that killing evening by age and possible disability in joining the staunch men? (Aston had looked the man quickly up and down, and had seen that he appeared to have something like a right club foot, severely turned inward, and a weirdly swollen left knee poking its protuberance out on a radically thin leg, keloid-marked in several places, beneath his dirty, raggedy-torn knee-length shorts — and, not surprisingly, he was shoeless.) Or had the man, this begging man, joined the crowd in screaming their chant of execution, *Fire pon de battyman, all battyman fi dead*? Had he closed his eyes and given thanks to Jesus when the house's windows had exploded and the last curling screams of the creature trapped within had confirmed that the flames had finally —?

He had not actually struck the man in the face, he would think sometime that evening, although he had, as he had also cursed him — something like *Fuck off* or *Tek you* blood*claat hand off mi car, you nasty dutty* — as the man, hearing those furies hurled inexplicably at him, jumped back from the suddenly revved car in both shock and horror. But no, that couldn't have been right, it couldn't have gone so, because after all, he had *not* started and then revved the car so abruptly, feeling the heat of panic well up behind his eyes and tighten in his hands and chest as he had shouted, yes, *shouted* at the man that it was because of people like you that he was dead, nasty dutty damn-blasted bloodclaat ignorant country bitches — no, he will reflect in a quiet moment that evening. No. He had *not* gone on bad before the poor man (although he had, enough so to draw stares from people walking past nearby), and cursed him — that poor old crippled man who, though he may indeed have been one of Carlton's executioners, never did receive in his cracked palms, from the dead man's dear friend (if only he had known!), the modest sum of twenty Jamaican dollars, *I beg you, sah.*

An hour or so later, he does not in fact realize exactly where he is driving, or why, until, suddenly aware of the Blue Mountains off to his left and the sea out to the right (though the mountains, at greater and lesser distances, have been there for much of his drive back), he apprehends with mild shock that he is just passing eastward through the Harbour View roundabout, taking the turn that will lead him out to Bull Bay and then St. Thomas — and of course, he knows now and hopes, to Brattie. Will Brattie be out there when he gets there? He actually does feel his heart beating faster, and so true what people write in all those books, he thinks, that the heart beats faster when . . . he will not think *when one is in love*, for that cannot be, he thinks: it is too ridiculous, he is a big grown married man with a wife and children, and anyway how could someone like himself possibly be in love with someone like Brattie, a *fisherman*? As one of his daughters might say these days, enraptured as the girls were with American television, *As if.* Yet he knows: striving to keep at bay all thoughts of Carlton and the place out of which, after cussing off the hapless elderly begging man, he fled, it is Brattie's face he wants to see now, not Carole's nor anyone else's in his circle, especially after having restrained, on the drive back to town, his urge to pull the car over and retch violently out the driver's window. Brattie's face, if only to confirm, to confirm . . . what? That it was still possible, after a beloved friend had been burned to death and vilified and threatened even as he burned, to feel love, *love*, for a man from whom he had only bought fish, about whom he knew more by way of his own fantasies than he did in reality? Yet he felt that seeing Brattie's face would calm him. Carole had never known about Carlton, not really, any more than she had ever known the truth, the real truth, about him. All at once, feeling the sudden and unexpected weight of too many unspoken and unspeakable things, he wondered How the rassclaat can I possibly go home tonight? Go home and face all of them? Carole, the girls? How am I going to do it without crying, without feeling sick inna mi stomach, dear God, and just talk with her about what happened today at work, or ask her if so-and-so from church is feeling any better? How —

Amazingly, though the afternoon had worn on, Carole had not phoned him, a quick call to his office revealed as he passed through Poor Man's Corner, a town whose name he had always liked; one of those evocative country names, he thought, like Old Woman's Point or the District of Look Behind. The road curved, dipped, and rose slightly; he sped through Yallahs, a town he had never particularly liked, and in a shorter time than he imagined it would take found himself slowing into the town just a few miles outside Morant Bay where, on a few afternoons, he had glimpsed Brattie in the square, chatting with one of the vendors if he had finished selling off the day's catch. And there, in the square just off the road, were, as usual, all the vendors selling everything from peanuts and plastic combs to box juice, not far from the aggressive men looking to stuff even more people into their hazardous route taxis or minivans en route to Morant Bay or back to Kingston. But no Brattie. Seeing all the quotidian activity somehow comforted him in the wake of what he had just left behind, even as its very quotidianness made what had happened to Carlton seem all the more profane. How *could* life possibly go on as normal, he thought, with the embers still cooling in St. Catherine? But it was with renewed dread that he then understood that the people in this parish would ultimately surely have shown the same reaction to Carlton, and perhaps to him, as the executioners had in St. Catherine. He drove quickly on, heading farther east, to the place where he was sure he would find Brattie.

After some more driving east on the increasingly pot-holed road, with the sea, calm on this afternoon and shimmering teal and azure off to his right, he slowed down to see a few fishing boats tied up on what passed for a shoulder on the right side of the road several yards ahead. Just beyond them, beneath the shade of a ratty-looking, dusty almond tree and nearly in the water herself, he saw a large woman cooking some meat over a low fire, speaking over her shoulder to one of the five men gathered there, three of them shirtless and all five bearing that sun-bronzed look on their skin and in their hair that marked lifelong fishermen — the people for whom boats such as those tied up by the roadside meant only work, and much of it. He recognized her as the same woman he had seen speaking with Brattie before, selling whatever she could from her fully-loaded, brightly painted vendor's cart. The cart was nowhere to be seen today. And then he saw him too. One of the shirtless men. Brattie.

Or rather, he first saw Brattie's eyes — those eyes, unmistakable even from this distance of some yards, above those cheekbones. The eyes that could have belonged to no one else, and that, because they suggested something and more of the sea, made perfect sense as a fisherman's. He looked and looked and *looked* at the eyes, at Brattie's change of facial expression that altered them; then fixed his own stare (one that he was careful even in that near-trancelike state to maintain as not hungry, as impassive) on that unbelievable mouth; then moved to the large, dark nipples, until he saw Brattie bend down, all five feet ten inches of him, laughing after some joke one of the others had made, and pull a white mesh tank top over himself. He saw Brattie's biceps, dark and velvety in the sun; he saw the muscles that formed the stunning V-shape that held proud reign from his smooth shoulders down to his narrow waist; he saw the top of the hard, lean backside that greeted the waist, because Brattie's underwear — boxer shorts, perhaps, or briefs? He could not tell at this distance, even though he could, from here, see the brightly colored waistband — crouched low on his hips, just barely peeking out from his knee-length, slightly ripped jeans — the clothes he obviously wore for work, but, Aston knew, would never even *think* to consider for use on a Sunday. He saw Brattie's hard stomach divided into those small cubes, what he had heard some people refer to as a "six-pack" — he liked the phrase — and wanted desperately to believe that, below the stomach, he could see the very thing that he had always wanted to see and feel of Brattie's — but it was not visible; Brattie's underwear, though low, concealed it well, and the man himself anyway, being a devout family man, was one of that rare breed of Jamaican male of his class who did not like to brag and shout about his hood and its majesty; Aston had divined that much in past conversations with him. He imagined Brattie's eyes lowering and his lips curling in faint derision coupled with mildly indulgent amusement at, even embarrassment over, what would surely have been his colleagues' bawdy jokes and assessments of the delight women took in their "cocky," how so many females begged for it, and how *good fi true* hood was the one thing that would keep them coming back. But Aston was certain Brattie would not comment on such randy matters himself; feeling his own heart beat even more furiously through these thoughts at the sight of all of *that*; it was altogether too much, in the stretching sunlight moving toward Negril, for his rapt gaze, even with the other men nearby as a sort of competition.

(And he did not even have sunglasses, he thought. Would they have helped both in Carlton's town and out here? But he would always want to look directly into Brattie's eyes, unimpeded, even if he wished not for Brattie ever to see too deeply into his own.)

In what felt to him like a slightly feverish state, but may have been only the burden of the day's waning heat unrelieved by the gentle breeze from the sea only some yards to his right, he felt certain that he could see, even from this distance, the curls of Brattie's eyelashes.

But how, he thought, leaving the thought unfinished as he felt himself first begin to tremble, then registered within himself the surge of a great wave that bore in its enormous crest a grief so piercing it threatened to suck out his entire insides. The wave pounded his insides, churning him to a point dangerously close, for the second time that day, to vomiting; then, for just a moment, its swirls turned everything utterly dark before him. Panicked, he lurched forward, sick to his stomach in the sudden grief-darkness, then thrust his head back against the driver's seat head support when — truly miraculously, it seemed — sight and a stable stomach returned. He felt suddenly as if Carlton were right there beside him; exactly what he wanted just then, he thought, and nothing more. No more desire, nor aching for the unobtainable. Just his beloved friend, the one who had almost fully understood him. *You, Carlton. You, to be here right now, beside me.*

Carlton, how the *rass* could God create a man like this Brattie so?

(Some time afterward, lying down next to a sleeping Carole, but himself awake at three-forty-five A.M., he would finally grasp that the deep grief and longing he had felt in that afternoon moment's initial glimpse, and then consuming, of Brattie's face and body was intricately connected to the fact that he finally truly understood that the end really had come; that Carlton really had died, was *dead*, and would be gone forever; that he would not, on the drive back to town, be able to ring his friend on the cell and share with him the joy that he could not share with a single other human being, not anyone at all: the joy of living, radiant beauty in a fishing man's face, and the *utter* joy of imagining that man on top of him, inside him, kissing him, licking him, moving into him and through him so slowly, like *that*, cradling his face with his rough fishing man's hands while calling out his name, not *Missa Aston* as Brattie had always called him, but *Aston*, as he, Aston, did some of those things to him in return and held him and called him by his name, Solomon, or *Brattie, my Brattie* . . . in such a sequence of events he knew that not only he, but the both of them, Brattie and Aston (and what a way oonu name sound nice together! Carlton might have teased), would be, finally, without question, completely free: the most impossible freedom of all, a radical freedom beyond all others. But Carlton could not hear that kind of joy from him about these sorts of things again. He would not cackle and shout *Mi love!* and slap his thigh at the latest report of joy because of beauty espied on the road or, out of the most cautious corner of the eye, glimpsed while swimming with Carole and the girls and their friends at the beach (the loveliness of a bored strolling policeman, perhaps, or of some young lithe men playing football on the sand). Carlton would no longer make slack comments to him about his own recent adventures. This was *it*, he would realize at three-forty-five that morning, and understand at last why the vision of Solomon "Brattie" James had produced such sorrow in him that afternoon. Everything was all over. Without Carlton, even with Brattie, there could not ever quite be joy again. He, Aston Patrick Leslie, husband of Carole Leslie and father of two daughters, was finally, truly, unimaginably alone.)

He did not quite know what to do. He was stopped in his car for the second time that day, arrested and frozen this time partly by recurring unbearable memories filled with smoke that bore a sickening stench, but also by the sight of all *that* before him: Brattie's beauty and the other men's, all gilded by Brattie's radiant smile, all of which would have made Carlton weep, he thought. He imagined how Carlton might have reacted if he had seen Brattie and the other men standing there and laughing, speaking their loud patois and so uninhibited and comfortable in their bodies by the roadside — a comfort *very* few men who actively, hungrily sought other men could ever experience in Jamaica. Only those completely beyond suspicion of perversion, for whatever reasons (the baritone depth of their voice, the deep blackness of their skin, the solidity of their hips when they walked, or their unimpeachable reputation for mashing up women), could experience it. If Carlton had been able to watch these men today so at ease with each other and themselves, these men so stunning to look at but, in the way of innumerable others like them, so completely unconcerned with the fact that they were, indeed, stunning, would that look of deepest lonesomeness have come into his face? The look that, had Carlton ever been aware of his face's betraying of his deepest vulnerability, would have mortified him? *All the blasted men in this damn country who look like* that, Carlton would have fumed, *dem just stand by the side of the road as if dem neva expect people fi look pon dem. Dem just a stand deh so,* Carlton would have hissed, *wid dem hand pon dem machete and dem hood inside dem pant big-big so.* Hands on their machetes, he thought, shifting in the car seat, and maybe also someday containers of kerosene — . . . He had just enough time to strike out the next thought, actually an image of a machete coming down hard on Carlton's agonized arm in one of the moments he must have tried to flee the collapsing house, when Brattie, turning and recognizing first the car, then him, walked over toward him, to greet him with a *Yes, sah, Missa Aston. How you do, sah?* That face, so near to his, bending down at the driver's window to smile in at him. (Now, he saw, Brattie had acquired one gold tooth, an upper. He was an archangel, Aston thought, with a tooth given him by Gabriel or Michael. What else could be the truth, looking into that face at which he could, today, barely look?) He smiled weakly in response, gave the expected reply — *Yeah, man, mi deh ya* — and touched his own fist to Brattie's fist extended for the man-to-man bredren connection, and followed the fist-touch with the nearly whispered words *Respect, respect*: not a form of speech, that kind of solidarity greeting, with which he, intensely aware out here of his upper St. Andrew origins and, next to Brattie, of his own color (all of the other men, and the woman cooking, were, like Brattie, very dark), had ever grown comfortable . . . then looked up again into Brattie's smiling face that was apologizing profusely because the fish run that day had been extremely low. *Not* one parrot *and only a* liccle *bit a snapper, Missa Aston . . . mi did lef' ya from two o'clock this morning, and mi neva catch more than twelve, thirteen fish, Missa Aston . . . the whole of we* (nodding his head back toward the other men), *we neva catch more than twenty liccle t'row-away fish, you see?*

Brattie continued apologizing, until, one hand still on the roof of the car and the other on the door, he looked more carefully at Aston and saw in his face what his own mind had already ascertained: *But what a way him look mash-up today, fi true, like tragedy catch him.* He saw the ashen cast in the other man's aspect, and the way his hand trembled and continued to shake, though slightly, on the steering wheel that it gripped; he saw Aston's wedding ring on that hand, and the fine-quality clothes. He felt a great surge of warmth for this brown man from town, immediately followed by a deep resentment that he did his best, calling automatically upon all the power of Christianity within himself, not to acknowledge. He felt affection for the man who came all the way out to this part of St. Thomas to buy fish from him and him alone (though he had sometimes wondered about this, about the sense of it: *how him get the fish all the way back to town before it spoil?* he had often wondered, but then remembered that Missa Aston's car did have air-conditioning) — Missa Aston who, after deciding on a given day whether he would take two parrot and three snapper or even some lobster in season, always took the time to listen to him chat briefly about the missus, the missus's and his pickney (they had three boys and two girls), what good things were happening in his church (a whole heap of new prayer books sent for the entire congregation by someone's grandpickney earning good money in foreign), and the local troubles in that part of St. Thomas which people from Kingston would not necessarily have seen or heard on the news: an elderly woman shot dead, right through the head, in a household robbery, or a six-year-old child beaten to death by his father because the boy had lost his new schoolbag on the first day of term. He was sure that Missa Aston from town would never scorn nor shame him with a particular look because the fish had not been running that morning; the look he knew well and had received before from people from town and especially people who came from that part of town where he knew Missa Aston came from. The look of scorn or simply of You-do-not-and-should-not-exist, bestowed on those like himself who were compelled in their ratty pants and old shoes to make their living selling fish from the roadside. *A good man dat, Missa Aston,* Brattie had often thought, struggling with his flashes of resentment as, on past occasions, after having wrapped up Missa Aston's fish good-good — he could only spare that special kind of paper for the few customers, like Missa Aston, who were regulars and bought quantities of fish — he watched the retreating shiny Pajero head back to town, after their brief conversations mostly within earshot of the other men also busy with selling their fish or giving it to the woman to fry up for those customers who wanted it fried just then. *A good man,* Brattie had thought, *but him always look like something trouble-trouble him.*

The man envisioned as "archangel" and "my Brattie" by the wrecked man sitting in his car does not know that, as he turns his gorgeous eyes down to him once more and asks, *Missa Aston, you all right?* and thinks *Becau' now him look kinda funny fi true,* something enormous and deeply necessary within the other man — vital for continued unimpeded light, perhaps, or merely the enlarging, in *tolerable* colors, of particular dreams — dies, even as, within him, something powerful and unknown — and, the man himself feels, potentially reckless — abruptly, without warning, springs into life. Brattie, aware of his colleagues not far behind him still engrossed in their conversation and work who may soon wonder, he knows, why he is taking so long in chatting with the brown man from town they have each seen before and remember (for the man's Pajero, as well as his clothes and manner, also are memorable) — Brattie wonders now if Missa Aston is simply feeling sun- and road-weary, maybe from the long drive, or —? when, in the next moment, Missa Aston grips Brattie's hand on the door, grips it, then looks up at him but not quite at him. The man of the sea cannot possibly know that this man who feels all those hidden things about him, for him, is looking not at him, Solomon "Brattie" James, but at a radiant archangel. He cannot understand why Missa Aston is suddenly gripping his hand so hard, *hard* where it rests on the car door in the window square, nor why it seems that Missa Aston cannot quite look at him. (On a future Sunday morning, his wife and children all in white beside him and each of them, like him, swaying to music and ecstatic shouted praises of His name, he will reflect and vaguely connect to this moment with Missa Aston, though uncertain why, the fact that it was once *known* that mere mortals could not ever bear to gaze directly into the faces of either earth-visiting angels or the Almighty Lord their God.) If he were a more outwardly harsh man, a man rather like many other men and not one of devout faith — the kind of faith that calms his wife when she frets and even storms a little about his dangerous work — he might utter a mild oath at this point, in the style of *rahtid* or something similar, in puzzlement and incipient exasperation about what exactly is happening here. *Missa Aston*, he thinks, feeling himself actually tense now, *him tek sick, or what?*

But then the visitor, looking up at what appears to be a combination of mild fear and confusion in the archangel's face, hears himself saying the words that his mouth is finally forming for him — his mouth doing all the work, knowing that he cannot possibly do it himself:

Brattie, his mouth says, *so sorry*. (He hears himself — is he actually beginning to snuffle, to choke back tears?) *Very sorry, man. But — but —*

Missa Aston? he hears Brattie respond. So softly, barely audible above the gentle refrains of the still-calm sea.

But why am I doing this? How the rassclaat can I be telling him this? Aston Patrick? You mad?

But in this moment, something — his brain, a voice, or a whisper, thickening from among the innumerable-and-counting dead, is telling him to *say it, tell it, speak it, uh huh, before it kills you, uh huh before you too* (he hears the words deep inside his head: " . . . end up like Carlton —"). *Speak it to the angel,* the voice-whisper tells him, *before —*

A friend of mine died recently, Brattie, he hears himself saying, in fact stuttering.

Only a few days ago, he hears himself say. They . . . they killed him, out in St. Catherine.

Missa Aston . . . he hears Brattie's voice trail off.

And then, just that quickly, feeling the waning sun warming him where he sits, he *knows.* Knows and feels that the archangel is not only looking at him, but *into* him.

He looks up and, in grief, in utter joy, takes in the vision's splendid face.

Like the gleaming sea just beyond the vision, it blinds him.

If only the archangel could know what he was truly thinking, he thinks. His hand still gripping the archangel's hand.

He hears himself saying so many things in the next minute or so that he knows he cannot possibly be saying, though some of them are indeed exiting his mouth: phrases like *Burned down his house, Burned him alive, They all wanted to kill him, No, they wanted to* exorcise *him, You could still smell the stink today, But what fucking harm did he ever do to anyone, I still can't believe it, This is a dear friend of mine I'm talking about, Brattie, I mean I could tell the man everything about every* rassclaat *thing, Brattie, The police aren't going to do a damn thing about it, There are times when I just want to mash up this entire country, Brattie, I can't*

believe that I'm still living in this country, Brattie, I'm sorry, Brattie,
I just had to tell someone about this, yes, mi did haffi talk bout it,
man, When mi tell you bout bu'n him dem did just bu'n him like
some old fire stick —

(hearing himself at the last achieve, finally, a smooth, effort-
less transition from English into patois)

And it is then — precisely now, the afternoon edging toward
four o'clock — that, shaken by his own rapid babble and by the
enormous and vitally necessary thing within him that just died
even as something else terrifying and new and powerful pulled
violently at his insides and sprang into life, he extends his grip to
the archangel's forearm, looking more clearly into the face and
registering there all at once the shock, bewilderment, and even
(now) fear, that disclose themselves so frankly. Yet the archangel's
face does not command him to release his grip on its arm. Along
with what he knows to be the vision's kindness, he begins to feel
its resistance to him: the forearm, so gripped in his desperate
clutch, now attempting to edge itself out of the grasp, back away
entirely to the body that owns it and to the men not far off who,
though busy at work selling the very little they have caught, have
begun to cast glances over to the quiet incipient struggle. Does
the vision in all its beauty know the depths to which he, both
penitent and witness, has sunk today? The archangel must surely
sense something of his desire for deliverance — sense the urgent
need for an embrace by the divine that would begin with those
arms about him that would both condemn him to and rescue
him from the beginning and complete end of all things, and
especially the yearning, vulnerable flesh, in fire . . . but the vision in struggle with him, he thinks, wants nothing to do with
any of it — the more unholy everlasting complications. All he,
the penitent, can do now is look directly up at him. Gaze upon
the radiant face, as, in a moment of what he *knows* is truly utter
madness, he hears himself begin to sob quietly; then, in genuine

horror — *this must be the moment of my death now,* he thinks, *I am really and truly going to die now* — he feels himself lower his sobbing face, his shoulders shaking, down to the archangel's hand still gripped so tightly in his own.

And he is falling, he knows, falling . . . with a pair of eyes looking down at him.

When one of the other fishing men comes nearer to them, quietly, to ask Brattie something about some earlier money exchange, this is exactly what he sees, that causes his eyebrows to raise and his glance, directed in one instant to the brown man sitting in the shiny Pajero, to narrow: he sees the brown man from town weeping, sobbing as if his heart truly would burst open upon the spot, with his face pressed down over Brattie's hand that he is gripping with what looks like all his strength. And then he sees Brattie's face — that expression in it. Somehow calm, if not truly completely at ease. Sorrowful, even something close to what could resemble grieving, as if all at once understanding a truth absolutely incomprehensible, even unthinkable. Brattie standing there with the brown man from town in such distress gripping his hand, and Brattie so evidently calm there now, though he had been close to the mildest form of quiet panic only one minute or so earlier. The other fishing man sees all of this, or sees at least the two men fixed in that strange and even disturbing, yet somehow arresting, position; for a reason that he will never either be able to explain to himself nor wish to, knowing that what he has seen is not something about which he will ever ask Brattie (though he will not ever be able to explain that decision to himself either), he decides not to disturb his friend. He leaves them both there and walks back to the others (the other two men in the meantime have walked over to the shop just farther down the road to buy cigarettes and some beer, leaving the woman energetically engaged with someone on her cell phone). He looks back over his shoulder only once, to see the man from town still sobbing, though more quietly now, as if nearly surrendered to or even welcoming of whatever it was that had wracked him so; and Brattie standing there, looking down at the man as if looking into him and seeing something that he recognizes, familiar but not entirely distinct; looking down at the distraught man that way. Permitting the brown man to continue holding him.

That evening, he will not tell Carole, weary with her own stories of irritation and disgust from her day of work, about what had happened to him that afternoon — *for* him? — out in St. Thomas; he certainly will not tell her about his earlier trip that day to St. Catherine and about Carlton, nor about the need that he might feel yet again, in a week's time, perhaps, to drive out there again, sit in his car once more near the house, and wonder how it could have happened, who exactly among the town's faces he had seen had done it, and what Carlton had felt in the searing last moments of his life before the house's flaming collapse on him. Their younger daughter, Rebecca, will be so happy that evening that she has finally mastered the intricacies of long division sums; he will certainly not tell her beaming face, when she calls to him *Look ya, Daddy* (he and Carole have been ambivalent about her speaking patois at home as if it and not English is her first language, but the tongue is difficult to undermine, given how many children and even several of the teachers in her school speak it, even in that very fine all-girls' school) — he will not tell either of his daughters that on days like this one he has sometimes considered very seriously the option of killing himself; of ending his life primarily, but not only, because his beloved friend above all others is gone. He will not tell his children how all the recent events have disclosed to him ever more clearly that Carlton had indeed been his friend even above Carole: Carole whom he had once loved and maybe still did love, or could;

could somehow try to love, whatever that might mean. Carole, whom he knew in her own way cared for him, whatever that might mean. Carole, who, amid the grayer, less frequent laughter of their evenings and weekends together, has been revealed less as a true friend than a colleague in the required business of correct coupledom and maintaining appearances, including the raising of two well-mannered children.

He glances at her from time to time — *my wife*, he thinks — as she scurries about the house before seeing to what she truly delights in: her slow, almost poetic (like a romantic dreamer, he has sometimes thought) watering of the hedges and flowering bushes just beyond the front verandah, not long after dusk. He notices again that, though she has begun to put on significant weight (his time, he knows, is coming, and in some parts of his body has already arrived), she is still actually quite lovely in the face. He knows — at least tonight — that he will never tell her that one of the reasons he sometimes thinks about killing himself centers on the fact that he does not wish to sneak around behind her back in desperate search of hood and batty, and even — especially — love, in the way of so many other men on the island, several of whom he either already knows or had heard about by way of Carlton or Carlton's several friends well connected to the wide, far-reaching battyman underground networks. He doesn't wish to come home to her, the girls sleeping only a few doors down the hallway, with the taste and strong scent of another man in his mouth, the feeling of another man's (protected, unprotected?) thrusts still throbbing in his backside, and the memory of another man's hand cupping his balls while whispering something in his ear — words such as those he would have wanted and still wanted the archangel he had left behind in St. Thomas to say to him, *over* him as blessing or incantation or merely . . . oh yes. (For just that moment, he closes his eyes, and shifts his hips where he sits in order to make room . . . to make room.) He does not want to come home to Carole of an evening secretly obsessed with Brattie to the point of agony, to the point at which everything she says becomes a target for his bitterest resentment because the fishing man's voice and words are not coming out of her mouth — although it may very well be far too late to help that; his resentment's harshness has been kept in strict check so far principally by the wrought-iron politeness drilled into him as a child, one of the lasting effects, for some, of a staunchly Jamaican middle-class upbringing. He knows this: that it is the formidable burden of his desire, coupled with the burden of his wish to honor at least the letter of the law of their marriage but also the warmth and care that surely had begun that journey for the both of them, that most encourages his frequent reach toward thoughts of ending everything, especially in the quietest, most still hours when Carole has drifted off to sleep beside him, sometimes touching him after muttering some sleep-syllable as he, out of reliable but now less easy habit, touches her: the steady calls of peepers outside and his own and Carole's shallow breaths the only noises filling the length of dead and deadening hours until morning . . . a drag of time sweetened by the feeling of Brattie held beside him, and holding him, in Carole's place. But he will not kill himself, he knows, as long as the archangel exists. He will know when Brattie has ceased to exist when Carlton comes to him in a dream and tells him that it is so: *Brattie gone*, he envisions Carlton telling him on that most unthinkable night, *him did dead two nights ago*. (He cannot know now that Solomon "Brattie" James, in spite of decades of an arduous daily life on the sea and the frequent stink and maw of poverty about him for his entire life will, like some country people living in the harshest of circumstances, live well past the age of one hundred with all of his faculties intact and even a good amount of his strength, outliving almost all of his friends and family and hailed by the media in that future time as one of the three oldest living people ever recorded, since records were kept of such things, in Jamaican history.) It is now, hearing Carole outside still watering the plants she loves and humming some tune he partly recognizes, then hearing the girls upstairs arguing about some pop star on American television, that he smiles, feeling what he knows without question to be Carlton's warm hand pressing gently on the back of his neck. This is no duppy, he knows; he feels no fear. Carlton would have been happy with everything that had happened in St. Thomas today, he thinks, even though he would have been unhappy to see how much I missed him. *How much I miss you, man.* But at least I know now that I'm going to stay here a little longer — in fact a lot longer. Yes, I do think so. I'm not sure exactly how, C., but if only because of what — what all of them, your *neighbors*, did to . . . knowing that some recollections still and for a long time will continue to bring trembling and chill, he does not finish the thought. He closes his eyes instead, once more, and feels the hand, comforting, on the back of his neck. Now unsure as to whether it is in fact Carlton's or the archangel's — and in that moment, to his own astonishment and sudden quiet joy, not caring either way — he closes his eyes once more and squeezes that caressing hand, then squeezes it again, more tightly; then, before getting up to join Carole in the garden, he pulls it in, *in*, toward his face for a kiss.